Wulfric the Weapon Thane
A Story of the Danish Conquest of East Anglia

Charles Whistler

PREFACE.

A word may be needed with regard to the sources from which this story of King Eadmund's armour bearer and weapon thane have been drawn. For the actual presence of such a close attendant on the king at his martyrdom on Nov. 20, 870 A.D. we have the authority of St. Dunstan, who had the story from the lips of the witness himself.

But as to the actual progress of events before the death of the king, the records are vague and imperfect. We are told that, after the defeat at Thetford, the king had intended to seek safety in the church, probably at Framlingham, where the royal household was, but was forced to hide, and from his hiding place was dragged before Ingvar the Danish leader, and so slain.

The two local legends of the "king's oak" in Hoxne woods, and of the "gold bridge", may fill in what is required to complete the story.

The former, identifying a certain aged oak as that to which the king was bound, has been in a measure corroborated by the discovery in 1848 of what may well have been a rough arrow point in its fallen trunk; while the fact that, until the erection of the new bridge at Hoxne in 1823, no newly-married couple would cross the "gold bridge" on the way to church, for the reasons given in the story, seems to show that the king's hiding place may indeed have been beneath it as the legend states. If so, the flight from Thetford must have been most precipitate, and closely followed.

There are two versions of the story of Lodbrok the Dane and Beorn the falconer. That which is given here is from Roger of Wendover. But in both versions the treachery of one Beorn is alleged to have been the cause of the descent of Ingvar and Hubba on East Anglia.

These chiefs and their brother Halfden, and Guthrum, are of course historic. Their campaign in England is hard to trace through the many conflicting chronicles, but the broad outlines given by the almost contemporary Anglo-Saxon Chronicle, supplemented with a few incidents recorded in the Heimskringla of Sturleson as to the first raid on Northumbria by Ingvar, are sufficient for the purposes of a story that deals almost entirely with East Anglia.

The legend of the finding of the head of the martyred king is given in the homily for November 20 of the Anglo-Saxon Sarum Breviary, and is therefore of early date. It may have arisen from some such incident as is given here.

Details of the death of Bishop Humbert are wanting. We only know that he was martyred at about the same time as the king, or perhaps with him, and that his name is remembered in the ancient kalendars on the same day. For describing his end as at his own chapel, still standing at South Elmham, the fate of many a devoted priest of those times might be sufficient warrant.

As to the geography of the East Anglian coast, all has changed since King Eadmund's days, with the steady gaining of alluvial land on sea at the mouth of the once great rivers of Yare and Waveney. Reedham and Borough were in his time the two promontories that guarded the estuary, and where Yarmouth now stands were sands, growing indeed slowly, but hardly yet an island even at "low-water springs". Above Beccles perhaps the course of the Waveney towards Thetford has altered little in any respect beyond the draining of the rich marshland along its banks, and the shrinking of such tributaries as the Hoxne or Elmham streams to half-dry rivulets.

With a few incidental exceptions, the modern spelling of place names has been adopted in these pages. No useful purpose would be served by a reproduction of what are now more or less uncouth if recognizable forms of the well-known titles of town and village and river.

C. W. W.

CHAPTER I. HOW LODBROK THE DANE CAME TO REEDHAM.

Elfric, my father, and I stood on our little watch tower at Reedham, and looked out over the wide sea mouth of Yare and Waveney, to the old gray walls of the Roman Burgh on the further shore, and the white gulls cried round us, and the water sparkled in the fresh sea breeze from the north and east, and the bright May-time sun shone warmly on us, and our hearts went out to the sea and its freedom, so that my father said:

"Once again is the spirit of Hengist stirring in me, and needs must that you and I take ship, and go on the swan's path even as our forefathers went; let us take the good ship somewhere--anywhere to be on the sea again. What say you, son Wulfric?"

And at that I was very glad, for I had longed for that word of his. For never, since I could remember, was a time when I knew not all that a boy might learn, for his years, of sea and the seaman's craft; and the sea drew me, calling me as it were with its many voices, even as it drew my father.

Yet, all unlike Hengist and his men, we sailed but for peaceful gain, and very rich grew Elfric, the thane of Reedham; for ours was the only ship owned by English folk on all our East Anglian shores, and she brought us wealth year by year, as we sailed to Humber and Wash northwards, and Orwell and Thames to the south, as seemed best for what merchandise we had for sale or would buy. But, more than all, my father and I alike sailed for the love of ship and sea, caring little for the gain that came, so long as the salt spray was over us, and we might hear the hum of the wind in the canvas, or the steady roll and click of the long oars in the ship's rowlocks, and take our chance of long fights with wind and wave on our stormy North Sea coasts.

So we went down to the shipyard, under the lee of Reedham Hill, and found old Kenulf our pilot, and with him went round our stout Frisian ship that my father had bought long ago, and at once bade him get ready for sailing as soon as might be. And that was a welcome order to Kenulf and our crew also; for well do the North Folk of East Anglia love the sea, if our Saxon kin of the other kingdoms have forgotten for a while the ways of their forbears.

Not so welcome was our sailing to my mother, who must sit at home listening to the song of the breezes and the roll of breakers, with her heart stirred to fear for us at every shift of wind and change of tide. And fair Eadgyth, my sister, beautiful with the clear beauty of a fair-haired Saxon lady, shared in her fears also, though I think that she believed that no storm could rage more fiercely than her father and brother and their crew could ride through in safety. Once she had sailed with us in high summer time to London, and so she held that she knew well all the ways of the ship and sea; fearing them a little, maybe.

Yet there was another dread in the heart of my mother, for this is what she said:

"What of the Danes, Elfric, my husband? Surely there is risk--aye, and great risk--of falling into their hands."

Thereat my father laughed easily, and answered:

"Not to an East Anglian ship now; for they have kept the pact we have made with them. And they watch not our shores for ships, but the long Frisian and Frankish coasts. There need be no fear of them."

So my mother was reassured, and in a fortnight's time we had gathered a mixed cargo, though no great one; and sailed, with a shift of wind to the southwest, into the Wash, and so put into the king's haven on its southern shore, where we would leave our goods with a merchant whom we knew.

On the second day after we came the wind shifted to the eastward, and then suddenly to the northeast, and blew a gale, so that we bided in the haven till it was over. For though it was not so heavy that we could not have won through it in open water with little harm, it was of no use risking ship and men on a lee shore for naught.

Our friend, the merchant, kept us with him gladly, and there we heard the last news of the Danish host, with whom we had made peace two years since; for nowadays that news had become of the first interest to every man in all England; though not yet in the right way. For we had not yet learnt that England must be truly one; and so long as he himself was unharmed, little cared an East Anglian what befell Mercian or Northumbrian, even as Wessex or Sussex cared for naught but themselves. Wherefore, all we longed to know was that the Danish host was not about to fall on us, being employed elsewhere.

We had found gain rather than hurt by their coming, for we had, as I say, made peace with them, and, moreover, sold them horses. Then they had honestly left our coasts, and had gone to York, and thereafter to Nottingham. Now Northumbria was theirs, and Mercia was at their feet. And now again we learnt that they bided in peace at

York, and we were content.

Three days it blew, and then the gale was spent; though the sea still ran high and swift. So we bade farewell to our friend the merchant and set sail, and if the passage homewards was rough, it was swifter than we had hoped.

So it came to pass that we reached the wide inlet of our haven at the Yare's mouth too soon for the tide to take us in over the sands which grow and shift every year, and must needs drop anchor in the roads and wait, with home in sight, hill and church and houses clear and sharp against the afternoon sky after rain; while past us the long surges the storm had raised raced in over half-hidden sands, and broke in snow-white foam along the foot of the sand dunes of the shore, sending the spindrift flying up and inland over their low crests.

Mostly the boats would have been out to meet us, and maybe to tow us in, sparing our crew a little; but today no boat might come, for the seas were too heavy over the bar, so that it would have been death to any man foolish enough to try to reach us; and we looked for none. So as the stout ship wallowed and plunged at her anchors--head to wind and sea, and everything, from groaning timbers to song of wind-curved rigging and creak of swinging yard, seeming to find a voice in answer to the plunge and wash of the waves, and swirl and patter of flying spray over the high bows--we found what shelter we might under bulwarks and break of fore deck, and waited.

My father and I sat on the steersman's bench aft, not heeding the showers of spray that reached us now and then even there, and we watched the tide rising over the sand banks, and longed for home and warm fireside, instead of this cold, gray sky and the restless waves; though I, at least, was half sorry that the short voyage was over, dreaming of the next and whither we might turn our ship's bows again before the summer ended.

My father looked now and then shoreward, and now seaward, judging wind and tide, and sitting patiently with the wondrous patience of the seaman, learnt in years of tide and calm; for he would tell me that sea learning never ends, so that though the sailor seemed to be idle, he must needs be studying some new turn of his craft if only his eyes were noting how things went around him. Yet I thought he was silent beyond his wont.

Presently he rose up and paced the deck for a little, and then came and sat down by me again.

"I am restless, son Wulfric," he said, laughing softly; "and I know not why."

"For the sake of supper," I answered, "for I am that also, and tide seems mighty slow therefore."

"Nay, supper comes to the patient; but it seems to me that I have to watch for somewhat."

"Surely for naught but the tide," I answered, not thinking much of the matter, but yet wondering a little.

"Not for tide or wind, but for somewhat new, rather--somewhat of which I have a fear.

"But this is foolishness," he said, laughing again at himself, for few men thought less of signs and forewarnings than he.

Then he looked out again to windward, under his hand, and all of a sudden turned sharply to me, pointing and saying:

"But, as I live, hither comes something from the open sea!"

I rose up and looked to where he showed me, and as the ship rose to a great wave, far off I saw a dark speck among white-crested rollers, that rose and fell, and came ever nearer, more swiftly than wreckage should.

Now some of the men who clustered under the shelter of the fore deck, with their eyes ever on us, rose up from their places and began to look out seaward over the bows through the spray to find out what we watched, and ere long one man called to his mates:

"Ho, comrades, here comes flotsam from the open sea!"

Slowly the men rose up one by one and looked, clustering round the stem head, and a little talk went round as to what this might be.

"It is a bit of wreck," said one.

"Hardly, for the gale has not been wild enough to wreck a ship in the open; 'tis maybe lumber washed from a deck," answered another.

"It is a whale--no more or less."

"Nay," said old Kenulf; "it behaves not as a whale, and it comes too swiftly for wreckage."

"Would it were a dead whale. Then would be profit," said another man again, and after that the men were silent for a long while, having said all that could be guessed, and watched the speck that drew nearer and nearer, bearing down on us.

At last my father, ever keen of sight, said to me:

"This thing is not at the mercy of wind and wave. Rather has it the rise and fall of a boat well handled. Yet whence should one come in this heavy sea, after three days' gale?"

Even as he spoke, old Kenulf growled, half to himself, that to his thinking this was a boat coming, and handled, moreover, by men who knew their trade. Thereat some of the men laughed; for it seemed a thing impossible, both by reason of the stretch of wild sea that so small a craft as this--if it were indeed a boat--must have crossed, and because the sea was surely too heavy to let one live.

Yet in the end we saw that it was a boat, and that in her, moreover, was but one man, whose skill in handling her was more than ours, and greater than we could deem possible.

Whereupon some of us were afraid, seeing how wondrously the tiny craft came through the swift seas, and a man called out, giving voice to our fears:

"Surely yon man is a Finn and the wizard who has raised this storm to drown us; now are we lost!"

And I--who had listened eagerly to all the wild stories of the seamen, since first I was old enough to wander curiously over the ships from overseas that put into our haven on their way up the great rivers to Norwich, or Beccles, or other towns--knew that the Finns have powers more than mortal (though how or whence I know not) over wind and sea, often using their power to the hurt of others, and so looked to see the lines of a great squall, drawn as it were astern of the wizard's boat, whitening as it rushed upon us to sink us in sight of home.

But old Kenulf cried out on the man, saying:

"Rather is it one of the holy saints, and maybe the blessed Peter the fisherman himself," and he bared his gray head, crossing himself, as he looked eagerly to catch sight of the glory of light round the seafarer; and that rebuked my fears a little.

But squall or crown of light was there none. Only the brown waves, foam crested, which we feared not, and the gray light of the clouded sun that was nigh to setting.

My father heeded naught of this, but watched the boat, only wondering at the marvellous skill of her steersman. And when the boat was so near that it was likely that the eyes of the man were on us, my father raised his arm in the seaman's silent greeting, and I thought that the boatman returned the salute.

Now the course that the boat was holding when that signal passed would have taken her wide of us by half a cable's length, but she was yet so far distant that but a little change would bring her to us. Some sort of sail she seemed to have, but it was very small and like nothing I had ever seen, though it was enough to drive her swiftly and to give her steering way before the wind. Until my father signed to him the man seemed to have no wish to near our ship, going on straight to what would be certain destruction amid the great breakers on our largest sand bar, and that made the men more sure that he was a wizard, and there were white faces enough among them.

"Now," said my father to me, "doubtless this is what was put in my mind when I felt I must watch. Had I not seen him, yon man would have been surely lost; for I think he cannot see the breakers from his boat," and again he signed to the boatman.

Then from the little craft rose a great, long-winged hawk that cried and hovered over it for a little, as if loth to leave it; and one man said, shrinking and pale, that it was the wizard's familiar spirit. But the wind caught the bird's long wings and drove it from the boat, and swiftly wheeling it must needs make for us, speeding down the wind with widespread, still pinions.

Then cried aloud that same terrified man:

"It is a sending, and we are done for!" thinking that, as Finns will, the wizard they deemed him had made his spells light on us in this visible form. But my father held out his hand, whistling a falconer's call, and the great bird flew to him, and perched on his wrist, looking bravely at us with its bright eyes as though sure of friendship.

"See!" said my father loudly; "this is a trained bird, and no evil sending; here are the jesses yet on its feet."

And Kenulf and most of the men laughed, asking the superstitious man if the ship sank deeper, or seas ran higher for its coming.

"Hold you the bird," said my father to me; "see! the boatman makes for us."

I took the beautiful hawk gladly, for I had never seen its like before, and loved nothing better when ashore than falconry, and as I did so I saw that its master had changed the course of his boat and was heading straight for us. Now, too, I could make out that what we had thought a sail was but the floor boarding of the boat reared up against a thwart, and that the man was managing her with a long oar out astern.

The great hawk's sharp talons were like steel on my ungloved wrist, piercing through the woollen sleeve of my jerkin, but I heeded them not, so taken up was I with watching this man who steered so well and boldly in so poorly fitted a craft. And the boat was, for all that, most beautiful, and built on such lines as no Saxon boat had. Well we know those wondrous lines now, for they were those of the longships of the vikings.

Now the men forward began to growl as the boat came on to us, and when my father, seeing that the man would seek safety with us, bade those on the fore deck stand by with a line to heave to him as he came, no man stirred, and they looked foolishly at one another.

Then my father called sharply to Kenulf by name, giving the same order, and the old man answered back:

"Bethink you, Thane; it is ill saving a man from the sea to be foe to you hereafter. Let him take his chance."

Thereat my father's brow grew dark, for he hated these evil old sayings that come from heathen days, and he cried aloud:

"That is not the way of a Christian or a good seaman! Let me come forward."

And in a moment he was on the fore deck, where the men made hasty way for him. There the long lines were coiled, ready for throwing to the shore folk on our wharf, both fore and aft. My father caught up one at his feet and stood ready, for now the boat was close on us, and I could see the white set face of her steersman as he watched for the line he knew was coming, and wherein lay his only slender hope of safety.

My father swung his arm and cast. Swift and true fled the coils from his hand--but fell short by two fathoms or less, and the boat swept past our bows, as the men held their breath, watching and ashamed.

But I also had caught up the coil from the after deck, fearing lest my father should not have been in time, while the hawk fluttered and gripped my arm in such wise that at any other time I should have cried out with the pain of the sharp piercing of its talons. Yet it would not leave me.

The boat flew on, but the man had his eyes on me--not looking vainly for the lost end of the first line among the foam as many another man would--and I saw that he was ready.

I threw; and the hawk screamed and clutched, as it lost its balance, and beat my face with its great wings, and I could not see for its fluttering; but the men shouted, and I heard my father's voice cry "Well done!" Then I made fast the end of the line round the mainsheet cleat, for that told me that the man had caught on.

Then the bird was still, and I looked up. I saw the boat pass astern as the man made fast the line round the fore thwart, with his eyes on the wave that came. Then he sprang to the steering oar, and in a moment the boat rounded to on the back of a great wave and was safe before the crest of the next roller ran hissing past me, to break harmless round her bows.

Then the man looked up, smiling to me, lifted his hand in greeting, and then straightway laid in the steering oar. Having found a bailing bowl in the stern sheets, he set to work to clear out the water that washed about in the bottom of the boat; then he replaced the floor boards, and all things being shipshape, sat down quickly in the stern, putting his head into his hands, and there bided without moving, as if worn out and fain to rest for a while.

Now it was like to be a hard matter to get the boat alongside in that sea, and we must needs wait till the man took in hand to help, so we watched him as he sat thus, wondering mostly at the boat, for it was a marvel to all of us. Sharp were her bows and stern, running up very high, and her high stem post was carved into the likeness of a swan's neck and head, and the wings seemed to fall away along the curve of the bows to the carved gunwale, that was as if feathered, and at last the stern post rose and bent like a fan of feathers to finish all. Carved, too, were rowlocks and the ends of the thwarts, and all the feathered work was white and gold above the black of the boat's hull. Carved, too, was the baling bowl, and the loom of the oar was carved in curving lines from rowlock leather to hand. And as I thought of the chances of our losing her as we crossed the bar among the following breakers, I was grieved, and would have asked my father to let us try to get her on deck if we could.

But now the man roused, and put his hands to his mouth, hailing us to ask if we would suffer him to come on board, and my father hailed him back to bid him do so. Then it would seem that our men were ashamed, having once disobeyed my father whom they loved, not to finish the work that we had begun, and so, without waiting for the order, saw to getting the boat up to our quarter, so that it was but a minute or two before the man leapt on our deck, and the boat was once more astern at the length of her line.

"Thanks, comrades," said the man; "out of Ran's {i} net have you brought me, and ill fall me if I prove foe to you, as the old saw bodes."

Now as one looked at this storm-beaten wanderer there was no doubt but that he was surely a prince among men, and I for one marvelled at his look and bearing after what he must have gone through. Drenched and salt crusted were his once rich clothes, tangled and uncared for were his hair and beard, and worn and tired he showed both in face and body, yet his eyes were bright and his speech was strong and free as he swung to the roll of the ship with the step of a sea king. His speech told us that he was a Dane, for though we of the East Angles had never, even before the coming of the great host of which I must tell presently, such great difference of tongue between our own and that of Dane and Frisian but that we could well understand them and speak therein, yet time and distance have given us a new way of handling our words, as one might say, and a new turn to the tones of our voices. Often had I heard the Danish way of speech on board the ships from over sea in our haven, and had caught it up, as I was wont to try to catch somewhat of every tongue that I heard.

So he and we looked at each other for a moment, we wondering at him and he seeking our leader. Nor did he doubt long, taking two steps to my father, holding out his hand, and again thanking him.

My father grasped the offered hand frankly, and, smiling a little, said:

"Rather should you thank Wulfric, my son, here; for it was his line that reached you."

"No fault that of yours," answered the Dane; and he turned to me with the same hearty greeting.

"Now, friend Wulfric, I owe you my life, and therefore from this time forward my life is for yours, if need be. Nor shall my men be behind in that matter--that is if I ever see them again," he added, looking quaintly at me, if gravely.

"Surely you shall do so," I said, "if it is in our power."

"I thank you--and it is well. I know coasts where a stranger would be a slave from the moment his foot touched shore. Now tell me whose ship this is that has given me shelter, and what your father's name is, that I may thank you rightly."

"Elfric, the Thane of Reedham, is my father," I said, "Sheriff of the East Anglian shore of the North Folk, under Eadmund, our king. And this is his ship, and this himself to whom you have spoken."

"Then, Thane and Thane's son, I, whose life you have saved, am Lodbrok, Jarl {ii} of a strip of Jutland coast. And now I have a fear on me that I shall do dishonour to the name of Dane, for I faint for want of food and can stand no more."

With that he sat down on the bench where I had been, and though he smiled at us, we could see that his words were true enough, and that he was bearing bravely what would have overborne most men. And now the falcon fluttered from my wrist to his.

Then my father bade me hasten, and I brought ale and meat for the jarl, and set them before him, and soon he was taking that which he needed; but every now and then he gave to the bird, stroking her ruffled feathers, and speaking softly to her.

"Aye, my beauty," he said once, "I did but cast you down wind lest you should be lost with me. And I would have had you take back the news that I was lost to my own home."

My father stood and watched the tide, and presently I joined him, for I would not hinder the Dane from his meal by watching him. I looked at the beautiful boat astern, tossing lightly on the wave crests, and saw that she would surely be lost over the bar; so I asked my father now, as I had meant before, if we might not try to get her on board.

For answer he turned to Lodbrok.

"Set you much store by your boat, Jarl?" he asked him.

"The boat is yours, Thane, or Wulfric's, by all right of salvage. But I would not have her lost, for my sons made her for me this last winter, carving her, as you see, with their own hands. Gladly would I see her safe if it might be."

"Then we will try to get her," answered my father; "for there are one or two things that my children have made for me, and I would not lose them for the sake of a little trouble. And, moreover, I think your sons have made you the best boat that ever floated!"

"Else had I not been here!" answered the Dane. "They are good shipwrights."

Then Kenulf and the men set to work, and it was no easy matter to come by the boat; but it was done at last, and glad was I to see her safely lashed on deck. Then the time had come, and we up anchor and plunged homewards through the troubled seas of the wide harbour mouth. It was I who steered, as I ever would of late, while the Dane stood beside me, stroking his hawk and speaking to it now and then. And once or twice he looked long and earnestly at the breakers, knowing now from what he had escaped; and at last he said to me:

"Many a man, I know, would have rather let me go on than have run the risk of saving one from the sea. Do you dare go against the saying?"

"Why not? I may not say that it came not into our minds," I answered; "but Christian men will put such ill bodes aside."

"Ah! I had forgotten your new faith," said Lodbrok. "Now from this time I, for one, have naught to say against it, for I think I owe it somewhat."

And he was silent for a while.

Now my father came aft, and sitting down by the Dane, asked him how he came to risk sailing in the little boat.

"I know not if you can believe me," answered Lodbrok, "but I will tell you in a few words. I have been blown from off the Jutland shore and have won through the gale safely. That is all. But it was by my own fault, for I must needs take the boat and put out to sea with my hawk there to find fresh sport. It seemed to me, forsooth, that a great black-backed gull or fierce skua would give me a fine flight or two. And so it was; but I rowed out too far, and before I bethought myself, both wind and tide were against me. I had forgotten how often after calm comes a shift of wind, and it had been over still for an hour or so. Then the gale blew up suddenly. I could have stemmed the tide, as often before; but wind and tide both were my masters then.

"That was three days and two nights ago. Never thought I to see another sunset, for by midday of that first day I broke an oar, and knew that home I could never win; so I made shift with the floor boards, as you saw, for want of canvas. After that there is little to tell, for it was ever wave after wave, and gray flying clouds ever over me, and at night no rest, but watching white wave crests coming after me through the dark."

"Some of us thought that you were a Finn, at least," said my father as the Dane paused.

"Not once or twice only on this voyage have I wished myself a Finn, or at least that I had a Finn's powers," said Lodbrok, laughing; "but there has been no magic about this business save watchfulness, and my sons' good handicraft."

Then I asked the jarl how he called his sons, with a little honest envy in my heart that I could never hope to equal their skill in this matter of boat building, wherein I had been wont to take some pride of myself.

"Three sons have I in Jutland, Wulfric, my friend, and they, when they hear my story, will hold you dear to them. Ingvar is the eldest, Hubba, the next, and the third, Halfden, is three-and-twenty, and so about your own age, as I take it, as he is also about your equal in build and strength. Yet I would sooner see a ship of mine steered by you than by him, for he is not your equal in that matter."

Now that praise pleased me well, as it did also my father. For we hold the Danes as first of all peoples in the knowledge of sea craft; and we had seen that this man was a master therein. But though at this time I thought of naught but the words of praise, hereafter I was to remember the words that Jarl Lodbrok spoke of the way in which these sons of his would hold me when the tale was told them.

At last we hailed the shore through the creeping dusk, and the shore lines were thrown out. Then were we alongside our staithe {iii}, and Lodbrok the Dane had come to Reedham.

Now it may seem but a little thing that a seafarer should be driven to a strange coast, and be tended there in friendly wise by those who saved him from the breakers, for such is a common hap on our island shores. Yet, from this day forward, all my life of the time yet before me was to be moulded by what came of that cast of line to one in peril. Aye, and there are those who hold that the fate of our England herself was in hand that day, though it seems to me that that is saying overmuch. Yet one cannot tell, and maybe those who will read this story of mine will be able to judge.

What I do know certainly is this, that all which makes my tale worth the telling comes from this beginning.

CHAPTER II. HOW LODBROK SPOKE WITH BEORN THE FALCONER.

So soon as we had stepped ashore there came in haste one of our housecarles with word from my mother that Eadmund, the king, had that day come to our house from Caistor; so at once my father bade the man return and bring changes of clothes for himself and me and Lodbrok to our steward's house, that we might appear in more decent trim before our guest and master.

So we waited for a little while, watching the men as they berthed the ship; and as we stood there a word went round among the knot of people watching with us, and they parted, making a little lane, as they said, "The king comes". And then I heard the well-known voice of Eadmund calling gaily to us:

"Ho, friend Elfric, here have I come to see what a man fresh from a stormy voyage looks like, if light will serve me."

And so saying, I being nearest to him, the king turned me round with his strong hands, and scanned my rough, wet garments and fur cap.

"Truly, son Wulfric," he cried, laughing, "I think these things suit you as well as war gear, and better than court finery, in this dim light at least. Now let me see the thane himself."

Then my father would have him come back to the house at once, out of the stormy weather, for the rain was coming now as the wind fell; and we went, not waiting for the change of garments, for that the king would not suffer.

As we turned away from the staithe, Lodbrok took my arm, asking me where he might find shelter.

"Why, come with us, surely!" I answered, having no thought but that he would have done so as our guest.

"Thanks," he said; "I knew not if your help could go so far as that to a man whose story might well be too strange for belief."

Now it had seemed to me that no one could doubt such a man, and so I told him that we had no doubt of him at all in that matter. And he thanked me gravely again, walking, as I thought, more freely beside me, as knowing that he was held to be a true man.

We followed my father, who walked with the king, at a little distance because of this small delay; and presently Lodbrok asked me if this was the King of all England.

"No," I answered; "though, indeed, he is the only king we know aught of. This is Eadmund of East Anglia."

"You know him well, as one may see by his way with you," said the jarl.

"Surely, for he is my father's close friend. They were comrades together in King Offa's court until the old king laid down his crown and gave the kingdom into Eadmund's hands; and they are the same to each other now as ever. He is my godfather; and I was in his court till I was eighteen. Moreover, I am one of his armour bearers yet when need is."

So I spoke plainly enough, for I think that I had, and ever shall have, reason to be proud of our nearness to the king, of whom no man had but good to say since he, almost as a boy, came to the throne.

"So then it seems that fate has brought me to court," said the Dane.

"Yes, in a way," I told him; "for the king will ever bide with us when he would visit this side of his kingdom."

"I think that I have seen this king before," said Lodbrok presently; "for he is a man the like of whom one sees not twice."

"Then," said I, "he will surely remember you, for he never forgets one whom he has had reason to notice."

Whereat the jarl laughed a little to himself; but I had no time to ask why, for now we were come to the great door; and when my father would have let the king go in first Eadmund laughed at him, and took his arm and drew him in with him, so that there was a little delay, and we drew close.

Very bright and welcome looked the great oaken hall as we came in from the dark, rainy night. A great fire burnt on its stone hearth in the centre, and the long tables were already set above and below it. The bright arms and shields on the walls shone below the heads of deer and wolf and boar, and the gust of wind that came in with us flew round the wall, making a sort of ripple of changing colour run along the bright woven stuffs that covered them to more than a man's height from the floor. No one in all East Anglia had so well dight a hall as had Elfric, the rich Thane of Reedham.

Well used was I to all this, but never seemed it more homelike to me than when I came in fresh from the the cold, gray sea.

And now there stood on the high place to welcome us those whose presence made the place yet more beautiful to me--my mother, and Eadgyth my sister, and beside them were Bishop Humbert, our own bishop, and many thanes of the court, and some of the bishop's clergy. Such a gathering my father, and, indeed, all of us, loved, for all were well known to us.

Now I went to greet these dear ones and friends, and there was pleasant jest and laughter at us for coming thus sea clad and spray stained into the midst of that gay company. So that for a little time I forgot Lodbrok, who had not followed me beyond the hearth.

Then Eadgyth said to me:

"Who is that noble-looking man who stands so sadly and alone by the fire?"

I turned, blaming myself for this forgetfulness, and there was the Dane gazing into the flames, and seeming heedless of all that was going on. Nor do I think that I had ever seen one look so sad as looked that homeless man, as he forgot the busy talk and movement around him in some thoughts of his own.

So I went to him, touching his arm gently, and he started a little. Then his grave smile came, and he said:

"Truly, Wulfric, I had forgotten all things but my own home, and when I woke from my dream at your touch, half thought I that you were Halfden--that youngest son of mine of whom I told you."

Then so wistfully looked he at me that I could not forbear saying to him:

"You must hold me as in Halfden's place, for this will be your house, if you will, until there comes a ship that will take you home. Gladly will some of the Frisians we know take you at least to the right side of the broad seas."

"Aye, gladly would some have Lodbrok the Jarl with them," he answered, smiling strangely.

What he meant, beyond that he might pilot them well, I knew not, nor, indeed, thought that any hidden meaning lay in his words. So that his saying passed from my mind, until one day when I should have cause to understand it well enough.

I would have taken him now to present him to my mother, but she was gone, and there came to us one of the steward's men, who stared at the Dane as if he were some marvel, having doubtless heard his story from one of the seamen, but covered his wonder by bowing low and bidding him to an inner room where the thane had prepared change of garment for him. For my father, having the same full belief and trust in the stranger's word, would no more than I treat him in any wise but as an honoured guest.

Then said Lodbrok:

"Good shall surely ever be to the house that will thus treat a wanderer. Hardly would a castaway meet with so great kindness in my own land. Nor do I think that we Danes have made our name so well loved among English folk that we should look for the like among them."

But I answered that we of East Anglia had no cause to blame his people, who had made peace with us and kept it faithfully.

So the man led Lodbrok away, and I too went to seek gear more courtly than salt-stained and tar-spotted blue cloth of Lavenham.

There are few thanes' houses which have so many chambers as ours, for because of the king's friendship with us, my father had added, as it were, house to house, building fresh chambers out around the great hall itself, till all one might see was its long roof among the many that clustered round and against its walls, so that the thanes who came with him, or to see him, might have no cause to complain of ill lodging with Elfric of Reedham. So it had come to pass that our house was often the place where the court lay, and I know that many of the poorer thanes thanked my father for thus using his riches, since he saved them many a time the heavy expenses of housing king and court when their turn should have come. Yet my father would ever put aside those thanks, saying that he loved to see his house full, though I myself know that this saving of others less rich was in his mind.

One part of all these buildings we called "the king's house", for it was set apart for him, and between that and the great hall was a square and large chamber which Eadmund would use for his private audiences, and sometimes for council room. And there we used to gather from all parts of the place that we might enter the great hall in his train at supper time, for there was a door which led to the high table thence, so that the king need not go through the crowd of housecarles and lesser folk who sat, below the salt, along the walls. And in that chamber was a chimney to the fire, so that the hearth was against the wall, which was a marvel to many, but made the place more meet for the king. Ingild the merchant, my other godfather, whose home was in London, had brought men thence to make it for us, having the like in his own house after some foreign pattern.

There were two men only in this room when I returned ready for the feast. Both stood before the fire, and both were brightly dressed, and hardly, but for the drowsy hawk which sat unhooded on his hand, should I have known Lodbrok in the rich dress my father had had prepared for him. The other was Beorn, the king's falconer, who went everywhere with his master. These two were speaking together as they stood before the fire, and I thought that what Beorn said was not pleasing to the Dane, for he turned away a little, and answered shortly.

When they saw me both turned, Lodbrok with a smile of welcome, and Beorn with a loud, rough voice crying to me:

"Ho, Wulfric, here is a strange thing! This gold ring have I offered to your stranger here for his falcon--which has three wing feathers missing, moreover--and he will not sell, though I trow that a man cast ashore must needs want gold more than a bird which he may not fly save I gain him leave from the king."

"The bird is Wulfric's," said Lodbrok quietly.

"Nay, Jarl," I answered, "I would not take so loving a hawk from her master, and over all our manors you may surely fly her."

"See you there!" cried Beorn, with a sort of delight, not heeding my last words, "Wulfric will not have her! Now will you sell?"

Then Lodbrok looked at me with a short glance that I could not but understand, and said that it would surely grieve him if I would not take the falcon.

Pleased enough I was, though half unwilling to take what seemed as a forced gift. Yet to quiet Beorn--whom I never liked, as he was both overbearing and boastful, though of great skill in his art of falconry--I thanked the Dane, and went to where a hawking glove hung on the wall, for my arm would feel the marks of those strong talons for many a day, already. As I put it on I said that I feared the bird would hardly come to me, leaving her master.

"Once I would have said that she would not," said Lodbrok; "for until today she would bide with no man but myself and her keeper. But today she has sat on your wrist, so that I know she will love you well, for reasons that are beyond my guessing."

And so he shifted the falcon lightly from his wrist to mine, and there she sat quietly, looking from him to me as though she would own us both.

Then said Beorn, holding out his hand, on which he wore his embroidered state glove of office:

"This is foolishness. The bird will perch on any wrist that is rightly held out to her, so she be properly called," and he whistled shrill, trying to edge the falcon from my hand.

In a moment she roused herself, and her great wings flew out, striking his arm and face as he pushed them forward; and had he not drawn back swiftly, her iron beak would surely have rent his gay green coat.

"Plague on the kite!" he said; "surely she is bewitched! And if her master is, as they say, a wizard, that is likely--"

"Enough, Master Falconer," I said, growing angry. "Lodbrok is our guest, and this, moreover, is the court for the time. Why, the bird is drowsy, and has been with me already. There is no wonder in the matter, surely?"

But Beorn scowled, and one might see that his pride of falconry was hurt. Maybe he would have answered again, but I spoke to Lodbrok, asking him what the falcon was, as she was like none of ours, for this was a thing I knew Beorn would be glad to know, while his pride would not let him ask.

And Lodbrok answered that she was an Iceland gerfalcon from the far northern ocean, and went on to tell us of her powers of flight, and at what game she was best, and how she would take her quarry, and the like. And Beorn sat down and feigned to pay no heed to us.

Presently the Dane said that he had known gerfalcons to fly from Iceland to Norway in a day, and at that Beorn laughed as in scorn.

"Who shouted from Norway to Iceland to say that a lost hawk had come over?" he said.

The Dane laughed a little also, as at a jest; though one could tell that Beorn rather meant insult.

"Why," he answered, "the bird got loose from her master's ship as he sailed out of port in Iceland, and he found her at home in Nidaros at his journey's ending; and they knew well on what day she came, which was the same as that on which she got free."

Then I said, lest Beorn should scoff again:

"Now, if this falcon got free from here, surely she will go home to your land."

"Aye, and so my sons will think me dead, seeing her come without me. Wherefore keep her safely mewed until she has learnt that this is her home, for I would not have that mischance happen."

That I promised easily, for I prized the bird highly. And that I might not leave him with the surly Beorn, I asked the jarl to come and see her safely bestowed, and left the room with him.

As we crossed the courtyard to the mews, where our good hawks were, Lodbrok said to me:

"I fear yon falconer is ill pleased with me."

"I have a mind to tell the king of his rudeness to our guest," I answered.

"That is not worth while," said Lodbrok. "The man's pride is hurt that he should be thus baffled for all his skill, which, from his talk, must be great," and we both laughed, for Beorn loved his own praises.

Now when we got back the guests were gathering, and it was not long before the king entered, and at once called me.

"All here I know but one, Wulfric, and that one is your seafarer. Let me know him also that speech may be free among us."

So Lodbrok came, and he and the king looked long at one another before Eadmund spoke.

"I have heard your story, friend, and it is a strange one," he said pleasantly. "Moreover, I know your name in some way."

"Well known is the name of Ragnar Lodbrok, my forefather," said the jarl. "Mayhap the king remembers the name thus!"

"Aye," answered Eadmund, "that is a well-known and honoured name, and I think that Ragnar's son has a share in his courage. But your face also seems known to me, and it was not of the great Ragnar that I thought. Have we met in years past?"

Then Lodbrok said that he had been in London at a time when Offa the King was there, and it was long years ago, but that the very day might be remembered by reason of a great wedding that he had been to see out of curiosity, knowing little of Saxon customs. And he named the people who were married in the presence of Offa and many nobles.

Then Eadmund laughed a little.

"Now it all comes into my mind," he said; "you are the leader of those strangers who must needs come into the church in helm and mail, with axe and shield hung on shoulders. Moreover, for that reason, when men bade you depart and you went not, they even let you bide. So I asked your name--and now I can answer for it that Lodbrok Jarl you are."

And he held out his hand for the Dane to kiss, after our custom. But Lodbrok grasped and shook it heartily, saying:

"Thanks, Lord King, for that remembrance, and maybe also for a little forgetfulness."

Nor was Eadmund displeased with the freedom, but at that last saying he laughed outright.

"Kings have both to remember and forget," he said, "and maybe, if the citizens had not expected you to behave as wild vikings, you would have gone peacefully as you came?"

"That is the truth," said Lodbrok.

So I suppose there had been some fray, of little moment, with the London folk.

Then we followed the king into the hall; and Lodbrok and I together sat at table over against him. Soon I knew all that an hour or two of pleasant talk would teach me of his home and sons and sports, and the king asked now and again of Danish customs, not yet speaking of the voyage.

"For," said he, "it is ill recalling hardships until the feast is over. Then may one enjoy the telling."

Presently the gleemen sang to us; and after that the harp went round, that those who could might sing, and all the talk in hall was hushed to hear Eadmund himself, the men setting down ale cups and knives to listen, for he had a wondrously sweet voice, and sang from the ancient songs of Caedmon {iv}. Then I sang of the sea--some song I had made and was proud of, and it pleased all. And at length we looked at Lodbrok, wondering if he could take his turn.

"Fain would I try to please my host," he said, looking a little wistfully at my father; "but a man swept far from home against his will is no singer."

Then Eadmund pitied him, as did we all, and rose up.

"Feasting is over, thanes," he said. "Let us sit awhile in the other chamber and hear Lodbrok's story."

For he would ever leave the hall as at this time, so that the housecarles and lesser guests might have greater freedom of talk when we were gone.

So we rose up, and as we did so I saw Beorn, the falconer, look sourly at Lodbrok; and it misliked me that he should harbour any ill will even yet against the Dane who had done him no wrong.

Round the fire we sat; some ten of us in all, for Bishop Humbert and his folk went to their lodgings in the town, and there Lodbrok told the king of his voyage.

And when he named his sons, Eadmund looked grave, and said:

"I have heard of those two chiefs, Ingvar and Hubba. Did they not make a raid into Northumbria two years ago? Maybe they are yet there with the host."

"Aye," answered Lodbrok, seeming to wonder at the grave face of our king; "they went to Northumbria with the host that is yet there. They fought well and bravely at the place men call Streoneshalch {v}, gaining much booty. And it was by Ingvar's plan that the place was taken, and that was well done. But they left the host with their men after that, saying that there were over many leaders already."

Now we all knew the cruel story of the burning of that place; but Northumbria was a far-off kingdom, and with it we had naught to do. So, except perhaps the king, the rest of us were as little moved as if he had spoken of the taking of some Frankish town; for if my father thought more of it, being in the king's counsels, he passed it over.

"These sons of yours have a mind to be first then," he said lightly.

"Seeing that the blood of Ragnar Lodbrok is in their veins it could not well be otherwise," answered the jarl somewhat grimly.

Then he ended his tale, and the king was greatly pleased with him, so that he bade him bide in the court for a while that he might take back a good report of us to his own people.

Now when the king was with us, I gladly took up my duties as his armour bearer for the time; and therefore slept across the doorway of his chamber when he went to rest. So my father bestowed Lodbrok with the thanes in the great hall, and I left him there, following the king.

Well did I sleep that night, though, sailorwise, not so heavily but that any noise would rouse me in a moment. And as it drew towards morning the king stirred uneasily, and I looked up at him. Seeing that I woke he called me softly. The gray light of dawn came through the window, and I could see that he sat up in his bed, though I might not make out his face.

"I am here, Lord King. Is aught amiss?" I said, rising up with my sword in my hand.

"Strange dreams have I had, my son," he said, in his quiet voice,

24

"and they trouble me."

"Let me know them, my master," I said, "and maybe the trouble will pass; for often that which seems sorely troublous in a dream is naught when one would put it into words."

"Sit on the bed and I will tell you," he answered; and when I was there close to him he went on:

"It was this: I thought that I was in some place where water gleamed beneath me, while overhead passed the tread of many feet with music of pipe and tabor as at a bridal. And I cannot tell what that place was. Then came to me the hand of this Lodbrok, and he, looking very sad and downcast, led me thence into the forest land and set me over against a great gate. And beyond that gate shone glorious light, and I heard the sound of voices singing in such wise that I knew it was naught but the gate of Heaven itself, and I would fain go therein. But between me and the gate sped arrows thick as hail, so that to reach it I must needs pass through them. Then said Jarl Lodbrok, 'Here is the entry, and it is so hard to win through because of me, yet not by my fault. But I think you will not turn aside for arrows, and when you come therein I pray you to remember me.' Then pressed I to the gate, unheeding of the arrow storm. And lo! the gate was an oak tree, tall and strong, yet beyond it was the light and the singing that I had reached. Then faded the face of Lodbrok, and after me looked sadly many faces, and one was yours, my son, and the nearest. So I woke."

"That is a wondrous dream," I said, not knowing what to make thereof, having no skill in reading these matters.

"Aye, my son," answered Eadmund; "nor can I read it; though I think I shall do so hereafter. Nevertheless it comes into my mind that the dream warns me that my time is short. Lie down again, my son. Let us sleep in peace while we may."

After that the king slept peacefully as a little child till full daylight came; but I for very sadness closed not my eyes again, for I thought that our king was fey {vi}.

But in the morning the dream had, as it seemed, passed from the mind of Eadmund, for he was very cheerful, as was his wont, and said naught of it. However, I told my father thereof, for the remembrance was heavy to me. And he, when he heard it, bit his lip a little, pondering, but at last laughed.

"Trouble not yourself about it, son Wulfric," he said; "were I to mind every dream that I have had, I think that I should take no joy in life. Why, every year, for the last five past, I have dreamed of sore shipwreck, and the old vessel's timbers are yet hanging together!"

I laughed also, and thought that maybe he was right--for my father's judgment was ever the best in my eyes--and so set my mind at rest, though the strangeness of the matter would not let it be altogether forgotten.

Now as days went on and we saw more of our guest, Lodbrok, there was, I think, no man of our household who would willingly have seen him take ship and leave us; for his ways and words were pleasant to all alike, and there seemed to be no craft of which he knew not something, so that he could speak to each man, in field or village or boat, of the things that he knew best. And that is a gift that may well be longed for by any man who would be loved by others.

Greatly pleased with him was Eadmund the King, so that he would talk long with him of the ways and laws and peoples beyond the seas; and also of hunting and hawking, which they both loved well. And in this last Lodbrok was the best skilled master I have ever known; and the king would ever have him ride beside him in the field while the court was yet with us. And that pleased not Beorn, though he kept his ill will to himself; and maybe I alone noted it, for I had not spoken of that meeting, of which I have told, even to my father.

Well, too, did my mother and Eadgyth like the courtly ways of the jarl, who was ever ready to tell them of the life in his household, and of the daughter, Osritha, who was its mistress since her mother died but a few years since, and her two elder sisters had been married to chiefs of their own land. Sometimes, too, they would ask him of the dress of the ladies of his land; but at that he would laugh and shake his head, saying that he only knew that they went wondrously clad, but that he could tell naught more of the matter.

"Weapons and war gear I may talk of by the hour," he said, "but women's gear is beyond me. But once my daughter and I wrought together in a matter that was partly of both, and that was when I needed a war flag. And so I drew out the great raven I would have embroidered on it, and they worked it in wondrous colours, and gold and silver round the form of the great bird, so that it seems to shift and flap its wings as the light falls on it and the breeze stirs it, as if there were magic therein."

Now Eadgyth was well skilled in this work, and thereat she must needs say that she would work me a flag for our ship, if the jarl would plan one. So it seems to me now that that evening was very pleasant, for they planned and shaped and began a flag whereon was drawn by the jarl a white falcon like the one he had given to me, and that was my thought, and it pleased him, as I think.

One day we came home early from our hunting, and Lodbrok and I sat in the great hall, while the summer rain swelled in torrents, with thunder and lightning sweeping over the river marshes and out to sea, and we looked at the weapons that hung on the walls.

"Little care I for your long spear and short sword, friend Wulfric," he said; "it seems to me that you must needs shorten the one and lengthen the other before you can be held well armed. And your bow is weak, and you have no axe."

For I had asked him what he thought of our Saxon weapons, else would he not have spoken so plainly. Then he thought for a little while, and said:

"Would you learn to use the axe?"

I answered that nothing would please me better; for of all things, I longed to excel in weapon play of all kinds.

"That is well," he said, "for I owe you my life, and I think that I can teach you that which will keep yours against any foe that you may meet; for you are of the right build for a good axeman, and not too old to learn."

Then we went to the smithy, and there, while the thunder raged outside, he forged me an axe of the Danish pattern.

"Thor's own weather!" he said, laughing; and as he spoke the blue lightning paled the red glow of the forge to a glimmer. "This should be a good axe, and were you not a Christian, I would bid you hold your beginning, as its wielder, of good omen."

Then the thunder crashed, and there was no need for me to answer. And in the end he taught me patiently, until, one day, he said:

"Now do you teach me to use your long spear. I can teach you no more axe play than you know. Some day you will meet an axeman face to face, and will find out what you know. Then, if I have taught you ill, say naught; but if well, then say 'Jarl Lodbrok taught me'."

Now I hold that the test of mastery of a weapon is that one wishes for no other, and I knew that I had learned that much. But I could not tell how much he had taught me, for axe play was new to me, and I had not seen it before.

After I had learned well, as he said, the jarl tempered the axe head, heating and cooling it many times, until it would take an edge that would shear through iron without turning. And he also wrought runes on it, hammering gold wire into clefts that he made.

"What say they?" I asked.

"Thus they read," he answered:

"Life for life. For Wulfric, Elfric's son, Lodbrok the seafarer, made me!"

Thereat I wondered a little, for I knew not yet what he had taught me. Yet when I asked why he wrote those first words, he only laughed, saying, "That you will know some day, as I think."

Now if I were to write all that went on until August came, I should speak of little but how the jarl and I were never apart; for though he was so much older than myself, I grew to be his fast friend. And many a long day did I spend with him in his boat, learning somewhat of his skill in handling her, both on river, and broad, and sea. Very pleasant those days were, and they went all too soon.

No ship came in that could help him homewards, and though the Danish host was in Northumbria, he cared not to go there, for his sons were gone home. And Eadmund would fain see more of him, so that, although I would willingly have taken our ship across the seas, for the first time, to his place, he would not suffer me to do so; for he said that he was not so restless here with us, and that his sons and Osritha, his daughter, had doubtless long thought him dead.

Now in June the king had gone to Framlingham, and in August came back to Thetford. Then he sent for my father, begging him to bring Lodbrok with him, that together they might hunt over the great heaths that stretch for many a mile north and west and south of the town. No better sport is there for hawk and hound than on Brandon and Croxton heaths, and the wilds to which our Saxon Icklings and Lakings have given their names, for they stretch from forest to fen, and there is no game in all England that one may not find there, from red deer to coney, wolf to badger, bustard to snipe, while there are otter and beaver in the streams.

So they would go, for the wish of a king is, as it were, a command, even had not both my father and Lodbrok loved to be with him, whether in hall or field. And I thought that I should surely go also.

However, my father had other plans for me, and they were none other than that I should take the ship round to London with some goods we had, and with some of the new barley, just harvested, which would ever find ready sale in London, seeing that no land grows better for ale brewing than ours of East Anglia.

Now that was the first time I had been trusted to command the ship unaided by my father's presence, though of late he would say that he was owner, not captain, and but a passenger of mine; so, though I was sorry not to go to Thetford, I was more proud of myself than I would show; and maybe I would rather have taken to the sea had there been choice.

I was to go to my godfather, Ingild the merchant, who would, as ever, see to business for me; and then, because the season was late, and wind and weather might keep me long in the river, my father bade me stay with him, if I would, and if need were lay up the ship in Thames for the winter, coming home by the great Roman street that runs through Colchester town to our shores; or if Ingild would keep me, staying in London with him even till spring came again.

"If I must leave the ship," I said, "I shall surely come back to hunt with the jarl and you."

"Nevertheless," answered my father, smiling, "Ingild will have many a brave show for you in town. Wait till you get to London, for the court of Ethelred himself will very likely be there, and there will be much to see. And maybe you will find some Danish ship in the river, and will send her captain here to take the jarl home with him; for we may not hold him as a prisoner with us."

Then Lodbrok added that, in any case, I might find means to send messages to his home by some ship sailing to ports that he named; and that I promised I would do. Thereon he gave me a broad silver ring, rune graven, to show as a token to any of his countrymen whom I might meet, for the ring was known.

"Do not part with it, Wulfric," he said, as I thanked him; "for it may be of use to you some day, if not on this voyage. Jarl Lodbrok is well known on the high seas, and he gives not rings for naught."

Now I would not take the falcon with me, but begged the jarl to use her; and I asked him also to train for himself a greyhound that I had bred, and of which he thought highly.

"Why," said he, "I shall have the best hawk and dog in all Thetford town, and Beorn the falconer will have naught to say to me."

Thereat we laughed, for Beorn's jealousy was a sport to us when we thought of it, which was seldom enough.

So these two went to Thetford, and in the last week of August I sailed for London, with a fair breeze over the quarter, from our haven.

CHAPTER III. WHAT CAME IN A NORTH SEA FOG.

Night saw our ship off Orfordness, and there the breeze failed us, and a thick fog, hiding the land and its lights, crept up from seaward and wrapped us round. But before it came, on Orfordness a fire burnt redly, though what it was, unless it might be some fisher's beacon, we could not tell.

The fog lifted as we drifted past the wide mouth of Stour and Orwell rivers with a little breeze, and the early daylight showed us the smoke of a fire that burnt on the higher land that shuts in the haven's mouth on its southern shores. But even as we saw it, the fog closed round us again and the wind died away, so that we lowered the sail, and the men got out the oars, and slowly, while Kenulf swung the lead line constantly, we crept on among the sand banks down the coast.

Presently the tide turned against us, and Kenulf thought well that we should drop anchor and wait for its turning again. The men gladly laid in the oars, and the anchor rattled out and held. The ship swung to her cable, and then there seemed deep silence after the even roll and creak of the great sweeps in their rowlocks. The fog was very dense, and beyond our stem head I could see nothing.

Then to break the silence came to us, over no great stretch of water as it seemed, the sound of a creaking block, the fall of a yard on deck, and a voice raised in some sharp order. Then I thought I heard an anchor plunge, and there was silence. Very ghostly it seemed to hear these familiar sounds and to see naught, and it was the more so that we might by no means judge from which side of us, or fore or aft, the noises came, for fog will confuse all things, and save a driving snowstorm, I dread nothing more at sea.

Now the men began to speak in whispers, for the silence and weirdness of the fog quieted us all. And, moreover, when the fog lifted we had seen no ship, though there must be one close to us now, and we wondered.

But Kenulf came to me presently with a scared face, and waiting till the men had gone forward to find their food, he asked me if I heard the voice that spoke.

"Aye, surely," I answered. "What of it?"

"Master," he said, "the voice was a Danish voice, as I think. And I mind me of the fires we saw."

"What then?" said I carelessly, though indeed I could see well what fear was in the old man's mind. Yet I would have him put the thing into words, being ready to look the worst in the face at any time.

"The vikings, master," he answered; "surely they were in Orwell mouth and saw us, and have given chase."

"We should have seen them also," I said.

"Not so, master, for the fog hung inland, and if a Dane lies in such a place he has ever men watching the sea--and they will sail two ship's lengths to our one."

"Supposing the ship is a viking, what should we do now?" I asked, for I knew of naught to do but bide where we were.

"Go back with tide and slip past them even now," said Kenulf, though I think he knew that this was hopeless, for if we rowed, the sound of our oars would betray us, and if not we should be on a shoal before long, whence any escape would be impossible.

"Hark!" I said in another moment, and we listened.

There was little noise beyond the lapping of the swift tide against our sides. The men forward were silent, and I had thought that I heard the distant sound of voices and oars.

It came again in the stillness; a measured beat that one could not well mistake, as of a ship's boat leisurely pulled.

Then one of our men began to sing in an undertone, and Kenulf smote his hands together in terror, for the sound would betray us, and he was going forward to stop the song.

"No matter," said I, "they know we are not far off, for I think they must have anchored when they heard us do so, as we heard them. If they seek us they will soon find us."

"They are coming nearer," said Kenulf, and I heard the oars more plainly yet.

Now the thought of calling my men to arms came over me, but I remembered how Lodbrok had told me that resistance to vikings, unless it were successful, meant surely death, but that seldom would the unresisting be harmed, even if the ship were wantonly burnt after plunder, and the crew set adrift in their boat.

Still the oars drew nearer, and I thought of the words that Lodbrok had spoken--how that shipmen would be glad of his presence--and I wished that he were indeed with me, for now I knew what he meant.

Now, too, I knew his gift of the ring to be our safety, and surely he had given it to me for this. So I grew confident, and even longed to see the sharp bow of the boat cleave the mist, if only her crew knew of our friend by name at least. Yet they might be Norse--not Danish.

But the sound of oars crossed our bows and died away again, and then a voice hailed from the ship, as I thought, and there was silence.

Kenulf and I breathed more freely then, and we too went forward and ate and drank, and afterwards spoke of the chance of slipping away when the tide turned, though I was sure that, if the ship were what we thought, she would up anchor and drift with us.

So the hours of flood tide passed, and then the ship began to swing idly as the slack came. Then with the turn of tide came little flaws of wind, and we hoisted the sail, and Kenulf hove the anchor short. Yet we heard no more sounds from the other ship.

Then all in a minute the fog thinned, lifted, and cleared away, and I saw the most beautiful sight my eyes had ever lighted on, and the most terrible.

For, not half a mile from us, lay a great viking snekr {vii}, with the sunlight full on her and flashing from the towering green and gold and crimson dragon's head that formed her stem, and from the gay line of crimson and yellow shields that hung along her rail from end to end of the long curve of her sides. Her mast was lowered, and rested, with the furled blue and white striped sail, on the stanchions and crossbars that upheld it, to leave the deck clear for swing of sword and axe; and over the curving dragon tail of the stern post floated a forked black and golden flag. And wondrously light and graceful were the lines on which she was built, so that beside her our stout cargo ship showed shapeless and heavy, as did our log canoes beside Lodbrok's boat. As soon should our kitchen turnspit dog fly the greyhound that I had given Lodbrok, as such a ship as ours from this swift viking's craft.

But her beauty was not that which drew the eyes of my men. Little they thought of wonder or pleasure in gazing on the ship herself. All her decks were crowded with scarlet-cloaked men, and the sunlight which made the ship so bright flashed also from helm and spear and mail coat from stem to stern. And at that sight every tale of viking cruelty they had heard came into their minds, and they were overcome with terror, so that I thought that several would have cast themselves into the sea, away from the terrible ship, choosing rather death by water than by the sword. But I saw some half dozen whose faces set hard with other thoughts than these, and they turned to seek their weapons from under the fore deck.

Then I spoke to them, for it was time; and I would have neither fear nor defiance shown, for I knew that we should be boarded.

"Yonder ship belongs, as I think, to the people of our guest, Lodbrok the Dane. So it seems to me that they will gladly hear news of him from us, as he is a great man in Denmark. And surely we have deserved well of his folk in every way, and we of East Anglia are at peace with the Danish host. Therefore, let us wait till they board us, and then let no man stir from his place or speak a word, that I may talk with them in peace."

Those words were listened to eagerly, and they wrought on the minds of my poor fellows as I wished. Moreover, to put our one chance of safety into form thus heartened me also, for I will not say that I feared nothing from these vikings, who might know and care naught concerning our sea-borne guest, even were they Danes.

Yet it seemed that none saw my fears, for in a little the men asked if they might take their weapons. And though it seemed hard to me and them alike to bide unarmed, I knew it was safer, and so bade them meet the Danes in all peaceful seeming.

Now we saw a boat lowered from the longship's side, and one by one armed men entered her, and she sank deeply in the water. Ten I counted, and at last one more, who, I supposed, was the leader.

So deep was she that, as she left the ship, I thought how that one sack of our grain, hove into her as she came alongside, would sink her and leave her crew to drown in our sight. But then the ship herself would close on us, and not one of us but would pay for that deed with his life.

So she came slowly over the glassy water of the slack tide, and my men watched her, saying nothing.

Soon she came alongside, and at a sign from me Kenulf threw a line which the bowman caught, and I thought that a word or two of wonder passed among her crew. They dropped to where the curve of our deck was lowest, and instantly the leader leapt on board and all but one of his men followed, axe or drawn sword in hand. As I had bidden them, not one of my men stirred save Kenulf, who made fast the line and stood watching.

The leader was a young man, of about my own age, clad in golden shining bronze scale armour and wearing a silver helm on which were short, black, curving horns; and he bore a double-headed axe, besides the sword at his side. He looked round on us--at the men standing silent, at Kenulf, and at me as I stood on the after deck resting on the tiller, and broke into a great laugh.

"Well," he cried, "are you all dumb, or fools, or wise men; or a little of all three?"

But my men answered nothing, even as I had bidden them, and I thought that my time was not yet come to speak.

"The fog has got into their throats," said a Dane; for with a great lifting of my heart I knew their tongue, and it was Lodbrok's and not Norse.

"Struck speechless with fear more like," said another.

"Ho, men," said the leader, "which is your captain?"

One of our crew pointed to me, and I came to the break of the deck saying:

"I am master of this ship."

And I spoke as a Dane, for my long company with Lodbrok had given me the very turn of his speech.

At that the viking stared at me, and one of his men said:

"When did Danes take to trading on this coast?"

"You are Saxon by all seeming," said the leader, "yet you speak like a Dane. Whence are you, and how learned you our tongue so glibly?"

"We are from Reedham in East Anglia, which is at peace with the Danish host," I said; "and I learnt the Danish speech from one who is my friend, Lodbrok the Dane, whom men call Jarl Lodbrok."

Now at that word the Danes all turned to me, and hardly one but let fall some word of wonder; and the young leader took two great steps towards me, with his face flushing and his eyes lit up with a new look.

Then he stopped, and his face changed, growing white and angry, and his teeth closed tightly as he looked at me. Then he said:

"Now if you are making a tale to save your skins, worse shall it be for you. What know you of Lodbrok?"

I held out my hand, on which the jarl's ring shone white against the sea-browned skin.

"Here is a token he gave me before I sailed, that some friend of his might know it and speak to me," I said.

The viking dropped his axe on the deck and seized my hand, gazing at the ring and the runes graven thereon.

"Lives he yet?" he said, breathless.

"Aye, Halfden Lodbroksson, your father lives and is well in our house," I answered; for now I knew that this was surely the youngest of those three sons of whom the jarl had told me so often.

Now at that word the Danes broke into a great cheer, but Halfden laid his hands on my shoulders and kissed me on both cheeks, while the tears of joy ran down his face.

"Well must Lodbrok my father love you if he has told you so much that you know me by name," he cried; "and well does he trust you since he has given you his ring. Tell me more and ever more of him."

Then sudden as before his mood changed, and he let me go and climbed on the rail with his arm round a backstay, and taking off his helm he lifted up a mighty shout to his ship:

"Found is Jarl Lodbrok, ahoy!"

And with uplifted weapons his men repeated the shout, so that it seemed as though the loved name was heard across the still water, for the men on board the ship cheered in answer.

Now nothing would serve Halfden but that I must go with him on board his own ship, there to tell him all I might; and he laughed gaily, saying that he had looked indeed for a rich booty, but had gained that which was more worth to him.

Then I told Kenulf that we would bide at anchor till we knew what should be done, thinking it likely that Halfden would wish us to pilot him back to Reedham.

"We shall lose our tide," grumbled the old man, who was himself again, now that he knew we had naught to fear.

"That is all we shall lose," I answered, "and what matters it? we have all our time before us."

"I like not the weather," he said shortly.

But I paid no more heed to him, for Halfden spoke to me.

"Let me leave a few men here," he said; "the boat is overladen, and the sea is rising with the breeze;" and then he added with a smile that had much grim meaning in it. "They bide as friends with you, and but for our safety; not to take charge of your ship."

So I bade Kenulf give the three who remained the best cheer that we might, treating them as Lodbrok's men; for the old pilot loved the jarl well, and I knew that for his sake he would do much.

Then in a few more minutes I stood on the deck of Halfden's ship, and word went round quickly of my news, so that I had a good welcome. Yet I liked not the look of the Danish men, after the honest faces of our own crew. It seemed to me that they were hard featured and cruel looking, though towards me were none but friendly looks. Yet I speak of the crew only, for Halfden was like his father in face and speech, and that is saying much for him in both.

They spread a great awning, striped in blue and white like the sail, over the after deck, and there they set food and wine for us, and Halfden and I sat down together. And with us one other, an older man, tall and bushy bearded, with a square, grave face scarred with an old wound. Thormod was his name, and I knew presently that he was Halfden's foster father, and the real captain of the ship while Halfden led the fighting men.

"Food first and talk after," quoth this Thormod, and we fell to.

So when we had finished, and sat with ale horns only before us, Halfden said:

"I have sought tidings of my father from the day when he was lost until this. Now tell me all his story from end to end."

And I did so; though when it came to the throwing of the line to the boat I said naught of my own part in that, there being no need, and moreover that I would not seem to praise myself. And I ended by saying how Lodbrok was even now at court with Eadmund, our king, and high in favour with him and all lesser men.

Many were the questions that the Danes asked me as I spoke, and I answered them plainly, for indeed I was glad to see the look in Halfden's eyes as I spoke to him of his father, I having naught but pleasant things to tell of him, which one may say of few men, perhaps. And by and by I spoke of his having taught me the use of the Danish axe.

"Ho!" said Thormod; "hold your peace for a while, and we will see what sort of pupil he had."

Then he rose up and took his axe, and bade me take Halfden's, which I did, not over willingly maybe, while Halfden stood by, smiling.

"I will not harm you," said Thormod shortly, seeing that I was not over eager. "See here!"

His ale horn stood on the low table where we had been sitting, and now he placed it on the gunwale, going from under the awning. The men who sat along the decks looked up at him and were still.

Then he heaved up the axe with both hands and whirled it, bringing it down with such force that I looked to see both horn and gunwale shorn through. But so skilful was he that he stayed that mighty stroke so that the keen edge of the axe rested on the horn's rim without marking it, and all the men who were watching cried out:

"Skoal {viii} to Thormod the axeman!"

"So," said he; "now stand up and guard a stroke or two; only strike not as yet, for maybe your axe would go too far," and he smiled grimly, as in jest.

But I had learned that same trick from the jarl.

Now Lodbrok had told me that when one has a stronger axeman to deal with than one's self the first thing is to guard well. So he had spent long hours in teaching me guard after guard, until I could not fail in them.

"I am ready," I said, standing out before him.

Thormod feinted once or twice, then he let fly at me, striking with the flat of his axe, as one does when in sport or practice. So I guarded that stroke as the jarl had taught me; and as I did so the men shouted:

"Well done, Saxon!"

"No need to go further," said Thormod, dropping his axe and grasping his wrist with his left hand; for that parry was apt to be hard on the arm of the man who smote and met it. "That is the jarl's own parry, and many an hour must he have spent in teaching you. It is in my mind that he holds that he owes you his life."

And from that time Thormod looked at me in a new way, as I felt.

Halfden was well pleased, and shouted:

"Nay, Thormod; your turn to guard now; let Wulfric smite at you!"

"No, by Thor, that will I not," he said; "he who taught to guard has doubtless taught to strike, and I would not have my head broken, even in play!"

Now he sat down, and I said, mindful of Lodbrok's words:

"It seems to me that I have been well taught by the jarl."

"Aye, truly," said Thormod; "he has taught you more than you think."

Halfden would have me keep his axe, but I told him of that one which the jarl had made for me, and straightway he sent the boat for it, and when it came read the runes thereon.

"Now this says that you are right, Thormod! Here has my father written 'Life for life'--tell us how that was!"

So I said that it was my good fortune to cast him the line that saved his boat, and that was all. But they made as much of that as did Lodbrok himself. And when the men came from our ship, they brought that tale from our men also; so that they made me most welcome, and I was almost fain to get away from them.

But we sat and talked while the tide went by and turned, and still we lay at anchor until the stars came out and the night wind began to sing in the rigging of the great ship.

Now I had thought that surely Halfden would have wished to sail back to Reedham at once, there to seek his father; but I knew not yet the power which draws a true viking ever onward to the west, and when I said that we would, if he chose, sail back with him on the next tide, he only laughed, saying:

"Why so? My father is well and in good case. Wherefore we will end our cruise well if we can, and so put in for him on our way home at the season's end."

"What would you do, then?" I asked, wondering.

"Raid somewhere," he answered carelessly. "We will not go home without some booty, or there will be grumbling among the wives; but for your sake we will go south yet, for you are bound for London, as I think."

I said that it was so, and that I would at once go back to Reedham when my business was done, there to prepare for his coming.

"That is well; and we will sail to Thames mouth together. And you shall sail in my ship to tell me more of my father, and because I think we shall be good friends, so that I would rather have you come and raid a town or two with me than part with you. But as you have your ship to mind, we will meet again at Reedham, and I will winter there with you, and we will hunt together, and so take you home with us in the spring."

Now this seemed good to me, and pleased me well enough, as I told him. Where Halfden and his crew went, south of Thames mouth, was no concern of mine--nor, indeed, of any other man in East Anglia in those days. That was the business of Ethelred, our overlord, if he cared to mind the doings of one ship. Most of all it was the concern of the sheriff in whose district a landing was made.

So messages were sent to old Kenulf, and glad was he to know that we should not have to give up our passage to London, and maybe still more to feel safe in this powerful company from any other such meetings. And before the tide served us, Halfden had said that he also would come to London, so that our ship should lead the way up the river.

When we weighed anchor Thormod must needs, therefore, reef and double reef his sail, else our ship had been hull down astern before many hours had passed, so swift was the longship.

Now I have said that old Kenulf had misliked the look of the weather, and now Thormod seemed uneasy. Yet the breeze came fresh from the southeast; and though it had shifted a good deal, I, for my part, thought little ill of that, for it held in that quarter till we were fairly among the sands of the Thames mouth at nightfall, and Kenulf lit lanterns by which we might follow him. No man knew the Thames-mouth channels better than our pilot, Kenulf the sea crafty, as we called him.

Then it fell dead calm, quite suddenly, and we drifted, with the sail flapping against the mast idly, for half an hour or so. Then fell on us, without warning, such a fierce gale as I had never before seen, blowing from north and west, with rain and bright lightning, and it raised in five minutes a sea that broke over us again and again as Thormod brought the ship head to wind.

Then I lost sight of Kenulf's lights, and as I clung to the rail, my mind was torn with longing to be back in my own ship in this danger, though I knew that Kenulf needed me not, and that, had I been there, it would but have been to obey him with the rest of our crew; yet I think that any man who loves his ship will know what I felt.

And of the fury and darkness of that night I will say little. This is what comes into my mind of all that happened--aye, and at night, when the wind roars round the house, I see it all again, waking in my dreams as I call to Kenulf. One flash of lightning showed me my ship dismasted and helpless, drifting broadside on to a sand over which the waves broke white and angry, and when the next flash came--she was gone!

Then I cried out on my folly in leaving her, and out of the blackness beside me as I clung to the gunwale, straining my eyes against the spray, Halfden's voice came, crying, as he gripped my arm:

"By Odin--it is well that I kept you here!"

And Thormod from the helm shouted to his men to stand by the sheet, and the helm went down, and the ship drove through the seas that broke clean over her as he saw the danger in time to stand away from it, heading her as free as he dared.

Naught of this I heeded, for I could think but of the stout sailor men with whom I had been brought up, and of whom I knew only too surely that I should see them not again. And for them I tried to pray, for it was all that I could do, and it seemed so little--yet who knows what help may come therefrom?

Now the longship fought alone with the storm. Hard was the fight, but I, who was willing to die with my own people who had gone before my eyes, cared nothing for whether we won through the gale or not. But Thormod called to me, bidding me pilot them as best I might, and so I was taken a little from my thoughts. Yet can I take no praise to myself that, when the gale slackened, we were safe and beyond the dangers of the shoals.

We were far down channel when morning broke, and on either bow were white cliffs, plain to be seen in the clear light that came after the short fury of the gale was spent. Never had I thought that a ship could sail so wondrously as this of Halfden's, and yet I took no pleasure therein, because of all that I had lost. And it seemed to me that now I knew from my own chance why it was that Lodbrok could sing no song to us at that feasting, when we came home to Reedham; for surely my case was even as his.

So I thought, leaning on the gunwale and staring ever at the white cliffs of England on our starboard; and there Halfden found me, and came, putting his hand on my shoulder very kindly.

"Now if you have lost friends and ship by the common chances of the sea," he said, "surely you have found both anew. You shall turn viking and go on this raid with us. Glad shall we be of your axe play and seamanship."

I turned to him and put my hand into his.

"I will go with you, Halfden," I said, for it seemed at that time that I had naught else left for me to do.

And ever since I was a child, listening to the songs of the gleemen, had I thought that some day I, too, would make a name for myself on the seas, as my forefathers had made theirs, so that my deeds should be sung also. Yet that longing had cooled of late, as the flying people from Mercia had found their way now and then to us with tales of Danish cruelties.

"That is well said," he answered, pleased enough. "Where shall we go?"

Then I had yet thought enough left me to say that against our Saxon kin I would not lift axe. And so came to me the first knowledge that what wiser men than I thought was true--that the old seven kingdoms were but names, and that the Saxon and Anglian men of England were truly but one, and should strive for that oneness, thinking no more of bygone strifes for headship.

"Why, that is fair enough, so you have no grudge to pay off," he said; "but I will help you to settle any, if you have them."

"I have no grudge against any man," I answered, truly enough.

"Then if we raid on English shores, you shall keep ship, as someone must; and so all will be satisfied," he answered; "but we will go first to the Frankish shores, for it is all one to me."

So that pleased me as well as anything would at that time; whereupon we went to Thormod, and he was very willing that I should take part and share with them. And as to my loss, he bade me take heart, for a seaman has ever risks such as these to run; and, as it seemed, this ship of ours had ever been lucky. Which was true enough, as my father had told me by the fireside many a time.

After this we headed over to the Frankish shore, and there I had my first fight. For we raided a town there, and the citizens stood up to us well. I fought in silence, while my comrades yelled to Thor and Odin as they smote, for those against whom we fought were Christian men, and to fight against them by the side of heathen went against me. Yet the lust of battle took hold on me, and fight I must. But I will tell no more of that business, save that Halfden and Thormod praised me, saying that I had done well. And after that the crew asked that I should lead the men amidships, for their head man had been slain, and Halfden was on the fore deck, and Thormod aft. So my boyish dreams were like to come to pass, for I was thus a viking indeed. Yet I had little pride therein.

Thence we raided ever eastward and westward along that shore, and I grew to love Halfden well, strange as were his wild ways to me. For he was in all things most generous; nor was he cruel, but would hold back the more savage of the men when he could--though, indeed, that was seldom--when they were mad with fighting.

So the weeks went on, until at last one day as we left a haven where we had bided for a while, taking ransom from the town that we might leave it in peace, we spied a sail far off coming from eastward, and Thormod would have us bear up for her, to see what she might be. But instead of flying, as a trading ship would, the strange vessel waited for us, lowering her sail and clearing for action, so that there was doubt if she was not Norse. Now between Dane and Northman is little love lost, though at times they have joined hands, loosely as one might say, or as if cat and dog should go together to raid a rabbit warren.

"If she be Norse," said Halfden, and his eyes shone, "we will fight her, and that will be a fight worth telling of by the crew that is left when we have done!"

But she turned out to be Danish, and a boat came from her to us. She was on the same errand as ourselves, and, moreover, belonged to one Rorik, who was a friend of Lodbrok's, so that again I must go through all the story of his perils.

Now if Halfden's men had seemed rough and ill-favoured to me when first I saw them, time and comradeship had worn off the feeling, but it came back to me as I looked on these men, and most of all on this Rorik; so that for a little I hated myself for being in their company to make war on peaceful Christian folk, though, indeed, I could well excuse myself, seeing what straits had thrown me thus among them to follow the ways of my own forefathers, Hengist's men.

These newcomers held long counsel with Halfden and Thormod, and the end of it was that they agreed to sail in company, making a raid on the English coast, and first of all on the South Saxon shores, behind the island that men call Wight. And that was the thing that I had feared most of all, so that as I sat silent and listened, taking no part, as I might, in the planning, my heart seemed like to break for the hardness of it.

Yet I set my face, saying naught, so that presently Rorik looked over at me and laughed, crying in a kind of idle jest:

"Silent is our friend here, though he looks mighty grim, so that I doubt not he will be glad to swing that big axe of his ashore."

Now I was in ill company, and must fit my speech to theirs, answering truly enough:

"It seems to me that some of us here were a little downcast when we found that you were no Northmen, for we looked for a fight."

Whereon they all laughed, and Rorik said that maybe his men had the same longing, but that we would make a great raid between us. And so the matter passed, and he and his men went back to their ship, and we headed over to the English shore together.

CHAPTER IV. THE SONG OF THE BOSHAM BELL.

There is a wondrous joy in the heart of a man who sees his own land again after long days at sea, but none of that joy might be mine as the long lines of the South Downs showed blue through the haze of the late September day. Only the promise of Lodbrok's son, that on English shores I should not fight, helped me a little, else should I have been fain to end it all, axe to axe with Rorik on the narrow deck just now, or in some other way less manful, that would never have come into my mind but for the sore grief that I was in. And these thoughts are not good to look back upon, and, moreover, I should have fully trusted my friend Halfden Lodbroksson.

Hardest of all was it to me when I knew where our landing was to be made; for if Glastonbury is the most holy place in Wessex, so should Bosham, the place of Wilfrith the Saint, be held in reverence by every South Saxon; because there, unmindful of his wrongs {ix}, he was content to labour with the wild heathen folk, teaching them, both in body and soul, the first lessons of our holy faith.

Well knew I the stories of those places which I saw as the ships crept up the haven, for Humbert our bishop had told me them many a time when as a child I sat on his knee and listened, wondering. There was Selsea with its pile of buildings--Wilfrith's own--there the little cliff over which the starving heathen had cast themselves in their despair, and there, at last, the village, clustering round the little monastery that Dicul, the Irish monk, had founded, and where Wilfrith had first taught. And now, maybe, I must see the roofs that had sheltered him, and heard the first praises of his converts, burnt before my eyes, and that while I myself was siding with the destroyers.

Then at last I took Halfden aside and told him my trouble, putting him in mind of the promise he had made me.

"Aye," said he, "I knew what made you so silent, and I have but waited for you to speak. Ill should I have thought of you had you not done so. But I have this plan for you. You shall go ashore with the first, and speak to the Saxons to give us ransom, if they have aught, or if any man is foolish enough to bide in the place when we come. Then, if you will, you shall leave us and make your way homeward, there to give messages to my father and yours, and to look for my coming to Reedham shortly. There will I winter with you, and we will sail to Jutland in the spring."

Then he looked long at me, and put his arm round my shoulder.

"Truly I shall miss you, Wulfric, my brother, yet it is but for a short time."

Now I knew not how to thank him, for this plan was all that I could wish. And he would have no delay, but gave me good Saxon arms and helm, and a chain-mail byrnie {x} of the best, such as Saxon or Dane alike would wear, for he had many such, gathered from the different lands he had raided with his father and brothers.

"Any man, seeing you in Danish arms and helm," he said, "might well mistrust you. So you must needs take these, for you have far to go."

Then, too, he pressed on me a heavy leathern bag, for he said truly enough that I should need gold withal to buy a horse. And this I took willingly, saying that it should be as a loan till he came to Reedham.

"Nay," quoth he, "this is your share of booty; we surely gained enough on yonder shores to bring you this much."

Then I was silent, for I was ashamed of those gains, and I did not look into the bag, but bestowed it inside my mail shirt, for I would not offend him. Then, when I was armed and ready, he gave me many messages for his father, and thanks to mine. A ring, too, he gave me for a sure token of his friendship to me; and so as the ship crept, under oars only, up Bosham haven, we talked of the hunting we would have together, when the leaves were fallen in our forests; and that was pleasant to look forward to.

Now began frightened men to run to and fro on the haven's banks, and then suddenly came the ringing of a bell from the low tower of the church, and the Danes began to look to their arms, stringing bows, and bringing up the pebble ballast for sling stones, in case the landing should be resisted.

But when we came to a little wharf, the other ship being perhaps a mile astern of us, there was no man. Only a small fishing vessel lay alongside, and that we cast adrift, taking its place.

Then Halfden and I and twenty men went quickly ashore and marched up among the trees of the village street. There was no man in sight, but the bell was still ringing.

A great fear for the holy men shut up in the little monastery came over me now, and I asked Halfden to let me warn them, for I knew that he was like his father and would not deny me in this.

"Go and do so if you can," he said, "and so farewell till we meet at Reedham. We shall bide here till Rorik's men join us, and you will have time."

So he took my hand and I went quickly thereafter, the men calling after me "Farewell, axeman!" heartily enough, knowing of my going to Reedham, and caring nothing for the monks, seeing that there would be no fighting.

Now, guided by the bell, I went on quickly, seeing no man. The houses stood open and deserted, and all along the road were scattered goods, showing that the people had fled in haste, so that they had soon cast aside the heavier things they had thought to save.

Soon I came to the gate of the little stone-walled monastery, over which rose the tower whence the bell yet rang; for the church seemed to make one side of the courtyard into which the gate would lead. A farm cart stood outside; but the gates were closed, and when I looked, I saw that the pin of the wheel was broken, so that the cart could go no further. And that made me fear that more than the monks were penned inside those four walls.

I knocked loudly on the gate, and for a while was no answer, though I thought the ringing of the bell grew more hurried. Then I beat on the gate with my axe, crying:

"Open, in the name of Eadmund the King."

And I used his name because, though a Dane might well call in subtlety on the name of Ethelred, none but a Saxon who knew how well loved was the under-king of East Anglia would think of naming him. And I was right, for at his name the little square wicket in the midst of the gate opened, and through its bars an old monk looked out, and at once I cried to him:

"Let me in, Father, for the Danes are at my heels."

He muttered a prayer in a voice that trembled, and let me in, holding the gate fast, and closing and barring it after me.

And all the courtyard was full of terrified men, women, and children, while among them stood the half-dozen monks of the place, pale and silent, listening to the clang of the bell overhead.

When they saw me some of the women shrieked and clung to children or husbands, scared at my arms. But one of the monks, a tall man on whose breast was a golden cross, came quickly to me, asking: "Is the sheriff at hand with the levy?"

I told him hastily how that the only hope for these helpless ones was in flight to the woods, urging him until he understood me. Gathering his monks around him, and rousing the people, he led them to the rearward gate that opened toward the forest land, calling at the same time to his swineherd, who was there, and bidding him take them by the forest tracks to Chichester.

Then he bade his monks go also; but they lingered, asking to be allowed to stay with him, and also what should become of the holy vessels if the heathen laid profane hands on them.

"Obey, as your vows bid you," said the prior; "I and this warrior will care for the holy things."

So they went, weeping, and were lost in the woods; for there was little cleared land round the village, and the trees came close to the monastery walls.

Now we two, the monk and I, stood at the open gate for a moment and listened. We could hear nothing of the Danes as yet.

Then we closed and barred that gate; and all this while the bell had tolled unceasingly, calling as it were for help that came not.

"Now do you go and call the sacristan from the bell," the prior said, "and bid him lead you to the chancel, where I shall be."

I went to the tower door, unhesitating, for this man seemed to have a wondrous power of command, so that I obeyed him without question, even as had the villagers. And even as I went there came the sound of many rushing feet up the street, and yells from Danish throats, while axe blows began to rain on the gate by which I had entered.

Then the prior bade me hold the gate when he heard that, and he spoke quietly and in no terror, turning and calling to the man in the tower himself; while I stood opposite the gate, looking to see it fall with every blow. Yet it was not so weakly made as that, and moreover I remembered that it was crossed with iron bands in squares so that the axes could not bite it fairly.

Now the bell stopped and the Danes howled the louder. A torch flew over the wall and fell at my feet blazing, and I hurled it back, and the Danes laughed at one whom it struck. Then came the two monks from the tower and ran into the church, while I watched the trembling of the sorely-tried gate, and had it fallen I should surely have smitten the first Dane who entered, even had Halfden himself been foremost, for in the four walls of that holy place I was trapped, and knew that I must fight at last. And now it seemed to me that I was to fight for our faith and our land; and for those sacred things, if I might do naught in dying, I would give my life gladly.

"Come," said the prior's voice, and he was smiling though his face was pale, while behind him the sacristan bore an oaken chest, iron bound, on his shoulders.

He drew me across the courtyard, but I ever looked back at the gate, thinking it would fall; and now they were at the other gate, and blows rained on it. Yet the monk smiled again and went on without faltering, though our way was towards it.

Then we turned under an arch into a second court, and the din was less plain as we did so. There was the well of the monastery, and without a word the sacristan hove the heavy chest from his shoulders into its black depths, and the splash and bubble of its falling came up to us.

"That is safe," said the prior; "now for ourselves."

He hooked the oaken bucket to its rope and let it down to its full length in the well, and at once the sacristan swung himself on it, slid down, and was gone. Then the rope swayed to one side, and stayed there, shaking gently in a minute or so.

The prior drew it up, and maybe fifteen feet from the top, there was a bundle tied--a rope ladder on which were iron hooks. These he fastened to the edge of the oaken platform that covered the well mouth, and let the other end fall down the well. Then he bade me go down to the sacristan.

That was easy to me, and I went, yet I feared for him who stood listening to the splintering of the nearer gate, for it would soon fall surely. I saw the sacristan's face glimmer white before me from a hollow in the well shaft, as I set my foot on the last rung of the ladder, and I held out my hand to him. Then in a moment I was beside him in a little chamber built in the walling of the well; and after me came the prior.

He jerked the ladder from side to side till the hooks above lost their hold and it fell, so that he drew it in. We were but a few feet above the water, and the well rope hung down into the blackness before us, but I was sure that no man could see the little doorway of the chamber from above, for the trapdoor in the well cover was small, and light there was hardly any.

"Now all is safe," said the prior; "and we may be careless again."

"They will burn the monastery," I said. "One torch has been thrown already."

He smiled a little, as I thought, for my eyes were growing used to the dim light.

"They may burn some things, but roof and benches are soon made afresh. There is oaken timber in plenty in Andredsweald, and ready hands to hew it. Our stone walls they cannot hurt."

Those were all the words we spoke of the matter at that time, for there came a great shouting. One of the gates had fallen at last, and the Danes were in the place.

"Father," said the sacristan, "surely they will find this place?"

The prior laughed a short laugh.

"That is a thought born of your fears, Brother," he answered; and I who had had the same fear was rebuked also, for indeed that I should go down the well had never come into my mind, even in our need of shelter, so why should the Danes think of it?

Then we were silent, listening to the feet and voices overhead. The Danes found the belfry presently, and began to toll the bell unskillfully while the men below jeered at those who handled the ropes. Then the bell clashed twice strangely, and the prior laughed outright.

"The clumsy churls have overthrown her," he said, "now I hope that one has had his head broken thereby."

I marvelled that he could jest thus, though maybe, after the strain and terror of the danger we had so far escaped, it was but natural that his mind should so rebound as it were.

Very soon after this the Danes came clattering into the little court where the well was, and straightway came to its mouth, casting stones down it, as no idle man can help doing. The sacristan crept to the furthest corner of our little den and sat there trembling, while I and the other monk listened with set teeth to the words that came down to us.

Nor will I say that I was not somewhat frightened also, for it seemed to me that the voices were unknown to me. They were Rorik's men, therefore, and not our crew--who likely enough would but have jeered at me had they found me hiding thus.

"Halfden's men have drunk all the ale in the place, and that was not much," said one man; "let us try the water, for the dust of these old storehouses is in my throat."

Then he began to draw up the bucket, and it splashed over us as it went past our doorway.

"There is naught worth taking in this place," growled another man. "Maybe they have hove their hoards down the well!"

Now at that the sacristan gave a stifled groan of terror, and I clutched my axe, ready for need.

"All right, go down and see!" answered one or two, but more in jest than earnest.

Then one dropped a great stone in, and waited to hear it bubble from the bottom, that he might judge the depth. Now no bubbles came, or so soon that they were lost in the splash, and the prior took some of the crumbling mortar from the cell walls, and cast it in after a few moments. And that was a brave and crafty thing to do, for it wrought well.

"Hear the bubble," said the Dane; "the well must be many a fathom deep--how long it seemed before they came up!"

So they drank their fill, saying that it was useless to go down therefore, and anyhow there would be naught but a few silver vessels.

"I have seen the same before," said one; "and moreover no man has luck with those things from a church."

No man gainsaid him, so they kicked the bucket down the well and went away.

Now I breathed freely again, and was about to whisper to the prior that his thought of making what would pass for bubbling was good; but more Danes came. And they were men of Halfden's ship; so we must wait and listen, and this time I thought that surely we were to be found. For the men began to play with one another as they drank from the bucket; pushing each other's heads therein, and the helm of one fell off and fled past us to the bottom; and some words passed pretty roughly. And after they had done quarrelling they crowded over the trapdoor, as one might know by the darkening of the shaft. Then one saw the helm, for it was of leather, iron bound, and had fallen rim upward, so that it floated. Now one was going to swarm down the rope to get it, but as he swung the rope to him, the bucket swayed in the water under the helm, and he saw that it did so. Whereon he wound both up, and they too went away.

"That was a lucky chance!" I whispered.

"No chance at all, my son; that was surely done by the same Hand that sent you here to warn us," answered the prior. And I think that he was right.

Now came a whiff of biting smoke down the well shaft, borne by some breath of wind that eddied into it. The Danes had fired the place!

"Father," I whispered, pulling the prior forward, for he had gone into the little cell to give thanks for this last deliverance.

He looked very grave as he saw the blue haze across the doorway, hiding the moss and a tiny fern that grew on the shaft walls over against us.

"This is what I feared, though I must needs make light of it," he said.

"It cannot harm us here," I answered.

"All round this court on three sides the buildings are of wood; sheds and storehouses they are and of no account, but if one falls across the well mouth--what then?"

"Then we are like to be stifled," said I; for even now the smoke grew thicker, even so far down as we were. And when I looked out and up there was naught but smoke across the well mouth, and with that, sparks.

"Pent up and stifled both," said the quavering voice of the sacristan from behind us. "How may we get out of this place till men come and raise the ruin that will cover us? And who knows we are here but ourselves?"

"Forgive me for bringing you to this pass," said the prior gravely, after a little silence.

The smoke grew even denser, and we must needs cough, while the tears ran from my eyes, for the stinging oak smoke seemed trapped when once it was driven down the well.

"I have known men escape from worse than this," I said, thinking of Lodbrok, and turning over many wild plans in my mind.

"I had forgotten this danger of wooden walls," said the prior to himself, as it were. "Doubtless when this well chamber was made it was without the inclosure."

Now it seemed to me that this could not be borne much longer, and that soon the walls he dreaded would fall. So as one might as well die in one way as another, I thought I would climb to the well's mouth and see if there were any chance of safety for these two monks. Yet I had no thought of aught but dying with them, if need were, though as for myself I had but to walk across the courtyard and go away. The Danes would but think I lingered yet for the sake of plunder.

"If we may not stand this smoke, neither can the Danes," I said. "I am going to see."

So I set down my axe and sword and leapt sailor-wise at the rope--which the men had dropped again when they had taken the helm from the bucket--catching it easily and swarming up to the trapdoor. I only raised myself to the height of my eyes and looked out.

I could see nothing. The dense smoke eddied and circled round the court, and the Danes were gone, leaving us in a ring of fire on three sides. The wooden buildings were blazing higher every moment, and the heat seemed to scorch my head and hands till I could scarcely bear it. But as the wind drove aside the smoke I could see that the way to the rear gate, the last we had barred, was clear. So I slid down and hung opposite the chamber. The monks looked out at me with white faces.

"It may be done," I said. "Come quickly! it is the only chance."

The prior gave me the rope-ladder end without a word, not needing to be asked for it; nor did I wait to say more, for at that moment a roof fell in with a great crash, and a red glare filled the well as the flames shot up, and the sparks and bits of burning timber came down the shaft and hissed into the water below me.

I clomb up, fixed the ladder, and called down to the prior to bring my arms with him. There was a burning beam not three feet from the well mouth, part of the fallen roof that had slipped sideways from it. The flames that shot up from the building were so hot that I could barely abide them, and I shaded my face with both my hands, crying again to the monks to come quickly.

In a few seconds came the sacristan, white and trembling--I had to help him out of the well mouth. The prior was close to him; he was calm, and even smiled at me as he saw me clutch my arms eagerly.

"To the rear gate," I said, turning and kicking the ladder into the well, and thinking how cool the splash was compared with this furnace of heat. "Kilt up your frocks and go swiftly, but run not," for in that smoke, save their long garments betrayed them, a man might be armed or unarmed for all that one could see.

So, walking quickly, we came to the court entrance, and even as we stood under its archway the building nearest the well fell with a crash and rumble, covering the well mouth with a pile of blazing timber. The smoke and flame seemed to wrap us round, while the burning timber flew, and the Danes from the great courtyard yelled with evil delight; but before that cloud had cleared away we three were outside the monastery gate, and were safe.

"Just in time," I said.

But "Deo gratias" said the monks in a breath.

"Now run," said I, and into the nearest spur of woodland we went, and stayed not till we were beyond reach of the yells of the destroyers, who, as it seemed, had not even seen us.

When we were sure that we were not pursued, the prior took my arm and pressed it.

"Thanks to you, my son, our people are safe, and we have come out of yon furnace unscathed. May you find help in time of need as near and ready. Now when I read the story of the Three Children, I think I shall know all that they suffered, for we have been in like case."

And I could make no answer, for it seemed to me that I had forgotten that I was a Christian of late. And that was true.

Now the prior bade the sacristan hasten to Chichester and tell all this to the sheriff, and he left us, while we went on alone. Presently I asked who made the chamber in the well, for the silence weighed on me, and my thoughts were not so lightsome.

"Doubtless by Wilfrith's men," he said, "and for the same turn it has served us. For in his days there were many heathen round him, and flight or hiding might be the last resort at any time."

Then I wondered, saying that I deemed that surely it was a greater thing to be a martyr and to die, than to save life.

"Not always so," he answered, and then he told me of the ways of holy men of old time. "We may by no means save life by denying our faith, but we are bidden to flee into another place when persecuted. We may not choose the place of our death, nor yet the time."

So he showed me at last what it was to be truly a martyr, fearing not, nor yet seeking death.

"Of a truth," he ended, "the Lord may need my death by the hand of the heathen at some time, and when the time comes I shall know it, and will die gladly. But while He gives me the power to save life blamelessly, I know that He needs me on earth yet, though I am of little worth."

So we were silent after that, ever going on through the woods. At last he laughed a little, and looked sidewise at me.

"We two are alone," he said, "therefore I do not mind saying that I have been fairly afraid--how felt you?"

"I would I might never be so frightened again," I answered, for truly I had made myself so at one with this brave man that I had forgotten that there was little fear for myself, as I have said, unless that it had been Rorik's crew who had found us, for only a few of them knew me.

We came now to a place where the trees thinned away on the brow of a hill, and I could see the broad waters of the haven through their trunks. We had reached the crest of that little cliff over which Wilfrith's heathen had cast themselves in the great famine from which he saved them.

"Let us see the last of Bosham," the prior said sadly. So we crept through the fern and long grass, and lying down looked out over haven and village. Even if a prying Dane looked our way he would hardly see us thus hidden, or if he did would take us but for villagers and care not.

Now I saw that the tide was on the turn, and that Halfden's ship--my own ship, as I have ever thought her--had hauled out, and her boats waited for the last of the crew at the wharf side. But Rorik's ship was there still, and her men were busy rigging a crane of spars as though they would lower some heavy thing on board her. Nor could I guess what that might be.

Then I looked at the village, which was burning here and there, and at the monastery. They had not fired the church, and the Danes clustered round the tower doorway, busied with something, and I could see them well, for the smoke from the burning buildings blew away from us.

Now I asked the prior what heavy things worth carrying away might be in the monastery.

"Naught," he said; "since they have drunk all the ale that was in the cask or two we had.

"But," he added, "there is the great bell, it is the only weighty thing else."

Then I knew what was toward, and said:

"I fear, Father, that your bell is going to be taken to become metal for mail shirts, and axe heads, and arrowheads, and helms."

"Holy St. Wilfrith!" cried the monk, in great grief; "would that we could have saved it. There is no such bell in all England, and if they take it, many a sailor will miss its call through fog and driving mist, and many a shepherd on yonder downs will wait for its ringing, and be the wearier for lack thereof."

"Never have I seen bell too large for one man to handle," I said; "this must be a wondrous bell!"

So it was, he told me, and while we watched the busy Danes, he began to sing to me in low tones the song of Bosham bell which his people would sing by the fireside.

"Hard by the haven,
Wilfrith the holy
Bade men a bell tower
Sturdily build.
Thence should a bell sound
Over the wide seas,
Homeward to hail
The hardy shipmen.
Thus was the bell wrought
By skilful workmen:
Into the fierce fire,
When it was founded,
Helm and harness
The warriors hove;
Willingly women,
The jewel wearers,
Golden and silver gauds
Gave for the melting;
And a great anchor
The seamen added.
Thus was a wealth
Of wondrous metal.
When all was molten
More grew its marvel!
Cast in a chalice,
Cuthred the priest."

"Aye, Father," said I, "that is a wondrous bell."

He nodded, and went on, with his eyes fixed on the monastery.

"Thus as the bell swings
Soothly it speaketh:
Churchward it calleth
With voice of the chalice,
Speaking to shipmen

With voice that is sea born.
Homeward the husband
Hailing with voices
Fresh from the fireside,
Where flashed the gold gifts--
Clashing the war call,
Clear with its warrior voice."

"That was the voice of the bell that sounded as we came," I thought; and even as I would have said it, the bell of Bosham spoke again, and the prior stopped with an exclamation, and pointed.

Out of the gateway came four Danes, bearing the bell between them, and as they crossed the threshold, one stumbled, and the bell clanged as they dropped it on the courtyard pavement. The tears ran down the holy man's face as he saw this mishap to his beloved bell, which was kept bright as when it was first founded, by the loving hands of his people.

Now the Danes put it on that farm cart I had seen, and which they had mended, and took the bell down to the wharf, and we watched them sling it to the crane they had rigged, and place it amidships on deck. Then they all went hastily on board, and put out into the haven, down which Halfden's ship was already a mile distant, and dancing on the quick waves of wind against tide where the waters broadened into a wide lake.

Now when the ship was fairly under way, the prior rose up from beside me, and lifting his hand, cursed ship and crew with so great and bitter a curse that I trembled and looked to see the ship founder at once, so terrible were his words.

Yet the ship held on her course, and the words seemed vain and wasted, though I know not so certainly that they were so. For this is what I saw when the ship met the waves of that wider stretch of water that Halfden had now crossed.

She pitched sharply, and there was a bright gleam of sunlight from the great bell's polished sides, and then another--and the ship listed over to starboard and a wave curled in foam over her gunwale. Then she righted again quickly, and as though relieved of some weight, yet when a heavier, crested roller came on her she rose to it hardly at all, and it broke on board her. And at that she sank like a stone, and I could hear the yell that her men gave come down the wind to me.

Then all the water was dotted with men for a little, and the bright red and white of her sail floated on the waves for a minute, and then all that was left of her were the masthead and yard--and on them a few men. The rest were gone, for they were in their mail, and might not swim. Only a few yet clung to floating oars and the like.

"Little have these heathen gained from Bosham," said the prior, and his eyes flashed with triumph. "Wilfrith the holy has punished their ill doing."

So, too, it seemed to me, and I thought to myself that the weight of that awesome curse had indeed fallen on the robbers.

Yet I know that, as I watched the ship in her trouble, in my own mind I had been going over what was amiss, as any seaman will, without thought of powers above. And I thought that the sharp pitching of the vessel had cast the great bell from amidships, where I had seen the Danes place it unsecured, against the frail gunwale, first to one side, and then, with greater force yet, against the other; so that it burst open gunwale and planking below, and already she was filling when the wave came and ended all. For these swift viking ships are built to take no heavy cargo, and planks and timbers are but bound together by roots and withies; so that as one stands on the deck one may feel it give and spring to the blow of a wave, and the ship is all the swifter. But though the outer planking is closely riveted together with good iron, that could not withstand the crashing weight of so great a bell when it was thus flung against it.

However that may have been--and thus I surely think it was--Bosham bell passed not into the power of the heathen, but destroyed them; and it lies at the bottom of the deepest reach of the haven whence the depth and swiftness of the tide will hardly let men bring it again. So I suppose that, profaned by heathen hands, it may no longer call men from across the water and woodland to the church of God.

Soon came the boats from Halfden's ship and picked up those who yet clung to what they might of the wreck, and then ship and Danes passed from Bosham haven, leaving the silent tower and burning village to mark where they had been.

Then the prior sighed, and turning away, said:

"Let us go to Chichester and find shelter. Night comes soon, and rest."

Sadly enough we went, though not for long: for when we came into the roadway from the forest land, the prior put his heavy thoughts aside, and spoke cheerfully to me.

"What is done is done; and but for you, my son, things would have been worse. And their greed for the bell has made them spare the church itself. Surely you must have fallen from the clouds to help us--borne hither from the East Anglian land whose tongue bewrays you."

"I marvel that you trusted me," I said.

"I trusted your face, my son, and when one is in a hard case the first help is ever the best. Yet now I would fain know somewhat of my good comrade."

Now I think that to any but this monk, with his friendly smile and way of quiet authority, I should have been ashamed to own my part with the Danes. But a few hours of companionship in danger knit closer than many a long day of idleness together, and he seemed to me as a near friend. Moreover, he had trusted me without question; so I told him all my tale and he listened patiently.

"Now I am glad that I cursed not your friend's ship--for I forgot her," he said, smiling.

At that I was glad, for how he would hold my being with the heathen I somewhat doubted, and I told him so.

"Why, my son, I know not that you had much choice. And as for fighting against outlanders--let me heft that axe of yours."

He took it, and it fell into his hands in a way that told me that he, too, had been a stark fighting man at some time.

"Take it away, my son, take it away!" he cried, thrusting it back on me; "I am not the man to blame you. And I know that much good has come to us from your being with them. And from your talk about martyrs I know that you have done no honour to their gods."

I said truly that the question had never come into my mind. For, save as oath or war cry, the names of Thor and Odin were not heard. They sacrificed on going to sea, and on return; and meanwhile cared naught, so far as I knew, for none had questioned my faith.

He said it was well, and so talking we went on. And he said that, as friend of his, none would question me, so that I should find all I needed for my journey in the town. And when we came there--meeting the sheriff's ill-armed levy on the way--we went to the house of a great thane, and there were well and kindly received.

Yet once and again as I slept I dreamed and woke with the cry of Rorik's men in my ears, and before me the bell seemed to flash again as it crashed through the ship's side. And once I woke thinking that the smell of burning was round me, and felt, half awake, for the stone walls of the well chamber. But at last I slept soundly and peacefully.

CHAPTER V. HOW WULFRIC, LODBROK, AND BEORN

HUNTED.

When morning came it was great wonder and joy to me to wake and find myself in England and free, for indeed I had begun to think of my comradeship with the Danes as a sort of thralldom that I knew not how to break. And now I longed to make my way back to Reedham as soon as I might, for I had been many weeks away, though I have said little of all that befell in that time beyond what was needful. One thing saved me from grief that might have been, and that was the knowledge that Ingild, the merchant, had not been told to look for my coming, and that none at home would wonder if I were long away, because of that plan of wintering our ship in the Thames. And I knew that not one of my poor crew could have lived to take news of the wreck.

That I must take back myself; and though I could not fairly be blamed for loss of ship and crew, the thought of having to break the tidings to those who would mourn for their lost ones was very hard to me. But it must be done, and there was an end.

Now came to me, as I thought of these things, my friend the Prior of Bosham, and he sat down beside me and asked how he could further my plans. He himself must go to Selsea, there to see the bishop and tell him all, not forgetting my part, as he said.

I told him that I only needed a horse, and that then I should ride to London, where I had friends: and he asked me if I had money wherewith to buy one, for he had none, else would he gladly do so for me. And that reminded me of the bag which Halfden gave me, and I opened it.

It was full of treasure--gold ornaments, and chains wherein were set precious stones, and some gold coins and silver, and these were the least value of all. But little pleasure had I in them, for I knew too well how they came, and a thought came to me.

"Father," I said, "this comes from ruined towns on yonder shore--take it and build up Bosham again. Aye, take it."

"Why, my son, here is treasure enough to build three villages like ours," he said quietly; "for timber houses cost but labour in this forest land, and there was naught else worth taking in the place."

"But your people are the poorer," I said; "I pray you take it for their need, and for a new bell, moreover."

And so I urged him till he took the greatest gold chain, saying that in honesty he could no more, for that would surely make Bosham wish for more burnings if they turned out as this.

"Keep the rest and buy a new ship," he said, "and forget not that always and every day your name will be remembered at the time of mass in Bosham; and that may help you in days to come."

So he blessed me and departed, and I think that both of us were light at heart, save for parting. And I have never seen the good prior again, though his face and words I cannot forget.

Soon came one to lead me to the presence of the thane and his wife, and from them I found kindness more than I could have looked for. We broke our fast together, and then the lady asked me if I would accept horse and gear for my journey from her, for she had heard from the prior that I had been shipwrecked, who had also told her all the story of our doings at Bosham.

Thanking her, I told her that though shipwrecked, I was yet rich, having a store of wealth with me; for I thought that it was in the minds of these kind people that I was in need.

"Be not proud," she said "bide with us for a while, and then take horse and go. We hold that you have deserved well of all of us."

But I told her of my mother and sister at home, and how I would fain be back with them, so she pitied me the more, saying that now for their sakes she would hasten me.

"Aye, lad," said the thane, "we have sons of our own at court, and the lady would that someone would pack them home on a good horse-- so she must not be denied."

Thus they persuaded me, and when I tried to thank them, the thane laughed, and the lady said:

"Thank me not but in one way, and that is by asking your mother to help homeward some other lady's son when need is. And that is all I would wish."

And the end of it was that I rode away from Chichester town on a good horse and with change of clothes in saddlebags, and those worthy people stood at the gate to give me good speed.

Yet that is not the end, for there are one or two who have ridden in like sort from Reedham since that day, and have borne home the like message; so that I know not where the ending of that kindly deed may be.

Past the old Chichester walls I went, and out on the long line of the Roman street that should take me to London. And as I went I sang, for the green beechen woods were wondrous fair to me after the long weeks of changing sea, and it seemed to me that all was going well, so that I put away for the time the grievous thought of my shipwreck, the one hard thing that I must face when I came home again.

There is nothing to tell of that ride; for well armed, and rich, and with a good horse, what should there be? And at last I came to London town, and rode straightway to the great house of my godfather, Ingild, that stood by London Bridge. Very strange it was to me to look out over the Pool as I crossed, and not to see our good ship in her wonted place, for this was the first time I had come to London except in her.

At the door of the courtyard, round which Ingild had his great storehouses and sheds for goods, I drew rein, and two serving men whom I knew well came out. Yet they knew me not, staring at my arms and waiting for my commands.

So I spoke to them by name, and they started and then laughed, saying that they must be forgiven for not knowing me in my arms, for surely I had changed greatly since two years ago, when I was last with them.

It was the same when Ingild himself came out, ample robed and portly; for he gazed long at my helmed face, and then cried:

"Why, here is a marvel! Wulfric, my son, you have grown from boy to man since last we met; and you come in helm and mail shirt and on horseback, instead of in blue homespun and fur cap, with an oar blister on either hand. How is this?"

Then he kissed me on both cheeks and led me in, running on thus till a good meal was before me, with a horn of his mighty ale; and then he let me be in peace for a little while.

Afterwards, as we sat alone together, I told him all that had befallen, even as I would have told my father, for in my mind Ingild, my godfather, came next to him and our king, and I loved him well.

Sorely he grieved for loss of ship and goods and men, but he told me that we were not the only seamen who had been hurt by that sudden gale. Nor did he blame me at all, knowing that Kenulf was in truth the commander of our ship. Rather was he glad that it had chanced that I had left her and so was safe.

Then when I told him of my turning viking thereafter, he laughed grimly, with a glitter of his eye, saying that he would surely have done the same at my age--aye, and any young man in all England likewise, were he worth aught.

So when I had told him all about my journey, I showed him the bag that Halfden gave me, and well he knew the value of the treasure therein.

"Why, son Wulfric," he cried; "here is wealth enough to buy a new ship withal, as times go!"

And I would have him keep it, not being willing to take so great a sum about with me, and that he did willingly, only asking me to let him use it, if chance should be, on my behalf, and making me keep the silver money for my own use going homeward.

"Yet I will keep you awhile, for Egfrid, the Thane's son of Hoxne, who is here at court, goes home for Yuletide, and so you can ride with him. And I think it will be well that we should send word to your father of how things have been faring with you, for so will you have naught of misfortune to tell when you come home."

I thought this wise counsel and kindly, for my people would best tell those wives and children of their loss, and so things would be easier for me. And Ingild sent writing to my father by the hand of some chapman travelling to the great fair at Norwich; and with his letter went one from me also, with messages to Lodbrok--for Eadmund had made me learn to write.

So after that I abode with Ingild, going to the court of Ethelred the King with him, and seeing the great feasts which the merchant guilds made for the king while he was in London; with many other wondrous sights, so that the time went quickly, and the more so that this Egfrid was ever with me. I had known him when we were little lads together at our own king's court, but he had left to go to that of our great overlord, Ethelred, so that I had not seen him for long years. And one may sail up our Waveney river to Hoxne, where his father's house is, from ours at Reedham, though it is a long way.

Now in the week before Yuletide we would start homewards, so with many gifts and words of good speed, Ingild set us forth; and we rode well armed and attended as the sons of great thanes should. So the way was light to us in the clear December weather, and if it were long the journey was very pleasant, for Egfrid and I grew to be great friends, and there is nothing more joyous than to be riding ever homeward through wood and over wild, with one whose ways fit with one's own, in the days of youth, when cares are none and shadows fall not yet across the path.

When we came to Colchester town we heard that Eadmund was yet at Thetford, and when we asked more we learnt that Lodbrok was there also with my father. So, because Hoxne was but twenty miles or thereby from Thetford, both Egfrid and I were glad that our way was yet together, and we would go there first of all.

One other thing we heard in Colchester, for we waited there for two days, resting our horses. There was a wandering gleeman who came into the marketplace on the hill top, and we stood and listened to him.

And first he sang of how Danes had come and burnt Harwich town. But the people told him to sing less stale news than that, for Harwich was close at hand. Now it was Halfden's ship which had done that, and the fires we saw before the fog came had been the beacons lit because of his landing.

Then he made a great outcry until he had many folk to listen, and they paid him well before he would sing. Whereon, forsooth, my ears tingled, for he sang of the burning of Bosham. And when he came to the stealing of the bell, his tale was, that it, being hallowed, would by no means bear that heathen hands should touch it, so that when it came to the deepest pool in the haven it turned red hot, and so, burning a great hole through the Danish ship, sank to the bottom, and the Danes were all drowned. Whereat the people marvelled, and the gleeman fared well.

I suppose that the flashing of the great bell that I had seen gave rise to this tale, and that is how men tell it to this day. And I care not to gainsay them, for it is close enough to the truth, and few know that I had so nearly a hand in the matter.

So we rode to Thetford, and how we were received there is no need for me to tell, for I came back as it were from the dead, and Egfrid after years of absence. And there with Eadmund were my father and mother, and Eadgyth, and Lodbrok, and Egfrid's folk also, with many more friends to greet us, and the king would have us keep Yuletide with him.

It had been in my mind that Halfden would have come to Reedham, and at first I looked for him, but he had not been heard of, so that now we knew that we should not see him before springtime came, for he must needs be wintering somewhere westward. Yet now Lodbrok was at ease with us, seeing the end of his stay, and being in high favour with our king, so that he was seldom away from his side in all the hunting that went on.

That liked not Beorn, the falconer, and though he would be friendly, to all seeming, with the Dane, it seemed to me that his first jealousy had grown deeper and taken more hold of him, though it might only be in a chance look or word that he showed it as days went on.

But one night my father and I rode in together from our hunting, and there was no one with us. We had been at Thetford for a month now, since I came home, and there was a talk that the king would go to the court of Ethelred at Winchester shortly, taking my father with him for his counsellor, and so we spoke of that for a while, and how I must order things at Reedham while he was away.

"Lodbrok, our friend, will go back with you," he said. "Now, have you noted any envy at the favour in which he is held by Eadmund?"

"Aye, Father," I answered, "from Beorn, the falconer."

"So you, too, have had your eyes open," went on my father; "now I mistrust that man, for he hates Lodbrok."

"That is saying more than I had thought."

"You have been away, and there is more than you know at the bottom of the matter. The king offered Lodbrok lands if he would bide with us and be his man, and these he refused, gently enough, saying that he had broad lands of his own, and that he would not turn Christian, as the king wished, for the sake of gain. He would only leave the worship of his own gods for better reasons. Now Beorn covets those lands, and has hoped to gain them. Nor does he yet know that Lodbrok will not take them."

Then I began to see that this matter was deeper than I had thought, and told my father of the first meeting of Lodbrok and Beorn. But I said that the falconer had seemed very friendly of late.

"Aye, too friendly," said my father; "it is but a little while since he held aloof from him, and now he is ever close to Lodbrok in field and forest. You know how an arrow may seem to glance from a tree, or how a spear thrust may go wide when the boar is at bay, and men press round him, or an ill blow may fall when none may know it but the striker."

"Surely no man would be so base!" I cried.

"Such things have been and may be again. Long have I known Beorn, and I would not have him for enemy. His ways are not open."

Then I said that if Beorn was ever near Lodbrok, I would be nearer, and so we left the matter.

There was one other thing, which was more pleasant, which we spoke about at that time. And it was about the betrothal of my sister Eadgyth. For it had come to pass that Egfrid, my friend, had sought her hand, and the match pleased us all. So before the king and my father went to Winchester there was high feasting, and those two were pledged one to the other. Then was a new house to be built for them at Hoxne, where the wedding itself should take place.

"Maybe Halfden will be here by that time," said Lodbrok to me. "I wish, friend Wulfric, that honest Egfrid had not been so forward, or that you had another fair sister."

Now though that saying pleased me, I could not wish for the wild viking as husband to our gentle Eadgyth, though I loved him well as my own friend. So I said that I thought Halfden's ship was his only love.

"Maybe," answered the jarl; "but one may never know, and I think it would be well for English folk and Danish to be knit together more closely."

But when I asked him why this should be so, he only smiled, and talked of friendliness between the two peoples, which seemed a little matter to me at that time.

Now when the time came, my father having gone, we two, Lodbrok and I, went back to Reedham, while my mother and Eadgyth stayed yet at Thetford for the sake of Egfrid's new house building, for he would have it built to suit her who should rule it.

Strange and grievous it was to me to see our shipyard empty, and sad to have to tell the story of the good ship's loss to those whose mourning was not yet over. Yet they were sailors' wives and children, and to them death at sea was honourable, as is to a warrior's wife that her husband should fall in a ring of foes with all his wounds in front. And they blamed me not; but rather rejoiced that I was safe returned.

Now without thought of any foe, or near or far, Lodbrok and I hunted and hawked over our manors, finding good sport, and in a little while I forgot all about Beorn, for I had seen him go in the king's train as they rode out to Winchester.

Out of that carelessness of mine came trouble, the end of which is hard to see, and heavily, if there is blame to me, have I paid for it. And I think that I should have better remembered my father's words, though I had no thought but that danger was far away for the time.

We hunted one day alone together, and had ridden far across our nearer lands to find fresh ground, so that we were in the wide forest country that stretches towards Norwich, on the south of the Yare. Maybe we were five miles from the old castle at Caistor. There we beat the woods for roebuck, having greyhounds and hawks with us, but no attendants, as it happened, and for a time we found nothing, not being far from the road that leads to the great city from the south.

Then we came to a thicket where the deer were likely to harbour, and we went, one on either side of it, so that we could not see one another, and little by little separated. Then I started a roe, and after it went my hounds, and I with them, winding my horn to call Lodbrok to me, for they went away from him.

My hounds took the roe, after a long chase, and I was at work upon it, when that white hound that I had given to Lodbrok came leaping towards me, and taking no heed of the other hounds, or of the dead deer, fawned upon me, marking my green coat with bloodstains from its paws.

I was angry, and rated the hound, and it fled away swiftly as it came, only to return, whining and running to and fro as though to draw me after it. Then I thought that Lodbrok had also slain a deer, starting one from the same thicket, which was likely enough, and that this dog, being but young, would have me come and see it. All the while the hound kept going and coming, being very uneasy, and I rated it again.

Then it came across me that I had not heard Lodbrok's horn, and that surely the dog would not so soon have left his quarry. And at that I hasted and hung the deer on a branch, and, mounting my horse, rode after the hound, which at once ran straight before me, going to where I thought Lodbrok would be.

When I came round the spur of wood that had first parted us I was frightened, for Lodbrok's horse ran there loose, snorting as if in terror of somewhat that I could not see, and I caught him and rode on.

When I could see a furlong before me, into a little hollow of the land that is there, before me was a man, dressed like myself in green, and he was dragging the body of another man towards a thicket; and as I saw this my horses started from a pool of blood in which lay a broken arrow shaft.

At that I shouted and spurred swiftly towards those two--letting the other horse go free--with I know not what wild thoughts in my mind.

And when I came near I knew that the living man was Beorn, and that the dead was Lodbrok my friend.

Then I took my horn and wound it loud and long, charging down upon that traitor with drawn sword, for I had left my hunting spear with the slain deer. He dropped his burden, and drew his sword also, turning on me. And I saw that the blade was red.

Then I made no more delay, but leapt from my horse and fell upon him to avenge myself for the death of him whom I loved. Would that I had had the axe whose use he who lay there had taught me so well, for then the matter would have been ended at one blow. But now we were evenly matched, and without a word we knew that this fight must be to the death, and our swords crossed, and blow and parry came quickly.

Then I heard shouts, and the noise of men running behind me, and Beorn cried:

"Stay us not, I avenge me of my friend," whereon I ground my teeth and pressed on him yet more fiercely, wounding him a little in the shoulder; and he cried out for help--for the men who came were close on us--and the well-cast noose of a rope fell over my shoulders, and I was jerked away from him well-nigh choked.

Two men ran past me and took Beorn, throwing up his sword with their quarterstaves, and it seemed to me that it was done over gently. Then they bound us both and set us on the ground face to face.

"Now here be fine doings!" said a man, who seemed to be the leader of the six or seven who had ended the fight.

"Aye, 'tis murder," said another, looking from Beorn to me and then to Beorn again; "but which is murderer and which true man?"

Now all these men were strangers to me, but I knew one thing about them from their dress. They were the men of mighty Earl Ulfkytel himself, and seemed to be foresters, and honest men enough by their faces.

"I am Wulfric, son of Elfric of Reedham," I said. "The slain man is Lodbrok, the Danish jarl, and this man slew him."

"He lies!" cried Beorn. "It was he who slew him, and I would revenge myself on him, for this Lodbrok was my friend."

Now I held my peace, keeping back my wrath as well as I might, for I began to see that Beorn had some deep plot on hand, thus to behave as if innocent.

"Why, so he cried out as we came," said one of the men when he heard Beorn's words.

"Maybe both had a hand in it," the leader said, and so they talked for a little.

Then came two of my own serfs, who had followed me to see the sport, I suppose, at a distance, as idle men will sometimes, when hunting is on hand, and with them came Lodbrok's dog, the same that had brought me. And when the dog saw Beorn he flew at him and would have mauled him sorely, but that the earl's men beat him off with their staves; and one took the leash that hung from my saddle bow and tied him to a tree, where he sat growling and making as though he would again fly at the falconer.

"Whose dog is this?" asked the leader.

"His," answered the serfs, pointing to Lodbrok.

"Dogs might tell strange tales could they talk," said the earl's man; "I misdoubt both these men. Let us take them to the earl for judgment."

"Where is the earl?" I asked.

"At Caistor," answered the man shortly, and I was glad that he was so near, for the matter would be quickly settled and I could go free.

"Unbind me, and I will go where you will," I said, but at that Beorn cried out.

"Loose him not, loose him not, I pray you!"

"Tie their hands behind them and let us be gone," was the answer, and they did so, loosing my feet, and setting us on my horse and Lodbrok's. And some of the men stayed behind with my serfs to make a litter on which to carry my friend's body, and follow us to Caistor. So as I went I cried quickly to those two men of mine that they should go in all haste to Reedham and tell what had befallen me to our steward, who would know what to do.

"Reedham is too far for a rescue to reach you in time," said the leader of the earl's men grimly; "think not of it."

"I meant not that, but to have witnesses to speak for me."

"That is fair," said the man, after a little thought, "we will not hinder their going."

Then they led us away, and presently reached that place where I had seen the broken arrow, and one picked it up, saying that here was surely the place where the deed was done, and that the arrow would maybe prove somewhat. And I think that here Beorn had shot the jarl, for all around those other marks on the grass were the hoofmarks of the rearing and frightened horse, and there were many places where an archer might lie unseen in the thickets, after following us all day maybe, as Beorn must have done, thus to find fitting chance for his plan when we two were far apart. And surely, had it not been for the dog, I think the fate of Lodbrok would have been unknown for many a long day, for but for him Beorn would have hidden his deed and ridden off before I had known aught.

Now, as the man handled the broken arrow, walking beside me, I saw it plainly, and knew it for one of my own, and one of four that I had lost at Thetford, though I did not know how.

At that I seemed to see all the plot, and my heart sank within me, for this Beorn was most crafty, and had planned well to throw doubt on me if things by ill chance fell out as they had, and so I rode in silence wondering what help should come, and whence. And I thought of Halfden, and what he should think when he heard the tale that was likely to be told him, and even as I thought this there was a rushing of light wings, and Lodbrok's gray falcon--which I had cast from my wrist as I fell on Beorn--came back to me, and perched on my saddle, for my hands were bound behind me. She had become unhooded in some way.

Then Beorn cried out to the men to take the falcon, for it was his, and that he would not have her lost; and that angered me so that I cried out on him, giving him the lie, and he turned pale as if I were free and could smite him. Whereon the men bade us roughly to hold our peace, and the leader whistled to the falcon and held out his hand to take her. But she struck at him and soared away, and I watched her go towards Reedham, and was glad she did so with a sort of dull gladness.

For I would have no man pass through a time of thoughts such as mine were as they took me to Caistor--rage and grief and fear of shame all at once, and one chasing the other through my mind till I knew not where I was, and would start as from a troubled dream when one spoke, and then go back to the same again as will a sick man. But by the time we reached Caistor I had, as it seemed to me, thought every thought that might be possible, and one thing only was plain and clear. I would ask for judgment by Eadmund the King, and if that might not be, then for trial by battle, which the earl would surely grant. And yet I hoped that Beorn's plot was not so crafty but that it would fail in some way.

So they put me in a strong cell in the old castle, leading Beorn to another, and there left me. The darkness came, and they brought me food, so I ate and drank, being very hungry and weary; and that done, my thoughts passed from me, for I slept heavily, worn out both in body and mind.

CHAPTER VI. THE JUSTICE OF EARL ULFKYTEL.

An armed jailor woke me with daylight, bringing me food again, and at first I was dazed, not knowing where I was, so heavy was my sleep. Yet I knew that I woke to somewhat ill.

"Where am I?" I asked.

"Under Caistor walls, surely," he said; and I remembered all.

The man looked friendly enough, so that I spoke again to him, asking if the great earl was here, and he said that he was.

"What do men say?" I asked then.

"That the matter is like to puzzle the earl himself, so that it is hard for a plain man to unriddle. But I think that half Reedham are here to see justice done you; even if it is naught but Earl Ulfkytel's justice!" And he grinned.

I knew why. For Ulfkytel was ever a just man, though severe, and his justice was a word with us, though in a strange way enough. For if a case was too hard for him to decide in his own mind, he would study to find some way in which the truth might make itself known, as it were. Nor did he hold much with trial by hot water, or heated ploughshares, and the like; finding new ways of his own contriving, which often brought the truth plainly to light, but which no other man would have thought of. So that if a man, in doing or planning some ill to another, was himself hurt, we would laugh and say: "That is like the earl's justice".

So though Ulfkytel was no friend of my father's, having, indeed, some old quarrel about rights of manor or the like, I thought nothing of that, save that he would the sooner send me to the king for trial.

The jailor told me that I should be tried at noonday, and went away, and so I waited patiently as I might until then, keeping thought quiet as best I could by looking forward and turning over what I could say, which seemed to be nothing but the plain truth.

At last the weary waiting ended, and they took me into the great hall of the castle, and there on the high seat sat the earl, a thin, broad-shouldered man, with a long gray beard and gray eyes, that glittered bright and restless under shaggy eyebrows. Beorn, too, was brought in at the same time, and we were set opposite to one another, to right and left of the earl, below the high place, closely watched by the armed guards, bound also, though not tightly, and only as to our hands.

And there on a trestle table before us lay the body of Jarl Lodbrok, my friend, in whose side was my broken arrow. All the lower end of the hall was filled with the people, and I saw my two serfs there, and many Reedham folk.

Then the court was set, and with the earl were many men whom I knew by sight, honest thanes and franklins enough, and of that I was glad.

First of all one read, in the ears of all, that of which we two who were there bound were accused, giving the names of those half-dozen men who had found us fighting and had brought us for judgment.

Then said Earl Ulfkytel:

"Here is a matter that is not easy in itself, and I will not hide this, that the father of this Wulfric and I are unfriendly, and that Beorn has been a friend of mine, though no close one. Therefore is more need that I must be very careful that justice is not swayed by my knowledge and thoughts of the accused. So I put that away from me; I know naught of these two men but what I hear from witnesses."

Some people at the end of the hall sought to praise the even handedness of that saying loudly, but the earl frowned and shouted:

"Silence!--shall a judge be praised for doing right?"

"Then," said he, growing quiet again, and speaking plainly and slowly that all might hear, "this is how the matter stands. Here are two men found fighting over the body of a third who is known, as men say, to have been friendly with both. No man saw the beginning of the business. Now we will hear what was seen, but first let this Wulfric speak for himself;" and he turned his bright eyes on me.

Now I told him all the truth from the time when I parted from Lodbrok until the men came.

Then the earl asked me:

"Why thought you that Beorn slew the man?"

"Because there was no other man near, and because I know that he bore ill will towards him for the favour shown him by the king."

"So," said Ulfkytel; "now let Beorn speak."

Then that evil man, being very crafty, did not deny my words, but said that he had found the body lying with my arrow in its side. And though he knew not why I had done the deed, for the sake of his friendship with my father and myself he would have hidden it, and even as he did so I came, falling on him. Whereon he grew wroth, and fought.

"It seems to me," said the earl, "that a word from you should rather have made Wulfric help you and thank you; not fall on you. Now let the witnesses say their say."

So they stood forward, telling naught but the truth, as honest men. And they seemed to think much of Beorn's having cried out for revenge. Also they showed the arrow, which fitted exactly to the headed end which was in Lodbrok's side, and was the same as two that were in my quiver with others. Now if Beorn shot that arrow he must have made away with both bow and quiver, for he had none when we were taken.

Then one of the other thanes said that the dead man had another wound, and that in the throat, and it was so, Whereon the jailer was bidden to bring our swords, and it was found that both were stained, for I had wounded Beorn a little, as I have said.

"Is Wulfric wounded then?" asked Ulfkytel.

And I was not.

"Whence then is Beorn's sword stained?" he asked.

Then came my two thralls, and spoke to the truth of my story, as did one of the men who had stayed with them, for he too had seen the deer hanging where I had left it, nearly a mile away from where the fight was. And my men added that they had seen me riding to that place, and had followed the call of my horn.

"Murderers do not call thus for help," said the earl. "What more?"

"Only that Lodbrok's dog flew at Beorn;" they said.

Then my steward and others told the story of my saving of Lodbrok, and there were one or two who knew how closely Beorn seemed to have sought his friendship. There was no more then to be said.

All the while Ulfkytel had watched my face and Beorn's, and now he said:

"The arrow condemns Wulfric, but any man might pick up a good arrow that he had lost. And the sword condemns Beorn, but there are many ways in which it might be bloodstained in that affair. Now, were these two robbers, I would hold that they were fighting over division of booty, but they are honourable men. Wherefore I will have one more witness who knows not how to lie. Fetch the dog."

So they brought Lodbrok's dog, which the serfs had with them, and they loosed it. It ran to his body first and cried over it, pulling his coat with its paws and licking his face, so that it was pitiful to see it, and there were women present who wept thereat.

Then it left him and came to me, thrusting its nose into my hand, but I would not notice it, for justice's sake; but when it saw Beorn, it bristled up, flying at his throat so that he fell under it, and the guards had much ado in getting it off, and one was bitten.

"The dog condemns Beorn," said the earl, "but Wulfric bred it."

After that he would have no more witness; but now should each of us lay hand on the body and swear that he was guiltless.

They brought a book of the Holy Gospels and put it on Lodbrok's breast, and first I laid my hand thereon, looking into the quiet face of the man whose life I had saved, and sware truly.

Then must Beorn confess or swear falsely, and I looked at him and his cheek was pale. But he, too, laid hand on the dread book in its awful place and sware that he was innocent--and naught happened.

For I looked, as I think many looked, to see the blood start from the wound that he had given the jarl, but it was not so. There was no sign. Then crossed my mind the first doubt that I had had that Beorn was guilty. Yet I knew he lied in some things, and the doubt passed away quickly.

Then Ulfkytel pushed away the table from before him so that it fell over.

"Take these men away," he said. "I have heard and seen enough. I will think!"

They led us away to the cells again, and I wondered how all this would end. In an hour they brought us back, and set us in our places again. The earl had more to say, as it seemed.

"Will you two pay the weregild {xi} between you?"

"No, Lord Earl," I said; "that were to confess guilt, which would be a lie."

Then Beorn cried:

"I pray you, Wulfric, let us pay and have done!"

But I turned from him in loathing.

"Ho, Master Falconer," said Ulfkytel, "the man is an outlander! To whom will you pay it? To Wulfric who saved his life?"

Now at that Beorn was dumb, seeing that the earl had trapped him very nearly, and he grew ashy pale, and the great earl scowled at him.

"Let me have trial by battle," I said quietly, thinking that it would be surely granted.

There was as good reason to suspect me as Beorn, as I saw.

"Silence, Wulfric!" said the earl. "That is for me to say."

"Let the king judge, I pray you, Lord Earl," I went on, for he spoke in no angry tone, nor looked at me.

However, that angered him, for, indeed, it was hard to say whether king or earl was more powerful in East Anglia. Maybe Eadmund's power came by love, and that of the earl by the strong hand. But the earl was most loyal.

"What!" he said in a great voice, "am I not earl? And shall the king be troubled with common manslayers while I sit in his seat of justice? Go to! I am judge, and will answer to the king for what I do."

So I was silent, waiting for what should come next.

But he forgot me in a minute, and seemed to be thinking.

At last he said:

"One of these men is guilty, but I know not which."

And so he summed up all that he had heard, and as he did so it seemed, even to me, that proofs of guilt were evenly balanced, so that once again I half thought that Beorn might be wronged in the accusation, as I was.

"So," he ended, "friend has slain friend, and friends have fought, and there is no question of a third man in the matter."

He looked round on the honest faces with him, and saw that they were puzzled and had naught to say, and went on:

"Wherefore, seeing that these men have had trial by battle already, which was stopped, and that the slain man was a foreigner from over seas and has no friends to speak concerning him, I have a mind to put the judgment into the hands of the greatest Judge of all. As Lodbrok the Dane came by sea, these men shall be judged upon the sea by Him who is over all. And surely the innocent shall escape, and the guilty shall be punished in such sort that he shall wish that I had been wise enough to see his guilt plainly and to hang him for treachery to his friend and the king's, or else to put him into ward until some good bishop asks for pardon for ill doing."

And with that half promise he looked sharply at us to see if any sign would come from the murderer.

But I had naught to say, nor did I seem to care just now what befell me, while Beorn was doubtless fearful lest the wrath of Eadmund the King should prevail in the end were he to be imprisoned only. So he answered not, and the earl frowned heavily.

Now one of the franklins there, who knew me well enough, said:

"Wulfric, be not ashamed to confess it, if for once you shot ill--if your arrow went by chance to Lodbrok's heart, I pray you, say so. It may well be forgiven."

Very grateful was I for that kind word, but I would not plead falsely, nor, indeed, would it have told aught of the other wound that had been made. So I shook my head, thanking the man, and saying that it was not so.

Now I think that the earl had planned this in order to make one of us speak at the last, and for a moment I thought that Beorn was about to speak, but he forbore. Then Ulfkytel sighed heavily and turned away, speaking in a low voice to the thanes with him, and they seemed to agree with his words.

At length he turned to us and spoke gravely:

"It is, as I said, too hard for me. The Lord shall judge. Even as Lodbrok came shall you two go, at the mercy of wind and wave and of Him who rules them. You shall be put into Lodbrok's boat this night, and set adrift to take what may come. Only this I lay upon you, that the innocent man shall not harm the guilty. As for himself, he need, as I think, have no fear, for the guilty man is a coward and nidring {xii}. Nor, as it seems to me, if all may be believed, can the guiltless say for certain that the other did it."

Then was a murmur of assent to this strange manner of justice of Earl Ulfkytel's, and I, who feared not the sea, was glad; but Beorn would have fallen on the ground, but for his guards, and almost had he confessed, as I think.

"Eat and drink well," said Ulfkytel, "for maybe it is long before you see food again."

"Where shall you set them afloat?" asked a thane.

"Am I a fool to let men know that?" asked the earl sharply. "There would be a rescue for a certainty. You shall know by and by in private."

The guards took us away, and unbinding our hands, set plenty of good food and drink before us. And for my part I did well, for now that I knew the worst my spirits rose, and I had some hopes of escape, for there was every sign of fair weather for long enough. And viking ways had taught me to go fasting for two days, if need be, given a good meal to start upon.

But Beorn ate little and drank much, while the guards bade him take example from me, but he would not; and after a while sat silent in a corner and ghastly to look upon, for no one cared to meddle with him.

As soon as it grew dusk they bade us eat again, for in half an hour we should set forth to the coast. At that Beorn started up and cried out, wringing his hands and groaning, though he said no word, except that I should surely slay him in the boat.

Then I spoke to him for the first time since he had claimed the falcon, and said that from me, at least, he was safe. And I spoke roughly, so that I think he believed me, so plain did I make it that I thought one who was surely cowardly in word and deed was not worth harming, and he ceased his outcry.

At last we were set on horseback, and with two score or more mounted spearmen round us, we rode quickly out of Caistor town. A few men shouted and ran after us, but the guards spurred their horses, and it was of no use for them to try and follow. And the night was dark and foggy, though not cold for the time of year.

I feared lest we were going to Reedham, for there my folk would certainly rise in arms to rescue me, and that would have made things hard for them; but we went on southward, riding very fast, until after many long miles we came to the little hill of the other Burgh that stands where Waveney parts in two streams, one eastward to the sea, and the other northward to join the Yare mouth.

The moon had risen by the time we came there, and I could see a large fishing boat at the staithe, and, alas! alongside of her a smaller boat that I knew so well--that in which Lodbrok had come, and in which I had passed so many pleasant hours with him. Then the thought crossed my mind that what he had taught me of her was like to be my safety now; but my mind was dazed by all the strange things that came into it, and I tried not to think. Only I wondered if Ulfkytel had got the boat without a struggle with our people.

The earl was there with a few more thanes and many more guards, and they waited by the waterside.

One man started from beside the earl as we came, and rode swiftly towards us. It was Egfrid, my brother-in-law to be--if this did not bring all that fair plan to naught.

He cried out to the men to stay, and they, knowing who he was, did so, and made no trouble about his coming to my side. There he reined up his horse, and laid his hand on my shoulder.

"Alas for this meeting, my brother!" he cried. "What can I do? Men came and told me of rumour that was flying about concerning this business, and I have ridden hard to get to Reedham, but I met the earl, who told me all. And I have prayed him to let the king judge, but he will not, saying that his mind is fixed on higher judgment--and you know what he is."

Then I said:

"So that you hold me not guilty, my brother, I mind not so much; for if I must die you will take my place, and my father will not be without a son.

"I think you guilty!" he cried; "how could that be? Shame on me were I to dream thereof--and on any man of all who know you who would deem you could be so."

"Have you heard all?"

"Aye, for the earl has told me very patiently, being kind, for all his strange ways. At last I told him that his wish for justice blinded his common sense. And at that, instead of being wrath, he smiled at me as on a child, and said, 'What know you of justice?'; so that I was as one who would beat down a stone wall with his fists---helpless. He is not to be moved. What can I do?" and almost did he weep for my hard case.

"Let things go their own way, my brother," I said gently. "I do not fear the sea, nor this man here--Beorn. Do you go to Reedham and tend Lodbrok's hawk for me, and send word to my father, that he may come home, and to the king, so that Lodbrok may have honourable burial."

He promised me those things, and then went back upon the slaying of Lodbrok, asking how it came about.

I told him what I thought thereof; and Beorn, who must needs listen to all this, ground his teeth and cursed under his breath, for there seemed to have come some desperate fury on him in place of his cold despair of an hour since.

And when Egfrid had heard all, he raised his hand and swore that not one stone of Beorn's house should be unblackened by fire by this time tomorrow night, and as he said it he turned to Beorn, shaking and white with wrath.

"Let that be," I answered him quickly; "no good, but much harm may come therefrom. Wait but six months, and then maybe I shall be back."

Now while we had thus spoken together, Ulfkytel had dismounted and was holding some converse with a man whose figure I could not well make out, even had I cared to try, in the dark shadow of horses and riders which stayed the moonlight from them. But at this time the stranger came towards us, and I saw that it was the priest who served the Church of St. Peter, hard by where we stood. He came to Beorn first, and spoke to him in a low voice, earnestly; but Beorn paid no sort of heed to him, but turned his head away, cursing yet. So after a few more words, the priest came to me.

"Wulfric," he said, "sad am I to see you thus. But justice is justice, and must be done."

"Aye, Father," I answered, "and right will prevail."

"Maybe we shall see it do so," he answered shortly, not seeming willing to hold much converse with me; "but it is likely that you go to your death on the wide sea. Many a man have I shriven at the point of death--and Ulfkytel the Earl will not hold me back from your side--an you will."

Thereat I was very glad, for I knew that the risks before me were very great, and I said as much.

Then he took the bridle of my horse and began to lead me on one side, and the guards hindered him until Ulfkytel shouted to them to draw aside in such wise as to prevent my riding off, though, bound as I was, it had been of little use to try to do so. Then they let the priest take me out of earshot, and maybe posted themselves in some way round us, though I heeded them not.

So then in that strange way I, bound and on horseback, confessed; and weeping over me at last, with all his coldness forgotten, the priest of Burgh shrived me and blessed me, bidding me keep a good heart; for, if not in this world, then at the last would all be made right, and I should have honour.

After that he went once more to Beorn, but he was deaf to his pleading, and so he went away to the church, speaking no word to any man, and with his head bent as with the weight of knowledge that must not be told, and maybe with sorrow that the other prisoner, if guilty, would not seek for pardon from the Judge into whose hand he was about to go.

But as for me, this thing was good, and a wondrous comfort to me, and I went back to Egfrid with a cheerful heart, ready to face aught that might come.

Now the earl called to the guards from the water's edge, saying that the time was come, and we rode towards him, and I made Egfrid promise that he would hold his hand, at least till my father came.

Now they drew my boat to the shore, and they took Beorn from his horse first, and often have I wondered that he did not confess, but he said no word, and maybe his senses had left him by reason of his terror. They haled him to the boat and unbound him, setting him in the bows, where he sank down, seeming helpless, but staring away from shore over the sparkling waters that he feared.

Then came my turn, and of my own will I stepped into the boat, looking her over to see that all was there as when Lodbrok came. And all was there, though that was little enough. The one oar, the baler, and a few fathoms of line on the floorboards.

Now as I had nothing to lose by speaking, I cried to the earl concerning the one matter that troubled me.

"Earl Ulfkytel, I pray you forgive my poor folk if they fought for me when you took the boat."

"They knew not why it was taken," he answered quietly. "I sent a messenger before I gave sentence. But I should not have blamed them had they fought, knowing all."

Then a rough man who tended the boat called out:

"Ho, Lord Earl, are these murderers to go forth with gold on arm and hand?" for we had been stripped of naught but our arms, and I suppose the man coveted these things.

But the earl answered:

"Which is the murderer? I know not. When his time comes stripped he will be of life itself. Let the men be," and then in a moment he asked one by him; "what weapons had Lodbrok when he came?"

"Only a dagger," answered the thane to whom he spoke. "Or so men say."

"That is true," I said plainly.

"Give the men their daggers," then said the earl; and when one told him that we should use them on each other, he answered:

"I think they will not; do my bidding!"

So they threw my hunting knife to me, and I girded it on. But Beorn's dagger fell on the floor of the boat, and he paid no heed to it, not even turning his head.

Then the earl and three thanes went on board the fishing boat, and Egfrid would fain have come with him. But I signed him back, and when the fishermen put out oars and pushed from the shore, towing us with them, he ran waist deep into the water, and clasped my hand for the last time, weeping.

Then the shore grew dim to my eyes, and I put my head in my hands and would look no more. Soon I heard only the wash and creak of the large boat's oars, and a murmured word or two from those on board her. Then from Burgh Tower came the tolling of the bell, as for the dying, and that was the last voice of England that I heard as we went from shore to sea.

But at that sound came hope back to me, for it seemed to me as the voice of Bosham bell calling for help that should come to myself, as I had been called in time of need by the like sound to the help of St. Wilfrith's men. And straightway I remembered the words of the good prior, and was comforted, for surely if St. Wilfrith's might could sink the pirate ship it would be put forth for me upon the waters. So I prayed for that help if it might be given, and for the Hand of Him who is over all things, even as the prior had bidden me understand.

Whereupon I was in no more trouble about myself, and now I began to hope that the still weather might even bring Halfden's ship to find me.

So we passed from river to broad, and from broad to sea, and went in tow of the fishing boat until we came to that place, as nearly as might be, where I had saved Lodbrok. I could see the sparkle of our village lights, or thought I could.

There they cast us off, and for a few minutes the two boats lay side by side on the gently-heaving water, for the wind was offshore, and little sea was running.

Then the earl rose up, lifting his hand and saying, very solemnly:

"Farewell, thou who art innocent. Blame not my blindness, nor think ill of me. For I do my best, leaving you in the Hand of God, and not of man!"

So he spoke; then the oars swung and fell, and in a few moments his boat was gone into the shoreward shadows and we were alone, and I was glad.

Now I looked at Beorn, and I thought him strangely still, and so watched him. But I soon saw that he was in some sort of fit or swoon, and paid no heed to aught. Yet I thought it well to take his dagger from where it lay, lest he should fall on me in some frenzy.

I took up the weapon, and straightway I longed to draw it and end his life at once, while all sorts of plans for escape thereafter came into my mind. But I could not slay a helpless man, even this one, though I sat fingering the dagger for a long while. At last the evilness of these thoughts was plain to me; so quickly I cast the dagger overboard, and it was gone.

Then I thought I would sleep while I might, for there was no sea to fear, and the tide set with the wind away from shore from the river mouth, as I knew well, for it was ebbing. It was weary work to watch the land growing less and less plain under the moon. Yet I feared Beorn's treachery, and doubted for a while, until the coil of rope that lay at my feet caught my eye as I pondered. With that I made no more ado, but took it and bound him lightly, so that at least he could not rise up unheard by me. Nor did he stir or do aught but breathe heavily and slowly as I handled him. When he roused I knew that I could so deal with him that I might unbind him.

After that I slept, and slept well, rocked by the gentle rise and fall of the waves, until daylight came again.

CHAPTER VII. HOW WULFRIC CAME TO JUTLAND.

It was Beorn who woke me. Out of his swoon, or whatever it was that had taken his senses, he woke with a start and shudder that brought me from sleep at once, thinking that the boat had touched ground. But there was no land in sight now, and all around me was the wide circle of the sea, and over against me Beorn, my evil companion, glowering at me with a great fear written on his face.

Now as I woke and saw him, my hand went at once to the dagger at my side, as my first waking thoughts felt troubled by reason of all he had done, though it was but for a moment. Thereat he cried out, praying me to have mercy on him, and tried to rise, going near to capsize the boat. Indeed, I cannot believe that the man had ever been in a boat before.

"Lie down," I said, speaking sharply, as to a dog, "or you will drown us both before the time!"

He was still enough then, fearing the water more than steel, as it seemed, or seeing that I meant him no harm.

Then I spoke plainly to him.

"I will harm you not. But your life is in my hands in two ways. I can slay you by water or dagger for one thing; or for another, I think I can take this boat to shore at some place where you are not known, and so let you live a little longer. And in any case I have a mind to try to save my own life; thus if you will obey me so that I may tend the boat, yours shall be saved with it, so far as I am concerned. But if you hinder me, die you must in one way or another!"

Now he saw well enough that his only hope lay in my power to take the boat safely across the water, and so promised humbly to obey me in all things if I would but spare him and get the boat to shore quickly. So I unbound him and coiled the rope at my feet again, bidding him lie down amidships and be still.

Many a time men have asked me why I slew him not, or cast him not overboard, thus being troubled no more with him. Most surely I would have slain him when we fought, in the white heat of anger--and well would it have been if Ulfkytel had doomed him to death, as judge. But against this helpless, cringing wretch, whose punishment was even now falling on him, how could I lift hand? It seemed to me, moreover, that I was, as it were, watching to see when the stroke of doom would fall on him, as the earl said it surely must on the guilty.

The wind freshened, and the boat began to sing through the water, for it needed little to drive her well. My spirits rose, so that I felt almost glad to be on the sea again, but Beorn waxed sick and lay groaning till he was worn out and fell asleep.

Now the breeze blew from the southwest, warm and damp, as it had held for a long time during this winter, which was open and mild so far. And this was driving us over the same track which Lodbrok had taken as he came from his own place. There was no hope of making the English shore again, and so I thought it well to do even as the jarl, and rear up the floorboards in such wise as to use them for a sail to hasten us wherever we might go.

So I roused Beorn, and showed him how to bestow himself out of my way, and made sail, as one might say. At once the boat seemed to come to life, flying from wave to wave before the wind, and I made haste to ship the long oar, so that I could steer her with it.

And when I went aft, there, in the sharp hollow of the stern that I had uncovered, lay two great loaves and a little breaker of water. Now I could not tell, and do not know even to this day, what kindly man hid these things for us, but I blessed him for his charity, for now our case was better than Lodbrok's in two ways, that we had no raging gale and sea to wrestle against, and the utmost pangs of hunger and thirst we were not to feel. Three days and two nights had he been on his voyage. We might be a day longer with this breeze, but the bread, at least, we need not touch till tomorrow. But Beorn slept heavily again, and I told him not of this store as yet, for I thought that he would but turn from it just now. Which was well, for he could not bear a fast as could I.

So the long day wore through, and ever the breeze held, and the boat flew before it. Night fell, and the dim moon rose up, and still we went east and north swiftly. The long white wake stretched straight astern of us, and Beorn slept deeply, worn out; and the sea ran evenly and not very high, so that at last I dared to lash the oar in its place and sleep in snatches, waking now and then to the lift of a greater wave, or catching the rushing in my ears as some heavier-crested billow rose astern of us. But the boat was swift as the seas, and there was nothing to fear. Nor was the cold great at any time, except towards early morning before the first light of dawn. Moreover, the boat sailed in better trim with two men in her.

Gray morning came, and the seas were longer and deeper, for we were far on the wide sea. All day long was it the same, wave after wave, gray sky overhead, and the steady breeze ever bearing us onward. Once it rained, and I caught the water in the bailer and drank heartily, giving his fill to Beorn, and with it I ate some of my loaf, and he took half of his. Then slowly came night, and at last I waxed lonely, for all this while I had kept a hope that I might see the sail of Halfden's ship, but there was no glint of canvas between sky and sea, and my hope was gone as the darkness fell.

So I sang, to cheer myself, raising my voice in the sea song that I had made and that Lodbrok had loved. And when that was done I sang the song of Bosham bell, with the ending that the gleeman on Colchester Hill had made.

Thereat Beorn raised his head and, snarling at me like an angry dog, bade me cease singing of shipwreck. But I heeded him not, and so I sang and he cursed, until at last he wept like an angry child, and I held my peace.

I did not dare sleep that night, for the wind freshened, and at times we might see naught but sky above us and the waves ahead and astern of the boat, though to one who knew how to handle his craft there was no danger in them. But from time to time Beorn cried out as the boat slid swiftly down the slope of a great wave, hovered, and rose on the next, and I feared that he would leap up in his terror and end all.

"Bide still or I will bind you," I said at last to him, and he hid his face in his arms, and was quiet again.

Worn out when day broke was I, and again I ate and gave to Beorn, and he would eat all his loaf, though I bade him spare it, for I knew not how long yet we might be before we saw land. And that seemed to change his mood, and he began to scowl at me, though he dared say little, and so sat still in his place, glowering at me evilly.

Presently came a whale, spouting near us, and that terrified him, so that he cried to me to save him from it, as though I had power on the seas more than had other men. But it soon went away, and he forgot his terror, beginning to blame me for not having gained the shore yet.

I could say nothing, for I knew not how far we had run; yet we had come a long way, and I thought that surely we must have sailed as swiftly as Lodbrok, for the sea had favoured us rather than given trouble. Even now I thought the colour of the water changed a little, and I began to think that we neared some land at last.

As the sun set, the wind shifted more to the westward, and I thought a change was coming. It was very dark overhead until the waning moon rose.

Now, soon after moonrise Beorn began to groan, in his sleep as I thought; but presently he rose up, stiffly, from long sitting, and I saw that his eyes were flashing, and his face working strangely in the pale moonlight. I bade him lie down again, but he did not, and then I saw that he was surely out of his mind through the terror of the sea and the long nothingness of the voyage to which he was all unused. Then he made for me with a shout, and I saw that I must fight for my life. So I closed with him and dragged him down to the bottom of the boat, and there we two struggled, till I thought that the end was come.

The boat plunged and listed, and once was nearly over, but at that new strength came to me, and at last I forced his shoulders under the midship thwart, and held him there so that he could by no means rise. Then all his fury went, and he became weak, so that I reached out with one hand for the line and bound him easily, hand and foot. I set him back in his place, and the water washed over his face as he lay, for we had shipped a good deal in the lurches our struggle caused. Then he was still, and as on the first night, seemed to sleep, breathing very heavily.

So I left him bound, and bailed the water out. Then knew I how weak I was. Yet I held on, steering from wave to wave as though I could not help it.

Once, towards morning, there came a booming in my ears, and a faintness, for I was all but done. But the boat dashed into a wave, and the cold spray flew over me and roused me to know the danger, so I took my last crust and ate it, and was refreshed a little.

But when the morning broke cold and gray over brown waves, there, against one golden line of sunlight, rose the black steady barrier of a low-lying coast, and round the boat the gulls were screaming their welcome.

Then came over me a dull fear that I should be lost in sight of land, and a great sorrow and longing for the English shore in place of this, for never had I seen sunrise over land before from the open sea, and hunger and thirst gnawed at me, and I longed for rest from this tossing of sea, and wave--and always waves. Then I looked in Beorn's evil face, and I thought that he was dead, but that to me seemed to matter not.

Swiftly rose up the coast from out the sea, and I saw that it was like our East Anglian shore, forest covered and dark, but with pine and birch instead of oak and alder. The boat was heading straight through a channel; past sands over which I could see the white line of the tide on either side, and that chance seemed not strange to me, but as part of all that was to be and must be.

Then the last rollers were safely past, and the boat's keel grated on sand--and I forgot my weakness, and sprang out into the shallow water, dragging her up with the next wave and out of reach of the surges.

Then I saw that the tide was falling, and that I had naught more to do, for we were safe. With that I gave way at last, and reeled and fell on the sand, for my strength could bear no more, and I deemed that I should surely die.

I think that I fell into a great sleep for a while, for I came to myself presently, refreshed, and rose up.

The tide had ebbed a long way, and the sun was high above me, so that I must have been an hour or two there upon the sand. I went and looked at Beorn.

His swoon seemed to have passed into sleep, and I unbound him, and as I did so he murmured as if angry, though he did not wake.

Then I thought that I would leave him there for some other to find, and try to make my way to house or village where I might get food. I could send men thence to seek him, but I cared not if I never set eyes on him again, hoping, indeed, that I should not do so.

So I turned and walked inland through the thin forest for a little way, stumbling often, but growing stronger and less stiff as I went, though I must needs draw my belt tight to stay the pangs of hunger, seeing that one loaf is not overmuch for such a voyage and such stern work as mine had been, body and mind alike unresting.

Nor had I far to go, for not more than a mile from shore I saw a good hut standing in a little clearing; and it was somewhat like our own cottages, timber-framed, with wattle and clay walls, but with thatch of heather instead of our tall reeds, and when I came near, I saw that the timber was carved with twisted patterns round door and window frames.

No dog came out at me, and no one answered when I called, and so at last I lifted the latch and went in. There was no one, but the people could not be far off, for meat and bread and a great pitcher of ale stood on the round log that served for table, as if the meal was set against speedy homecoming, and the fire was banked up with peats, only needing stirring to break into a blaze.

Rough as it all was, it looked very pleasant to me, and after I had called once or twice I sat down, even as I should have done in our own land, and ate a hearty meal, and drank of the thin ale, and was soon myself again. I had three silver pennies, besides the gold bracelet on my arm that I wore as the king's armour bearer and weapon thane, and was sure of welcome, so when I had done I sat by the fire and waited till someone should come whom I might thank.

Once I thought of carrying food to Beorn, but a great hatred and loathing of the man and his deed came over me, and I would not see him again. And, indeed, it was likely that he would come here also, as I had done, when he woke; so that when at last I heard footsteps I feared lest it should be he.

But this comer whistled cheerfully as he came, and the tune was one that I had often heard men sing when I was with Halfden. It was the old "Biarkamal", the song of Biark the Viking.

Now at that I was very glad, for of all things I had most feared lest I should fall on the Frisian shores, for if so, I should surely be made a slave, and maybe sold by the lord of the coast to which I came. But Danes have no traffic in slaves, holding freedom first of all things. And that is one good thing that the coming of the Danish host has taught to us, for many a Saxon's riches came from trading in lives of men.

Then the door was pushed open, for I had left it ajar, and in came a great dog like none we have in England. I thought him a wolf at first, so gray and strong was he, big enough and fierce enough surely to pull down any forest beast, and I liked not the savage look of him. But, though he bristled and growled at first sight of me, when he saw that I sat still as if I had some right to be there, he came and snuffed round me, and before his master came we were good friends enough, if still a little doubtful. But I never knew a dog that would fly at me yet, so that I think they know well enough who are their friends, though by some sign of face or voice that is beyond my knowledge.

Now came the man, who edged through the door with a great bundle of logs for the fire, which he cast down without looking at me, only saying:

"Ho, Rolf! back again so early? Where is the Jarl?"

Now I knew that he was a Dane, and so I answered in his own way:

"Not Rolf, but a stranger who has made free with Rolf's dinner."

Whereat the man laughed, setting hands on hips and staring at me.

"So it is!" he said; "settle that matter with brother Rolf when he comes in, for strangers are scarce here."

Then he scanned my dress closely, and maybe saw that they were sea stained, though hunting gear is made for hard wear and shows little.

"Let me eat first," he said, sitting down, "and then we will talk."

But after he had taken a few mouthfuls, he asked:

"Are there any more of you about?"

"One more," I said, "but I left him asleep in the boat that brought us here. We are from the sea, having been blown here."

"Then he may bide till he wakes," the man said, going on with his meal.

Presently he stopped eating, and after taking a great draught of ale, said that he wondered the dog had not torn me.

"Whereby I know you to be an honest man. For I cannot read a man's face as some can, and therefore trust to the dog, who is never wrong," and he laughed and went on eating.

Now that set me thinking of what account I might give of myself, and I thought that I would speak the truth plainly, though there was no reason to say more than that we were blown off the English coast. What Beorn would say I knew not; most likely he would lie, but if so, things must work themselves out.

I looked at the man in whose house I was, and was pleased with him. Red haired and blue eyed he was, with a square, honest face and broad shoulders, and his white teeth shone beneath a red beard that covered half his face.

When he had eaten even more than I, he laughed loudly, saying that brother Rolf would have to go short this time, and then came and sat by the fire over against me, and waited for me to say my say.

So I told him how we had come, and at that he stared at me as our folk stared at Lodbrok, and started up, crying that he must go and see this staunch boat that had served me so well.

"Bide here and rest," he said, "and I will bring your comrade to you," and with that he swung out of the house, taking the dog with him. And at once the thought of leaving the hut and plunging into the forest came into my mind, but I knew not why I should do so, except that I would not see Beorn again. However, there was a third man now, and I would see what befell him.

Now I waited long, and had almost fallen asleep beside the warm fire, when I heard a horn away in the woods, and roused up to listen. Twice or thrice it sounded, and then I heard it answered from far off. So I supposed that there was a hunt going on.

Then I heard no more, and fell asleep in earnest; for I needed rest badly, as one might well suppose.

Something touched my hand and I awoke. It was the great dog, who came and thrust his nose against me, having made up his mind to be friendly altogether. So when his master came in I was fondling his head, and he looked puzzled.

"Say what men will," he said, "I know you are an honest man!"

"Do you hold that any will doubt it?" I asked, wondering what he meant; for he looked strangely at me.

"Aye; the jarl has found your boat, and has sent me back to keep you fast. Know you whose boat you have?"

"It belonged to Jarl Lodbrok, who came ashore in it, as I have come here--and he gave it me."

"Hammer of Thor!" said the man. "Is the jarl alive?"

"What know you of him?" I asked.

"He was our jarl--ours," he answered.

"Who is the other jarl you speak of?" I asked him, with a hope that Halfden had come home, for now I knew that we had indeed followed Lodbrok's track exactly.

"How should it be other than Ingvar Lodbroksson? for we have held that Lodbrok, his father, is dead this many a long day."

"Let me go to the jarl," I said, rising up. "I would speak with him," for I would, if possible, tell him the truth, before Beorn could frame lies that might work ill to both of us, or perhaps to me most of all. Yet I thought that I saw the shadow of judgment falling on the murderer.

"Bide quiet," said the man; "he will be here soon."

And then he said, looking from me to the dog, "Now I hold you as a true man, therefore I will tell you this--anger not the jarl when he speaks to you."

"Thanks, friend!" I answered heartily, "I think I shall not do that. Is he like his father?"

The man laughed shortly, only saying:

"Is darkness like daylight?"

"Then he is not like Jarl Halfden."

Now the honest man was going to ask in great wonder how I knew of him, when there came the quick trot of horses to the door, and a stern voice, which had in its tones somewhat familiar to me, called him:

"Raud, come forth!"

My host started up, and saying, "It is Jarl Ingvar," went to the door, while I too rose and followed him, for I would not seem to avoid meeting the son of Lodbrok, my friend.

"Where is this stranger?" said the jarl's voice; "bring him forth."

Raud turned to beckon me, but I was close to him, and came out of the hut unbidden.

There sat a great man, clad in light chain mail and helmed, with his double-headed axe slung to his saddle bow, but seeming to have come from hunting, for he carried a short, broad-pointed boar spear, and on the wrist of his bridle hand sat a hooded hawk like Lodbrok's. His face had in it a look both of his father and of Halfden, but it was hard and stern; and whereas they had brown hair, his was jet black as a raven's wing. Maybe he was ten years older than Halfden.

There were five or six other men, seemingly of rank, and on horseback also, behind him, but they wore no armour, and were in hunting gear only, and again there were footmen, leading hounds like the great one that stood by Raud and me. And two men there were who led between them Beorn, holding him lest he should fall, either from weakness or terror, close to the jarl.

So I stood before Ingvar the Jarl, and wondered how things would go, and what Beorn had said, though I had no fear of him. And as the jarl gazed at me I raised my hand, saying in the viking's greeting:

"Skoal to Jarl Ingvar!"

At that he half raised hand in answer, but checked himself, saying shortly:

"Who are you, and how come you by my father's boat?"

I was about to answer, but at that word it seemed that for the first time Beorn learnt into whose hands he had fallen, and he fell on his knees between his two guards, crying for mercy. I think that he was distraught with terror, for his words were thick and broken, and he had forgotten that none but I knew of his ill deed.

That made the jarl think that somewhat was amiss, and he bade his men bind us both.

"Bind them fast, and find my brother Hubba," he said, and men rode away into the forest. But I spoke to him boldly.

"Will you bind a man who bears these tokens, Jarl?"

And I held out my hand to him, showing him the rings that Lodbrok and Halfden had given me.

"My father's ring--and Halfden's!" he said, gripping my hand, as he looked closely at the runes upon them, so tightly that it was pain to me. "By Odin's beard, this grows yet stranger! Who are you, and whence, and how came you by these things?"

"I am Wulfric, son of Elfric, the Thane of Reedham, 'the merchant' as men call him. I have been Jarl Lodbrok's friend, and have fought by the side of Halfden, his son, as these tokens may tell you. As for the rest, that is for yourself alone, Jarl. For I have no good tidings, as I fear."

"Who is this man, then, and why cries he thus in terror?"

"Beorn, falconer to Eadmund, King of the East Angles," I said.

But I would not answer at once to the other question, and Ingvar seemed not to notice it.

Then there was silence while the great jarl sat on his horse very still, and looked hard at me and at Beorn; but when the men would have bound us he signed them back, letting Beorn go free. Whereupon his knees gave way, and he sank down against the house wall, while I leant against it and looked at the mighty Dane, somewhat dreading what I had to tell him, but meaning to go through all plainly.

Now the ring of men closed round us, staring at us, but in silence, save for the ringing of the horns that were blowing in the woods to call Hubba from his sport. And Jarl Ingvar sat still, as if carved in oak, and seemed to ponder, frowning heavily at us, though the look in his eyes went past me as it were.

Glad was I when a horseman or two rode up and reined in alongside Ingvar. I think that the foremost rider was the most goodly warrior to look on that I had ever seen, and one might know well that he was Lodbrok's son.

"Ho, brother!" he cried; "I thought you had harboured the greatest bear in all Jutland in Raud's hut. And it is naught but two strangers. What is the trouble with them?"

"Look at yon man's hand," said Ingvar.

I held out my hand, and Hubba looked at the rings, whereupon his face lit up as Halfden's had lighted, and he said:

"News of our father and brother! That is well; tell us, friend, all that you know."

"Stay," said Ingvar; "I took yon man from the boat we made for our father; he was half dead therein, and his wrists have the marks of cords on them; also when he heard my name he began to cry for mercy, and I like it not."

"This friend of our folk will tell us all," said Hubba.

"Aye," said I, "I will tell you, Jarls. But I would speak to you alone."

"Tell me," said Ingvar shortly; "came my father to your shores in yon boat alive?"

"Aye," I answered.

"And he died thereafter?"

"He died, Jarl," I said; and I said it sadly.

Then said Hubba:

"Almost had I a hope that he yet lived, as you live. But it was a poor hope. We have held him as dead for many a long day."

But Ingvar looked at Beorn fixedly, and the man shrank away from his gaze.

"How did he die, is what I would know?" he said sternly.

"Let the man to whom Halfden and Lodbrok gave these gifts tell us presently. We have enough ill news for the time. Surely we knew that the jarl was dead, and it is ours but to learn how;" said Hubba.

"How know you that these men slew not both?"

"Jarl Ingvar," I said; "I will tell you all you will, but I would do so in some less hurried way than this. For I have much to tell."

"Take the men home, brother," said Hubba; "then we can talk."

"Bind the men," said Ingvar again.

"Nay, brother, not the man who wears those rings," said Hubba quickly.

"Maybe, and it is likely, that they are ill come by, and he will make up some lie about them," answered Ingvar.

"It will be easily seen if he does," answered his brother; "wait till you know."

Ingvar reined his horse round and rode away without another word. Then Hubba bade the man Raud and his brother, a tall man who had come with the Jarl Ingvar, take charge of us until word should come from him, and then rode after Ingvar with the rest of the folk.

"Come into the house," said Raud to me. "I fear you have ill news enough, though only what we have expected."

So we went inside, and I sat in my old place beside the fire. Rolf, the brother, helped Beorn to rise, and set him on a seat in a corner where he could rest, and then we were all silent. The great dog came and sat by me, so that I stroked him and spoke to him, while he beat his tail on the floor in response.

"See you that," said one brother to the other.

"Aye; Vig says true, mostly."

"One may trust him," said Raud; telling of how Vig the dog had made friends with me at first, and he nodded in friendly wise to me, so that I would not seem to hold aloof, and spoke to him.

"That is Jarl Hubba, surely?"

"Aye, and the best warrior in all Denmark," said Raud. "We fear Ingvar, and we love Halfden; but Hubba is such a hero as was Ragnar himself."

And once set on that matter, the two honest men were unwearied in telling tales of the valour and skill of their master, so that I had no room for my own thoughts, which was as well.

Then came a man, riding swiftly, to say that the jarls had left their hunting, and that we were to be taken to the great house. Moreover, that Rolf and Raud were to be held answerable for our safe keeping. When I heard that I laughed.

"I will go willingly," I said, rising up.

"What of this man who sits silent here?" asked Rolf.

"Little trouble will be with him," said his brother.

And indeed Beorn almost needed carrying forth.

CHAPTER VIII. HOW WE FARED WITH INGVAR THE DANE.

We came to the shores of a haven at a river mouth, and there we saw the town clustering round a large hall that rose in the midst of the lesser houses, which were mostly low roofed and clay walled, like that of Raud, though some were better, and built of logs set upon stone foundations. The hall stood on higher ground than the rest of the houses, so that from the gate of the heavy timber stockade that went all round it one could see all the windings of the haven channel and the sea that lay some half mile or more away at its mouth. And all the town had a deep ditch and mound round it, as if there was ever fear of foes from shoreward, for these came down to the haven banks, and the only break they had was where a wharf and the ship garth were. There were several ships housed in their long sheds, as I could see.

All round the great hall and the buildings that belonged to it was a stockade of pointed logs, so that it stood in a wide courtyard on all four sides, and the great gate of the stockade was opposite the timber porch of the hall itself. There were other doors in the side of the hall, but they were high up, and reached by ladders; and there seemed to be only one more gate in the stockade, leading landward, and both were such as might not easily be broken down, when once they were closed and barred with the square logs that stood beside the entrances ready. And all the windows of the hall were very high up and narrow, and the roof was timbered, not thatched.

This was the strongest house that I had ever seen, and I said to Raud as I looked at it:

"This place is built to stand some fierce fighting. What need have you of such strength?"

He laughed, and answered:

"Why, much need indeed! For when the ships are gone a-viking we are weak in men, so needs must have strong walls to keep out all comers from over seas. And we have an ill neighbour or two, who would fain share in our booty. However, men know in Sweden, and Finmark, and Norway also, that it is ill meddling with Jarl Ingvar and his brothers."

We passed through the stockade gate, and went straight to the porch; all the woodwork of which was carved and gaily painted, and so were eaves and rafter ends and tie beams.

Two sturdy axemen stood at the doorway, and they spoke freely to the brothers, asking questions of us and of our tale.

Then roared the voice of Jarl Ingvar from within, bidding the men cease prating and bring us in, and so we entered.

A great fire burnt in the centre of the hall, and the smoke rose up and found its way out under the eaves; and there were skins and heads of wild beasts on the wall, amid which arms and armour hung everywhere, bright in the firelight. Yet the hall, though it was carved on wall, and rafter, and doorway, was not so bright as ours at Reedham, nor so pleasant.

Ingvar and Hubba sat on one side of the fire, where the smoke was driven away from them, and before them was set a long bench where we should be placed. There Hubba bade us sit down, telling the two men to go without and wait.

So we were left face to face with those two, and I saw that Ingvar's face was dark with doubt, but that Hubba seemed less troubled. Yet both looked long and sternly at us.

"Tell us this tale of yours," said Ingvar at last; "and lie not."

Now it seemed to me that it were well to get the worst over at once without beating about beforehand. And now that the jarls knew that Lodbrok was dead, the hardest was to tell them how he died, and why I was here thus.

"Well loved I Lodbrok the Jarl, and well do I love Halfden his son," I said. "Have patience with me while I tell all from the first."

"Go on," said Ingvar, knitting his brows.

"Safely came Jarl Lodbrok to the English shores," I went on; "steering his boat through the storm as I think no other man might. And my father and I, lying at anchor for tide in our coasting ship, took him from the breakers. Some of his craft taught he me, else had I not been here today. So he bided with us until I went to sea, and there I met Halfden, and went on a raid with him, coming back from the South Saxon shores to wait at our place for his coming to take Lodbrok home. But he came not last winter, and so we waited till this spring should bring him. For my ship was lost, and no other came."

"What!" said Ingvar; "he died not of stress of storm, but lived so long! Then he has been slain!" and he half started from his seat in rage.

But Hubba, though his teeth were set, drew him back.

"Hear all," he said.

I went on without bidding, not seeming to note these things.

"The jarl and I hunted together, and the chance of the day parted us, and he was slain; nor can I say by whom. But this man and I, being found with his body, were accused of the deed. And because there was no proof, our great earl, who loves even-handed justice, would have us cast adrift, even as was Lodbrok; that the guilty might suffer, and the innocent escape."

Then Ingvar rose up, white and shaking with wrath, and drew out his sword. Whereon Beorn yelled and fell on the floor, grovelling with uplifted hands and crying for mercy.

But the great jarl paid no heed to him, and hove up the sword with both hands over my head, saying in a hoarse voice:

"Say that you lie--he is not dead--or you slew him!"

Now I think the long struggle with the sea, or my full trust in the earl's words, or both, had taken away my fear of death, for I spoke without moving, though the great blade seemed about to fall, and the fierce Dane's eyes glared on mine.

"It were easy for me to have lied; I would that I did lie, for then Lodbrok would be living, and I beside him, waiting for Halfden my friend even yet."

"Odin!" shouted Ingvar; "you speak truth. Woe is me for my father, and woe to the land that has given him a grave thus foully."

With that he let his sword fall, and his passion having gone, he sat down and put his face in his hands, and wept tears of grief and rage. And I, as I watched him, was fain to weep also, for my thoughts were akin to his.

Now Hubba had sat very still, watching all this, and he kept his feelings better than did his fierce brother, though I might well see that he was moved as deeply. But now he spurned Beorn with his foot, bidding him get up and speak also. But Beorn only grovelled the more, and Hubba spurned him again, turning to me.

"I believe you speak truth," he said quietly, "and you are a brave man. There was no need for you to tell the accusation against yourself; and many are the lies you might have told us about the boat that would have been enough for us. We never thought to hear that our father had outlived the storm."

"I speak truth, Jarl," I said, sadly enough, "and Halfden will come to our haven, seeking us both, and will find neither--only this ill news instead of all we had planned of pleasure."

Then Hubba asked me plainly of Beorn, saying:

"What of this cur?"

"No more than I have told you, Jarl," I said.

"How came he into the forest?" asked Hubba, for he saw that there was more than he knew yet under Beorn's utter terror.

"Let me tell you that story from end to end," I answered.

And he nodded, so that I did so, from the time when I left the jarl until Ulfkytel sentenced us, giving all the words of the witnesses as nearly as I could. Then I said that I would leave them to judge, for I could not.

Now Ingvar, who had sat biting his nails and listening without a word, broke in, questioning me of Halfden's ship for long. At last he said:

"This man tells truth, and I will not harm him. He shall bide here till Halfden comes home, for he tells a plain story, and wears those rings. And he has spoken the ill of himself and little of this craven, who maybe knows more than he will say. I have a mind to find out what he does know," and he looked savagely at Beorn, who was sitting up and rocking himself to and fro, with his eyes looking far away.

"Do what you will with him he will lie," said Hubba.

"I can make him speak truth," said Ingvar grimly.

"What shall be done with this Wulfric?" asked Hubba.

"Let him go with Raud until I have spoken with Beorn," answered Ingvar, "then we shall be sure if he is friend or not."

Hubba nodded, and he and I rose up and went out to the porch, where Raud and Rolf waited with the two guards. We passed them and stood in the courtyard.

"I believe you, Wulfric," said Hubba, "for I know a true man when I see him."

"I thank you, Jarl," I answered him, taking the hand that he offered me.

I looked out over the sea, for the frank kindness moved me, and I would not show it. There was a heavy bank of clouds working up, and the wind came from the north, with a smell of snow in it. Then I saw a great hawk flying inland, and wondered to see it come over sea at this time of year. It flew so that it would pass over the house, and as it came it wheeled a little and called; and then it swept down and came straight towards me, so that I held out my hand and it perched on my wrist.

And lo! it was Lodbrok's gerfalcon; and pleased she was to see me once more, fluttering her wings and glancing at me while I smoothed and spoke to her.

But Hubba cried out in wonder, and the men and Ingvar came out to see what his call meant. Then they, too, were amazed, for they knew the bird and her ways well.

I had spoken of the falcon once or twice, telling the jarls how she had taken to me, and I think they had doubted it a little. Now the bird had got free in some way, and finding neither of her masters, had fled home, even as Lodbrok said she would.

"Now is your story proved to be true," said Hubba, smiling gravely at me, but speaking for Ingvar's ear.

"Aye, over true," answered his brother; "serve this man well, Raud and Rolf, for he has been a close friend of Jarl Lodbrok."

"Then should he be in Lodbrok's house as a guest," said Raud stoutly, and free of speech as Danes will ever be.

"Maybe he shall be so soon," said Ingvar.

"I will bide with my first hosts," I said, not being willing to speak much of this just now.

"That is well said," was Hubba's reply, and so we went to have the falcon--who would not leave me--hooded and confined; and then I went with the two men back to their hut, and there they vied with each other in kindness to me until night fell, and I gladly went to rest; for since that night within Caistor walls I had had no sleep that was worth considering. So my sleep was a long sleep, and nothing broke it until I woke of myself, and found only the great dog Vig in the hut, and breakfast ready set out for me, while outside the ground was white with snow.

I was glad to find that no watch was kept on me, for it seemed as if Hubba's words were indeed true, and that the jarls believed my story. And my dagger was left me also, hanging still on the wall at my head where I had slept. Then I thought that the great dog was maybe bidden to guard me, but he paid no heed when I went outside the hut to try if it were so.

Ere an hour had passed Raud came back, and he had news for me.

"Now, friend Wulfric, I am to part with my guest, and not in the way that was yesterday's. The jarls bid me say that Wulfric of Reedham, Lodbrok's preserver, is a welcome guest in their hall, and they would see him there at once."

"Nevertheless," I answered, "Raud the forester was the first to shelter me, and I do not forget."

Whereat Raud was pleased, and together we went to the great house, and entered, unchallenged. Hubba came forward and held out his strong hand to me frankly, smiling a little, but gravely, and I took it.

"Beorn has told the truth," he said; "forgive me for doubt of you at any time."

"Aye, let that be forgotten," said Ingvar, coming from beyond the great fire, and I answered that I thought it not strange that they had doubted me.

"Now, therefore," said Hubba, "you yourself shall question Beorn, for there are things you want to know from him. And he will answer you truly enough."

"After that you shall slay him, if you will," said Ingvar, in his stern voice, "I wonder you did not do so in the boat. Better for him if you had."

"I wonder not," said Hubba. "The man is fit for naught; I could not lay hand on such a cur."

I had no answer to make after that, for the warrior spoke my own thoughts, and I held my peace as they took me to the further side of the hearth, past the fire, beyond which I had not yet been able to see.

Then I knew how Beorn had been made to speak the truth. They had tortured him, and there was no strength left in him at all, so that I almost started back from the cruel marks that he bore. Yet I had things to hear from him, now that he had no need to speak falsely, and I went to his side. The two jarls stood and looked at him unmoved.

"The justice of Ulfkytel is on you, Beorn," I said slowly; "there is no need to hide aught. Tell me how you slew Lodbrok, and why."

Then came a voice, so hollow that I should not have known it for the lusty falconer's of past days:

"Aye; justice is on me, and I am glad. I will tell you, but first say that you forgive me."

Then I could not but tell this poor creature that for all the harm he had done me I would surely forgive him; but that the deed of murder was not for me to forgive.

"Pray, therefore, that for it I may be forgiven hereafter," he said, and that I promised him.

Then he spoke faintly, so that Hubba bade Raud give him strong drink, and that brought his strength back a little.

"I took your arrows at Thetford, and I followed you to Reedham. There I dogged you, day by day, in the woods--five days I went through the woods as you hunted, and then you twain were far apart, and my chance had come. Lodbrok reined up to listen, and I marked where he would pass when he went back, hearing your horn. Then I shot, and the arrow went true; but I drew sword, being mad, and made more sure. That is all. Surely I thought I should escape, for I told no man what I would do, and all men thought me far away, with the king."

Then he stopped, and recovered his strength before he could go on.

"I hated Lodbrok because he had taken my place beside the king, and because his woodcraft was greater than mine, though I was first in that in all our land. And I feared that he would take the land the king offered him, for I longed for it."

Then Beorn closed his eyes, and I was turning away, for I need ask no more; but again he spoke:

"Blind was yon dotard Ulfkytel not to see all this; would that you had slain me in the woods at first--or that he had hanged me at Caistor--or that I had been drowned. But justice is done, and my life is ended."

Those were the last words that I heard Beorn, the falconer, speak, for I left him, and Raud gave him to drink again.

"Have you no more to ask?" said Ingvar gloomily, and frowning on Beorn, as he lay helpless beyond the hearth.

"Nothing, Jarl."

"What was the last word he said. I heard not."

"He said that justice was done," I answered.

"When I have done with him, it shall be so," growled Ingvar, and his hand clutched his sword hilt, so that I thought to see him slay the man on the spot.

"Has he told you all?" I asked of Hubba.

"All, and more than you have told of yourself," he answered; "for he told us that it was your hand saved my father, and for that we thank you. But one thing more he said at first, and that was that Eadmund the King set him on to slay the jarl."

On that I cried out that the good king loved Lodbrok too well, and in any case would suffer no such cowardly dealings.

"So ran his after words; but that was his first story, nevertheless."

"Then he lied, for you have just now heard him say that his own evil thoughts bade him do the deed."

"Aye--maybe he lied at first; but we shall see," said Ingvar.

Now I understood not that saying, but if a man lies once, who shall know where the lie's doings will stop? What came from this lie I must tell, but now it seemed to have passed for naught.

"Now shall you slay the man in what way you will, as I have said.

There are weapons," and Ingvar pointed to the store on the walls.

"I will not touch him," I said, "and I think that he dies."

"Then shall you see the vengeance of Ingvar on his father's murderer," the jarl said savagely. "Call the men together into the courtyard, Raud, and let them bring the man there."

"Let him die, Jarl," I said boldly; "he has suffered already."

"I think that if you knew, Wulfric of Reedham, how near you have been to this yourself, through his doings, you would not hold your hand," answered Ingvar, scowling at Beorn again.

"Maybe, Jarl," I answered, "but though you may make a liar speak truth thus, you cannot make an honest man say more than he has to speak."

"One cannot well mistake an honest saying," said Ingvar. "And that is well for you, friend."

And so he turned and watched his courtmen, as the Danes called the housecarles, carry Beorn out. Then he went to the walls and began to handle axe after axe, taking down one by one, setting some on the great table, and putting others back, as if taking delight in choosing one fittest for some purpose.

Even as we watched him--Hubba sitting on the table's edge, and I standing by him--a leathern curtain that went across a door at the upper end of the hall was pulled aside, and a lady came into the place. Stately and tall, with wondrous black hair, was this maiden, and I knew that this must be that Osritha of whom the jarl was wont to speak to Eadgyth and my mother, and who wrought the raven banner that hung above the high place where she stood now. She was like Halfden and Hubba, though with Ingvar's hair, and if those three were handsome men among a thousand, this sister of theirs was more than worthy of them. She stood in the door, doubting, when she saw me. Sad she looked, and she wore no gold on arm or neck, doubtless because of the certainty of the great jarl's death; and when she saw that Hubba beckoned to her, she came towards us, and Ingvar set down the great axe whose edge he was feeling.

"Go back to your bower, sister," he said; "we have work on hand."

And he spoke sternly, but not harshly, to her. She shrank away a little, as if frightened at the jarl's dark face and stern words, but Hubba called her by name.

"Stay, Osritha; here is that friend of our father's from over seas, of whom you have heard."

Then she looked pityingly at me, as I thought, saying very kindly:

"You are welcome. Yet I fear you have suffered for your friendship to my father."

"I have suffered for not being near to help him, lady," I said.

"There is a thing that you know not yet," said Hubba. "This Wulfric was the man who took Father from the breakers."

Then the maiden smiled at me, though her eyes were full of tears, and she asked me:

"How will they bury him in your land? In honour?"

"I have a brother-in-law who will see to that," I said. "And, moreover, Eadmund the King, and Elfric, my father, will do him all honour."

"I will see to that," growled Ingvar, turning sharply from where he sought another weapon on the wall.

Not knowing all he meant, this pleased me, for I thought that we should sail together to Reedham for this, before very long. But Osritha, knowing his ways, looked long at him, till he turned away again, and would not meet her eyes.

"Now go back to your place, my sister," he said. "It is not well for you to bide here just now."

"Why not? Let our friend tell me of Father also," she said wilfully.

"Because I am going to do justice on Lodbrok's slayer," said Ingvar, in a great voice, swinging an axe again.

Then the maiden turned pale, and wrung her hands, looking at Ingvar, who would not meet her eyes; and then she went and laid her hands on his mighty arm, crying:

"Not that, my brother; not that!"

"Why not?" he asked; but he did not shake off her little hands.

"Because Father would not have men so treated, however ill they had done."

"Aye, brother; the girl is right," said Hubba. "Let him die; for you gave him to Wulfric, and that is his word."

"Well then," said Ingvar, setting back the axe at last, "I will not carve him into the eagle I meant to make of him. But slay him I must and will, if the life is yet in him."

"Let Odin have him," said Hubba; and I knew that he meant that the man should be hanged, for so, as Halfden's vikings told me, should he be Odin's thrall, unhonoured.

Then the maiden fled from the hall, glad to have gained even that for the man, instead of the terrible death that the Danes keep for traitors and cowards.

Now Ingvar put back the axes he had kept, saying that the girl ever stood in his way when he would punish as a man deserved. After that he stood for a while as if in thought, and broke out at length:

"We will see if this man can sing a death song as did Ragnar our forefather."

And with that he waited no more, but strode out into the courtyard, we following. And I feared what I should see; until I looked on Beorn, and though he was yet alive, I saw that he was past feeling aught.

They bore him out of the village to a place just inside the trenched enclosure, and there were old stone walls, such as were none elsewhere in the place, but as it might have been part of Burgh or Brancaster walls that the Romans made on our shores, so ancient that they were crumbling to decay. There they set him down, and raised a great flat stone, close to the greatest wall, which covered the mouth of a deep pit.

"Look therein," said Ingvar to me.

I looked, and saw that the pit was stone walled and deep, and that out of it was no way but this hole above. The walls and floor were damp and slimy; and when I looked closer, the dim light showed me bones in one corner, and also that over the floor crawled reptiles, countless.

"An adder is a small thing to sting a man," said Ingvar in his grim voice. "Nor will it always hurt him much. Yet if a man is so close among many that he must needs tread on one, and it bites him, and in fleeing that he must set foot on another, and again another, and then more--how will that end?"

I shuddered and turned away.

"In such a place did Ella of Northumbria put my forebear, Ragnar Lodbrok; and there he sang the song {xiii} we hold most wondrous of all. There he was set because he was feared, and Northumbria knows what I thought of that matter. But Beorn goes here for reasons which you know. And East Anglia shall know what my thoughts are of those reasons."

Then two men seized Beorn and cast him into that foul pit, stripped of all things, and the stone fell.

But Beorn moved not nor cried out, and I think that even as Ulfkytel had boded, stripped of life itself was he before the bottom of the pit was reached.

So the justice of Ulfkytel the Earl came to pass. But the lies spoken by Beorn were not yet paid for.

CHAPTER IX. JARL HALFDEN'S HOMECOMING.

From the time when Beorn was made to speak the truth, I was a welcome guest in the hall that had been Lodbrok's, to Hubba at least, and we were good friends. As for Ingvar, he was friendly enough also, and would listen when I spoke with his more frank and open brother of my days with Halfden and his father. But he took little pleasure in my company, going silent and moody about the place, for the snow that began on the day after I landed was the first of a great storm, fiercer and colder than any we knew in England, and beyond the courtyard of the great house men could scarcely stir for a time.

This storm I had but just escaped, and it seemed to me, and still seems, that the terror and pain thereof was held back while I was on the sea, for those nights and days had had no winter sting in them.

Hubba and I would wrestle and practise arms in the hall or courtyard during that time, and he was even beyond his father, my teacher, in the matter of weapon play; so that it is no wonder that now, as all men know, he is held the most famous warrior of his time.

These sports Ingvar watched, and took part in now and then when his mood was lighter, but it was seldom. Yet he was skilful, though not as his brother.

Then at night was the fire of pine logs high heaped, and we feasted while the scalds, as they call their gleemen, sang the deeds of the heroes of old. And some of those of whom they sang were men of the Angles of the old country; and one was my own forefather, and for that I gave the scald my gold bracelet, and thereafter he sang lustily in my praise as Lodbrok's rescuer.

Very pleasant it was in Ingvar's hall while the wind howled over the roof, and the roar of the sea was always in our ears. And these Danes drank less than our people, if they ate more largely. But Ingvar would sit and take pleasure in none of the sport, being ever silent and thoughtful.

But to me, best of all were the times when I might see and speak with Osritha, and soon the days seemed heavy to me if by chance I had no word with her. And she was always glad to speak of her father and Halfden; for she was the youngest of all Lodbrok's children, and Halfden, her brother, was but a year older than herself, so that she loved him best of all, and longed to see him home again.

So longed I, grieving for the news he must hear when he came to Reedham, but yet thinking that he would be glad to find me at least living and waiting for him.

Now, as the snow grew deeper and the cold strengthened, the wolves began to come at night into the village, and at last grew very daring. So one night a man ran in to say that a pack was round a cottage where a child would not cease crying, and must be driven off, or they would surely tear the clay walls down.

Then Hubba and I would go; but Ingvar laughed at us, saying that a few firebrands would settle the matter by fraying the beasts away. However, the man was urgent, and we went out with Raud and his brother, and some twenty men, armed with spears and axes.

The night was very dark, and the snow whirled every way, and the end of it was that Raud and I and two more men, with the dog Vig, lost the rest, and before we found them we had the pack on us, and we must fight for our lives. And that fight was a hard fight, for there must have been a score of gaunt wolves, half starved and ravenous.

And I think we should have fared badly, for at last I was standing over Raud, who was down, dragged to the earth by two wolves, of which the dog slew one and I the other, while the other two men were back to back with me, and the wolves bayed all round us. But Hubba and his party heard our shouts in time and came up, and so ended the matter.

Now Raud must have it that I had saved his life, though I thought the good dog had a share in it, and both he and the dog were a little hurt. However, my shoulder was badly torn by a wolf that leapt at me while my spear was cumbered with another, and I for my part never wished it had not been so.

For Osritha, who was very skilful in leech craft, tended my hurt; and I saw much of her, for the hurts were a long time before they healed, as wolf bites are apt to be, and we grew very friendly. So that, day by day, I began to long to see the maiden who cared for my wound so gently, before the time came.

Now Raud must needs make me a spear from a tough ashen sapling that he had treasured for a long time, because that which I had used in the wolf hunt was sprung by the weight of one of the beasts, and while his hurts kept him away at his own house he wrought it, and at last brought it up to the hall to give to me.

When I looked at it--and it was a very good one, and had carved work where the hand grips the shaft, and a carved end--I saw that the head was one of Jarl Ingvar's best spearheads, and asked Raud where he got it.

"Why," he said, "a good ash shaft deserves a good head, and so I asked the jarl for one. And when he knew for whom it was, he gave me this, saying it was the best he had."

Now I was pleased with this gift, both because I liked the man Raud, who was both brave and simple minded, and because it showed that the surly jarl had some liking for me. Yet I would that he showed this openly, and telling Osritha of the gift, I dared say so.

Then she sighed and rose up, saying that she would show me another spear on the further wall, so taking me out of hearing of her maidens, who sat by the fire busied over their spinning and the like.

There she spoke to me of Jarl Ingvar.

"Moody and silent beyond his wont has he been since we have heard all about our father's death, and I fear that he plans some terrible revenge for it, even as he took revenge on the Northumbrian coasts for the long-ago slaying of Ragnar."

Then I remembered the story of the burnt town, Streoneshalch, and knew what Ingvar's revenge was like. But as yet I could not think that he would avenge Beorn's deed further than I had seen already.

"But he has no enmity with you, our friend," she went on; "though he speaks little to you, he listens as you talk to us. But there has grown up in his heart a hatred of all men in your land, save of yourself alone. And once he said that he would that you were a Dane, and his comrade as you had been Halfden's."

Then I told Osritha of how Halfden had let me go from him rather than have me fight against my own land. I had said nothing of this to the jarls, for there was no reason. And this was the first time that I had had private speech with Osritha.

"That is Halfden's way," she said, "he is ever generous."

"I would that he were back," I answered, and so we ceased speaking.

Yet after this, many were the chances I found of the like talk alone with Osritha before the weather broke, and we could once more get into the woods, hunting, and the men began to work in the ship garths on a great ship that was being built.

Now we had good hunting in the forests, and on the borders of the great mosses of Ingvar's lands. But there were many more folk in this land than in ours, and I thought that they were ill off in many ways. In those days of hunting, Ingvar, seeing me ride with the carven spear that was partly his gift, and with Lodbrok's hawk on my wrist, would speak more often with me, though now and again some chance word of mine spoken in the way of my own folk would seem to turn him gloomy and sullen, so that he would spur his horse and leave me. But Hubba was ever the same, and I liked him well, though I could not have made a friend of him as of Halfden.

In March messengers began to come and go, and though I asked nothing and was told nothing, I knew well that Ingvar was gathering a mighty host to him that he might sail in the May time across the seas for plunder--or for revenge. The hammers went all day long in the ship garths, where the air was full of the wholesome scent of tar; and in their houses the women spun busily, making rope and weaving canvas that should carry the jarl's men "over the swan's bath;" while in the hall the courtmen sat after dark and feathered arrows and twined bowstrings, and mended mail. And now and then some chief would ride into the town, feasting that night, and riding away in the morning after long talk with the jarls. And some, Bagsac and Guthrum, Sidrac and his son, and a tall man named Osbern, came very often as the days lengthened.

I would ask nothing of this matter, even of Osritha, having my own thoughts thereon, and not being willing to press her on things she might have been bidden to keep from me. She would ask me of my mother and Eadgyth, as they would ask the jarl of her, and I told her all I could, though that was not much, for a man hardly notes things as a woman will. Then she would laugh at me; until one day I said that I would she could come over to Reedham and see for herself.

At that I thought that I had offended her, for her face grew red, and she left me. Nor could I find a chance of speaking to her again for many days, which was strange to me, and grieved me sorely.

Now the southwest wind shifted at last to the west and north, and that shift brought home him whom I most wished to see, my comrade, Halfden. And it chanced that I was the first to see his sail from the higher land along the coast, south of the haven, where I was riding with my falcon and the great dog Vig, which Raud and his brother would have me take for my own after the wolf hunt.

Gladly I rode hack with my news to find Ingvar in the ship garth, and there I told him who came.

"A ship, maybe. How know you she is Halfden's?" he said carelessly.

"Why, how does any sailor know his own ship?" I asked in surprise.

Then he turned at once, and smiled at me fairly for the first time.

"I had forgotten," he said. "Come, let us look at her again."

And I was not mistaken, though the jarl was not so sure as I for half an hour or more. When he was certain, he said:

"Come, let us make what welcome for Halfden that we may."

And we went back to the hall, and at once was the great horn blown to assemble the men; and the news went round quickly, so that everywhere men and women alike put aside their work, and hurried down to the wharf side. And in Ingvar's house the thralls wrought to prepare a great feast in honour of Jarl Halfden's homecoming.

Soon I stood with the jarls and Osritha at the landing place, and behind us were the courtmen in their best array. And as we came to the place where we would wait, Halfden's ship came past the bar into the haven's mouth.

All men's faces were bright with the thought of welcome, but heavy were my thoughts, and with reason. For Halfden's ship came from the sea on no course that should have borne him from Reedham, and I feared that it was I who must tell him all. Yet he might have been drawn from his course by some passing vessel.

The long ship flew up the channel, and now we could see that all her rail was hung with the red and yellow shields that they use for show as well as to make the gunwale higher against the arrows, and to hinder boarders in a fight. And she was gaily decked with flags, and shone with new paint and gilding in all sea bravery. Not idle had her crew been in the place where they had wintered, and one might know that they had had a good voyage, which to a Dane means plunder enough for all. But surely if Halfden had been to Reedham, the long pennon had been half masted.

It were long to tell how the people cheered, and how they were answered from the ship, and how I spied Halfden on the fore deck, and Thormod at the helm, as ever. And when Osritha saw Halfden's gay arms and cloak and all the bright trim of the ship and men, she said to me, speaking low and quickly:

"They have not been to Reedham, or it would not have been thus."

And it was true, for there would have been no sign of joy among those who had heard the news that waited them there.

I knew not how to bear this meeting, but I was not alone in my trouble, for nearer me crept Osritha, saying to me alone, while the people cheered and shouted:

"How shall we tell Halfden?"

The two jarls were busy at the mooring place, and I could only answer her that I could look to her alone for help. Now at that I knew what had sprung up in my heart for Osritha, and that not in this only should I look for help from her and find it, but if it might be, all my life through. For now in my trouble she looked at me with a new look, answering:

"I will help you, whatever betide."

I might say no more then, nor were words needed, for I knew all that she meant. And so my heart was lightened, for now I held that I was repaid for all that had gone before, and save for that which had brought me here, gladly would I take my perilous voyage over again to find this land and the treasure it now held for me.

At last the ship's keel grated on the sand, and the men sprang from shore waist deep in water, to take her the mighty cables that should haul her into her berth; and then the long gangplank was run out, and Halfden came striding along it, looking bright and handsome--and halfway over, he stopped where none could throng him, and lifting his hand for silence cried for all to hear.

"Hearken all to good news! Lodbrok our Jarl lives!"

Then, alas! instead of the great cheer that should have broken from the lips of all that throng, was at first a silence, and then a groan--low and pitiful as of a mourning people who wail for the dead and the sorrowful living--and at that sound Halfden paled, and stayed no more, hurrying ashore and to where his brothers stood.

"What is this?" he said, and his voice was low, and yet clear in the silence that had fallen, for all his men behind him had stopped as if turned to stone where they stood.

Then from my side sprang Osritha before any could answer, meeting him first of all, and she threw her arms round his neck, saying:

"Dead is Lodbrok our father, and nigh to death for his sake has been Wulfric, your friend. Yet he at least is well, and here to speak with you and tell you all."

Then for the great and terrible sorrow that came at the end of the joyous homeward sailing, down on the hard sand Halfden the Jarl threw himself, and there lay weeping as these wild Danes can weep, for their sorrow is as terrible as their rage, and they will put no bounds to the way of grief of which there is no need for shame. Nor have they the hope that bids us sorrow not as they.

And while he lay there, all men held their peace, looking in one another's faces, and only the jarls and Osritha and myself stood near him.

Very suddenly he raised himself up, and was once more calm; then he kissed the maiden, and grasped his brothers' hands, and then held out both hands to me, holding mine and looking in my face.

"Other was the meeting I had planned for you and me, Wulfric, my brother-in-arms. Yet you are most welcome, for you at least are here to tell me of the days that are past."

"It is an ill telling," said Ingvar.

"That must needs be, seeing what is to be told," Hubba said quickly.

But those wise words of Osritha's had made things easier for me, for now Halfden knew that into the story of the jarl's death, I and my doings must come, so Ingvar's words meant little to him.

"You went not to Reedham?" I said, for now the men were at work again, and all was noise and bustle round us.

"I have come here first by Orkneys from Waterford, where we wintered," he answered. "And I have been over sure that no mishap might be in a long six months."

"What of the voyage?--let us speak of this hereafter," said Hubba.

And Halfden, wearily, as one who had lost all interest in his own doings, told him that it had been good, and that Thormod would give him the full tale of plunder.

Then came a chief from the ship whose face I knew, though he was not of our crew. It was that Rorik whose ship the Bosham bell had sunk, and who had been saved by Halfden's boats. He knew me, after scanning me idly for a moment, and greeted me, asking why I was not at Reedham to make that feast of which Halfden was ever speaking, and so passed on.

So we went up to the great hall in silence, sorely cast down; and that was Halfden's homecoming.

Little joy was there on the high place at the feast that night, though at the lower tables the men of our crew (for so I must ever think of those whose leader I had been for a little while, with Halfden) held high revelling with their comrades. Many were the tales they told, and when a tale of fight and victory was done, the scald would sing it in verse that should be kept and sung by the winter fire till new deeds brought new songs to take its place.

Presently Halfden rose up, after the welcome cup had gone round and feasting was done, and the ale and mead began to flow, and he beckoned me to come with him. Hubba would have come also, but Ingvar held him back.

"Let Wulfric have his say first," he growled; and I thanked him in my mind for his thought.

So we went to the inner chamber, where Osritha would sit with her maidens, and Halfden said:

"This matter is filling all my thoughts so that I am but a gloomy comrade at the board. Tell me all, and then what is done is done. One may not fight against the Norn maidens {xiv}."

There I told him all my story, and he remembered how I had told him, laughing, of Beorn's jealousy at first. And when my tale was nearly done Osritha crept from her bower and came and sat beside Halfden, pushing her hand into his, and resting her head on his shoulder.

Then I ended quickly, saying that Ingvar had done justice on Beorn. And at that remembrance the maiden shivered, and Halfden's face showed that he knew what the man's fate was like to have been at the great jarl's hands.

"So, brother," he said, when I left off speaking, "had I gone to Reedham there would have been burnt houses in East Anglia."

"In Reedham?" said I.

"Wherever this Beorn had a house; and at Caistor where that old fool Ulfkytel lives, and maybe at one or two other places on the way thither. And I think your father and Egfrid your brother would have helped me, or I them."

So he doubted me not at all, any more than I should have doubted his tale, were he in my place and I in his.

Then I said that I myself had no grudge against Earl Ulfkytel, for he had sent me here.

"Why then, no more have I," answered Halfden; "for he is a wiseacre and an honest one, and maybe meant kindly. Ingvar would have slain both guilty and innocent, and told them to take their wrangle elsewhere, to Hela or Asgard as the way might lead them."

Now as he said that, I, who looked ever on the face of her whom I loved, saw that a new fear had come into Osritha's heart, and that she feared somewhat for me. Nor could I tell what it was. But Halfden and I went on talking, and at last she could not forbear a little sob, and at that Halfden asked what ailed her.

"May I speak to you, my brother, very plainly, of one thing that I dread?" she asked, drawing closer to him.

"Aye, surely," he answered in surprise.

"Remember you the words that Ingvar said to the priest of the White Christ who came from Ansgar at Hedeby {xv}, while our father was away in the ships?"

"Why, they were like words. He bade him go and settle the matter with Odin whom he would not reverence, and so slew him."

"Aye, brother. And he said that so he would do to any man who would not honour the gods."

"Why do you remember that, Osritha?"

"Because--because there will be the great sacrifice tomorrow, and Wulfric, your friend, is not of our faith."

Then Halfden was silent, looking across at me, and all at once I knew that here was a danger greater than any I had yet been through. Fire I had passed through, and water, and now it was like to be trial by steel. And the first had tried my courage, and the next my endurance, as I thought; but this would try both, and my faith as well.

"That is naught," said Halfden, lightly. "It is but the signing of Thor's hammer, and I have seen Wulfric do that many a time, only not quite in our way, thus;" and he signed our holy sign all unknowing, or caring not. "And to eat of the horse that is sacrificed--why, you and I, Wulfric, did eat horse on the Frankish shores; and you thought it good, being nigh starved--you remember?"

I remembered, but that was different; for that we did because the shores were so well watched that we ran short of food, and had to take what we could under cover of night at one time. But this of which Osritha spoke was that which Holy Writ will by no means suffer us to do--to eat of a sacrifice to idols knowingly, for that would be to take part therein. Nor might I pretend that the holy sign was as the signing of Thor's Hammer.

"Halfden," I said, having full trust in him, "I may not do this. I may not honour the old gods, for so should I dishonour the White Christ whom I serve."

"This is more than I can trouble about in my mind," said Halfden; "but if it troubles you, I will help you somehow, brother Wulfric. But you must needs come to the sacrifice."

"Cannot I go hunting?"

"Why, no; all men must be present. And to be away would but make things worse, for there would be question."

Then I strengthened myself, and said that I must even go through with the matter, and so would have no more talk about it. But Osritha kept on looking sadly at me, and I knew that she was in fear for me.

Now presently we began to talk of my home and how they would mourn me as surely lost. And I said that this mourning would be likely to hinder my sister's wedding for a while. And then, to make a little more cheerful thought, I told Halfden what his father had said about his wishing that he had been earlier with us.

"Why, so do I," said my comrade, laughing a little; "for many reasons," he added more sadly, thinking how that all things would have been different had he sailed back at once.

Then he must needs go back to the question of the sacrifice.

"Now I would that you would turn good Dane and Thor's man, and bide here with us; and then maybe--"

But Osritha rose up quickly and said that she must begone, and so bade us goodnight and went her way into the upper story of that end of the great hall where her own place was. Whereat Halfden laughed quietly, looking at me, and when she was quite gone, and the heavy deerskins fell over the doorway, said, still smiling:

"How is this? It is in my mind that my father's wish might easily come to pass in another way not very unlike."

That was plain speaking, nor would I hesitate to meet the kindly look and smile, but said that indeed I had come to long that it might be so. But I said that the jarl, his father, had himself shown me that no man should leave his old faith but for better reasons than those of gain, however longed for. For that is what he had answered Eadmund the king when the land was offered him, and he was asked to become a Christian.

"Yet if such a thing might be," said Halfden, "gladly would I hail you as brother in very truth."

So we sat without speaking for a while, and then Halfden said that were I to stand among the crowd of men on the morrow there would surely be no notice taken of me.

Yet as I lay on my wolf skins at the head of the great hall, and prayed silently--as was my wont among these heathen--I asked for that same help that had been given to men of old time who were in the same sore strait as I must very likely be in tomorrow.

Then came to me the thought: "What matters if outwardly I reverence Thor and Odin while I inwardly deny them?" and that excuse had nigh got the better of me. But I minded what our king had told me many a time: how that in the first christening of our people it had ever been held to be a denying of our faith to taste the heathen sacrifices, or to bow the head in honour, even but outward, of the idols, so that many had died rather than do so. And he had praised those who thus gave up their life.

Then, too, I remembered the words of the Prior of Bosham concerning martyrs. And we had been led to speak of them by this very question as to sacrifice to the Danish gods. So I made up my mind that if I might escape notice, I would do so--and if not, then would I bear the worst.

So I fell asleep at last. And what it may have been I know not--unless the wind as it eddied through the high windows clashed some weapon against shield on the walls with a clear ringing sound--but I woke with the voice of Bosham bell in my ears--and Rorik and Halfden each in his place started also, and Rorik muttered a curse before he lay down again, for he sat up, looking wildly.

But greatly cheered with that token was I, for I knew that help was not far from me, and after that I had no more fear, but slept peacefully, though I thought it was like to be my last night on earth.

CHAPTER X. WHAT BEFELL AT THE GREAT SACRIFICE.

Very early in the gray morning Halfden woke me, and he was fully armed, while at the lower end of the hall the courtmen were rising and arming themselves also, for Vikings must greet Odin as warriors ready to do battle for him when Ragnaroek {xvi} and the last great fight shall come.

"Rise and arm yourself," he said; "here are the arms in which you fought well in your first fight, and axe and sword beside. Now you shall stand with our crew, and so none of them will heed you, for they love you, and know your ways are not as ours. So will all be well."

Then I thanked him, for I surely thought it would be so; and I armed myself, and that man who had been my own shield man when I led the midship gang helped me. One thing only I wished, and that was that I had the axe which Lodbrok made for me, for then, I told the man, I should feel as a Viking again, and that pleased him.

"However," he said, "I think I have found an axe that is as near like your own as may be."

And he had done so, having had that kindly thought for me. Then we went out, for the horns were blowing outside the town in the ash grove where the Ve, as they call the temple of Odin and Thor and the other gods, was. And overhead, high and unseen in the air, croaked the ravens, Odin's birds, scared from their resting places by the tramp of men, yet knowing that their share in the feast was to come.

I shivered, but the sound of the war horns, and the weight and clank of the well-known arms, stirred my blood at last, and when we fell in for our short march, Halfden and Thormod, Rorik and myself leading our crew, I was ready for all that might come, if need for a brave heart should be.

Silently we filed through the bare trunks of the ashes, the trees of Thor, where many a twisted branch and dead trunk showed that the lightning had been at work, until we came to the place of the Ve in its clearing.

There stood the sanctuary, a little hut--hardly more--built of ash-tree logs set endwise on a stone footing, and roofed with logs of ash, and closed with heavy doors made of iron-bolted ash timber also. This temple stood under the mightiest ash tree of all, and there was a clear circle of grass, tree bordered, for a hundred yards all round it, and all that circle was lined with men, armed and silent.

Before the temple was a fire-reddened stone, the altar. And on it were graven runes, and symbols so strange that neither I nor any man could read them, so old were they, for some men said that stone and runes alike were older than the worship of Odin himself, having been an altar to gods that were before him. And a pile of wood was ready on the altar.

Beside it stood Ingvar, clad in golden shining scale armour, and with a gilded horned helm and scarlet cloak that hung from shoulders to heel; for as his forefathers had been before him, beyond the time when the Danes and Angles came from their far eastern home {xvii}, led by Odin himself, he was the "godar", the priest of the great gods of Asgard, and his it was to offer the sacrifice now that Lodbrok his father was dead.

Now, as I stood there I thought how my father had told me that our own family had been the godars of our race in the old days, so that he and I in turn should have taken our place at such an offering as Ingvar was about to make. And straightway I seemed to be back in the long dead past, when on these same shores my forbears had worshipped thus before seeking the new lands that they won beyond the seas. And that was a strange thought, yet now I should know from what our faith had brought us.

In a little while all Ingvar's following had come, and there were many chiefs whose faces I had seen of late as they came to plan the great raid that was to be when the season came. And the men with them were very many, far more than we could have gathered to a levy on so short notice; and all were well armed, and stood in good order as trained and hardened warriors. No longer could I wonder at all I had heard of the numbers of the Danish hosts who came to our shores, and were even now in Northumbria, unchecked.

There was silence in all the great ring of men; and only the rustle of the wind in the thick-standing ash trees around us--that seemed to hem us in like a gray wall round the clearing--and the quick croak and flap of broad wings as the ravens wheeled ever nearer overhead, broke the stillness.

We of the crew for whose good voyage and safe return the offering was made stood foremost, facing the altar stone and the sanctuary door, and I, with Halfden and Thormod before me, and men of the crew to right and left, stood in the centre of our line, so that I could see all that went on.

Then, seeing that all was ready, Ingvar swung back the heavy door of the shrine, and I saw before me a great image of Thor the mighty, glaring with sightless eyes across the space at me. It was carved in wood, and the god stood holding in one hand Mioelner, his great hammer, and in the other the head of the Midgaard serpent, whose tailed curled round his legs, as though it were vainly trying to struggle free.

Then Ingvar turned and lighted the altar fire, and the smoke rose straight up and hung in the heavy morning air in a cloud over the Ve; and that seemed to be of good omen, for the men shouted joyfully once, and were again silent.

From behind the sanctuary two armed men led the horse for the sacrifice that should be feasted on thereafter; and it was a splendid colt, black and faultless, so that to me it seemed a grievous thing that its life should thus be spilt for naught. Yet I was the only one there who deemed it wasted.

Then Ingvar chanted words to which I would not listen, lest my heart should seem to echo them, so taking part in the heathen prayer. Over the horse he signed Thor's hammer, and slew it with Thor's weapon, and the two men flayed and divided it skilfully, laying certain portions before the jarl, the godar.

He sprinkled the blood upon doorway and statue, and then again chanting, laid those portions upon the altar fire, and the black smoke rose up from them, while all the host watched for what omens might follow.

The smoke rose, wavered, and went up, and then some breath of wind took it and drifted it gently into the open temple, winding it round the head of Thor's image and filling all the little building. And at that the men shouted again.

Then Ingvar turned slowly towards the shrine, and drawing his sword, lifted up the broad shining blade as if in salute, crying as he turned the point north and east and south and west:

"Skoal, ye mighty Ones!"

And at once, as one man all the host, save myself only, lifted their weapons in salute, crying in a voice that rolled back from the trees like an answering war shout:

"Skoal to the mighty Ones!"

But as for me, I stirred not, save that as by nature, and because I fixed my thoughts on the One Sacrifice of our own faith, I signed myself with the sign of the cross, only knowing this, that Thor and Odin I would not worship.

Suddenly, even as the echo of the shout died away, and while the weapons were yet upraised, the thick cloud of smoke rolled back and down, wrapping round Ingvar the godar as he stood between shrine and altar, and across the reek glared the sightless eyes of the idol again, cold and heedless.

Now of all omens that was the worst, for it must needs betoken that the sacrifice was not pleasing; and at that a low groan as of fear went round the host. Then back started Ingvar, and I saw his face through the smoke, looking white as ashes. For a long time, as it seemed to me, there was silence, until the smoke rose up straight again and was lost in the treetops. Even the ravens, scared maybe by the great shout, were gone, and all was very still.

At last Ingvar turned slowly to us and faced our crew.

"The sacrifice is yours," he said, "and if it is not accepted the fault is yours also. We are clear of blame who have bided at home."

Then Halfden answered for his men and himself:

"I know not what blame is to us."

But from close behind me Rorik lifted his voice:

"No blame to the crew--but here is one, a stranger, who does no honour to the gods, neither lifting sword or hailing them as is right, even before Thor's image."

Then I knew that the worst was come, and prepared to meet it. But Halfden spoke.

"All men's customs are not alike, and a stranger has his own ways."

But Ingvar's face was black with rage, and not heeding Halfden, he shouted:

"Set the man before me."

No man stirred, for indeed I think that most of our crew knew not who was meant, and those near me would, as Halfden told me, say nought.

Then said Ingvar to Rorik: "Point the man to me."

Then Rorik pointed to me. So I stood forth of my own accord, not looking at him, but at Ingvar.

"So," said the jarl, harshly, "you dare to dishonour Thor?"

I answered boldly, feeling very strong in the matter.

"I dishonour no man's religion, Jarl, neither yours nor my own."

"You did no honour to the Asir," he said sternly.

"Thor and Odin are not the gods I worship," I answered.

"I know. You are one of those who have left the gods of your fathers."

Then one of our men, who had stood next to me, spoke for me, as he thought.

"I saw Wulfric sign Thor's hammer even now. What more does any man want from a Saxon?"

Thereat Ingvar scowled, knowing, as I think, what this was.

"You claim to be truth teller," he said; "did you sign Thor's hammer?"

"I did not," I answered.

Then Halfden came to my side.

"Let Wulfric go his own way, brother. What matters it what gods he worships so long as he is good warrior and true man, as I and my men know him to be?"

So he looked round on the faces of my comrades, and they answered in many ways that this was so. And several cried:

"Let it be, Jarl. What is one man to Thor and Odin?"

Now I think that Ingvar would have let the matter pass thus, for the word of the host is not lightly to be disregarded. But Rorik would not suffer it.

"What of the wrath of the gods, Godar?" he said. "How will you put that aside?"

Then was a murmur that they must be appeased, but it came not from our crew; and Ingvar stood frowning, but not looking at me for a space, for he was pulled two ways. As godar he must not pass by the dishonour to the gods, yet as the son of the man whom I had saved, how could he harm me? And Rorik, seeing this, cried:

"I hold that this man should live no longer."

"Why, what dishonour has he done the gods?" said Halfden. "If he had scoffed, or said aught against them--that were a different thing. And what does Thor there care if one man pays no heed to him? Surely he can keep his own honour--leave it to him."

"It is dishonour to Thor not to hail him," said Rorik.

Now Ingvar spoke again to me:

"Why do you no honour to the gods?"

"My fathers honoured them, for the godarship was theirs, and would have been my father's and mine, even as it is yours, Jarl Ingvar. For good reason they left that honour and chose another way and a better. And to that way I cleave. I have done despite to no man's faith-- neither to yours nor my own."

At that Rorik lost patience, and lifting his axe, ground his teeth and said savagely:

"I will even make you honour Thor yonder."

Now at that Halfden saw a chance for me, and at once stayed Rorik's hand, saying in a loud voice:

"Ho! this is well. Let Wulfric and Rorik fight out this question--and then the life of him who is slain will surely appease the gods."

That pleased our crew well, for they had no great love for Rorik, who had taken too much command on him, for a stranger on board. Now, too, Ingvar's brows cleared, for he cared nothing for the life of either of us, so that the gods were satisfied with blood. And he said:

"So shall it be. Take axes and make short work of it. If Wulfric can slay Rorik, we know that he is innocent of aught to dishonour the gods. But if he is slain--then on his head is the blame."

Then he looked round and added:

"Let Guthrum and Hubba see fair play."

Now came Hubba, pleased enough, for he knew my axe play, and that chief whom they called Guthrum, a square, dark man with a pleasant, wise face, and took four spears, setting them up at the corners of a twelve-pace square, between the line of our crew and the altar.

So now it seemed to me that I must fight for our faith, for truth against falsehood, darkness against light. And I was confident, knowing this, that the death of one for the faith is often the greatest victory. So I said:

"I thank you, Jarl. I will fight willingly for my faith."

"Fight for what you like," said Ingvar, "but make haste over it."

Then Hubba and Guthrum placed me at one side of the square, and Rorik at the opposite. And I faced the image of Thor, so that under the very eyes of the idol I hated I must prove my faith.

Then came a longing into my mind to lift my axe in Thor's face and defy him, but I put it away, for how should an idol know of threat or defiance? Surely that would be to own some power of his.

When we were ready, Hubba and Guthrum, each with drawn swords, stood on either side of the spear-marked square, and signed to Ingvar to give the word. At once he did so.

Then I strode forward five paces and waited, but Rorik edged round me, trying to gain some vantage of light, and I watched him closely.

And all the host stood silent, holding breath, and the altar smoke rose up over our heads, and the ravens croaked in the trees, and over all stared the great statue of Thor, seeing naught.

Then like a wolf Rorik sprang at me, smiting at my left shoulder where no shield was to guard me. And that was Rorik's last stroke, for even as I had parried Thormod's stroke in sport, the man's wrist lit on the keen edge of my axe, so that hand and weapon flew far beyond me with the force of his stroke. Then flashed my axe, and Rorik fell with his helm cleft in twain.

Then roared our crew, cheering me:

"Skoal to the axeman! Ahoy!"

But I looked at Ingvar, and said:

"Short work have I made, Jarl."

Whereat he laughed a grim laugh, only answering:

"Aye, short enough. The gods are appeased."

Then I went back to my place beside Halfden, and our men patted my back, praising me, roughly and heartily, for it is not a viking's way to blame a man for slaying a comrade in fair fight and for good reason.

Now Ingvar stood before the shrine, and called to the gods to be heedful of the blood spilt to purge whatever dishonour or wrong had been done. And he hung up the weapons of the slain man in the shrine, and after that closed its doors and barred them; and we marched from the Ve silently and swiftly, leaving the body of Rorik alone for a feast to the birds of Odin before the dying altar fire.

Now was I light hearted, thinking that the worst was past, and so also thought Halfden, so that we went back and sought Osritha, who waited, pale and anxious, to know how things should go with me, and when we found her I saw that she had been weeping.

"Why, my sister," said Halfden, "hardly would you have wept for my danger--or weeping you would be from my sailing to return."

But she answered not a word, and turned away, for his saying made her tears come afresh.

"Now am I a blunderer," said Halfden. "If there is one thing that I fear it is a weeping maiden."

And with that he went from the room, leaving me.

Then I took upon me to comfort Osritha, nor was that a hard task. And again I would have gone through this new danger I had faced, for it had brought the one I loved to my arms.

Not long might we be together, for now the feasting began, and I must go to Halfden and his brothers in the great hall. And then came remembrance to me. For now must I refuse to eat of the horse sacrifice, and maybe there would be danger in that. Yet I thought that no man would trouble more about me and my ways, so that I said naught of it to Osritha.

So I sat between Halfden and Thormod at the high place, and the whole hall was full of men seated at the long tables that ran from end to end, and across the wide floor. The womenfolk and thralls went busily up and down serving, and it was a gay show enough to look on, for all were in their best array.

Yet it seemed to me that the men were silent beyond their wont, surly even in their talk, for the fear of the omen of that eddying smoke was yet on them. And presently I felt and saw that many eyes were watching me, and those in no very friendly wise. Some of the men who watched were strangers to me, but as they sat among our crew, they must be the rest of the saved from Rorik's following. Others were men from beyond the village walls, and as Rorik's men had some reason and the others knew me not, I thought little of their unfriendly looks.

At last they brought round great cauldrons, in which were flesh hooks; to every man in turn, and first of all to Ingvar himself. He thrust the hook in, and brought up a great piece of meat, cutting for himself therefrom, and at once every man before whom a cauldron waited, did likewise, and it passed on. They signed Thor's hammer over the meat and began to eat.

Now after Ingvar had helped himself, the cauldron came to Guthrum, and then to Halfden, and then it must come to me, and I had heaped food before me that I might pass it by more easily, knowing that this was the sacrificed meat of which I might not eat. But the men stayed before me, and I made a sign to them to pass by, and honest Thormod leaned across me to take his share quickly, and they passed to him, wondering at me a little, but maybe thinking nothing of it. They were but thralls, and had not been at the Ve.

But Rorik's men had their eyes on me, and when the cauldron passed Thormod, and I had not taken thereout, one rose up and said, pointing to me:

"Lo! this Saxon will not eat of the sacrifice."

At that was a growl of wrath from the company, and Ingvar rose, looking over the heads of my comrades, saying:

"Have a care, thou fool; go not too far with me."

Then Guthrum laughed and said:

"This is foolishness to mind him; moreover, he has fought for and won his right to please himself in the matter."

So too said Halfden and Thormod, but against their voices were now many raised, saying that ill luck would be with the host for long enough, if this were suffered openly.

Now a Dane or Norseman takes no heed of the religion of other folk unless the matter is brought forward in this way, too plainly to be overlooked. But then, being jealous for his own gods, whom he knows to be losing ground, he must needs show that he is so. Nor do I blame him, for it is but natural.

So to these voices Ingvar the godar must needs pay heed, even if his own patience were not gone, so that he might not suffer that one should sit at the board of Thor and Odin, untasting and unacknowledging.

He called to two of his courtmen.

"Take this man away," he said, very sternly, "and put him in ward till tomorrow. Today is the feast, and we have had enough trouble over the business already."

The two men came towards me, and all men were hushed, waiting to see if I would fight. As they came I rose from my place, and they thought I would resist, for they shifted their sword hilts to the front, ready to hand. But I unbuckled my sword belt, and cast the weapon down, following them quietly, for it was of no good to fight hopelessly for freedom in a strange land.

Many men scowled at me as I passed, and more than one cried out on me. But Halfden and Thormod and Hubba, and more than were angry, seemed glad that this was all the harm that came to me just now. And Ingvar leaned back in his great chair and did not look at me, though his face was dark.

They put me into a cell, oak walled and strong, and there left me, unfettered, but with a heavily-barred door between me and freedom; and if I could get out, all Denmark and the sea around me held me prisoner.

Yet I despaired not altogether, for already I had gone through much danger, and my strength had not failed me.

Now, how I spent the daylight hours of that imprisonment any Christian man may know, seeing that I looked for naught but death. And at last, when darkness fell, I heard low voices talking outside for a little while, and I supposed that a watch was set, for the cell door opened to the courtyard from the back of the great house.

Now I thought I would try to sleep, for the darkness was very great, and just as I lay down in a corner the barring of the door was moved, and the door opened gently.

"Do you sleep, Wulfric?" said Halfden's voice, speaking very low.

"What is it, brother?" I asked in as low a voice, for I had not been a viking for naught.

I saw his form darken the gray square of the doorway, and he came in and swung to the door after him; then his hand sought my shoulder, and I heard a clank of arms on the floor.

"See here, Wulfric," he said, "you are in evil case; for all Rorik's men and the men from outside are calling for your death; they say that Rorik had no luck against you because the Asir are angry, and that so it will be with all the host until you have paid penalty."

"What say you and our crew?"

"Why, we had good luck with you on board, and hold that Rorik had done somewhat which set Thor against him, for he got shipwrecked, and now is killed. So we know that your ways do not matter to Thor or Odin or any one of the Asir, who love a good fighter. But we know not why you are so obstinate; still that is your business, not ours."

"What says Ingvar?" I asked.

"Naught; but he is godar."

"Aye," said I. "So I must die, that is all. What said Ragnar Lodbrok about that?"

And I spoke to him the brave words that his forefather sang as he died, and which he loved:

"Whether in weapon play
Under the war cloud,
Full in the face of Death
Fearless he fronts him,
Death is the bane of
The man who is bravest,

> He loveth life best who
> Furthest from danger lives.
> Sooth is the saying that
> Strongest the Norns are.
> Lo! at my life's end
> I laugh--and I die."

"Nay, my brother," said Halfden earnestly; "think of me, and of Osritha, and seem to bow at least."

That word spoken by my friend was the hardest I ever had to bear, for now I was drawn by the love that had been so newly given me. And I put my hands before my face and thought, while he went on:

"If I were asked to give up these gods of ours, who, as it seems to me, pay mighty little heed to us--and I knew that good exchange was offered me--well then--I should--"

I ended that word for him.

"You would do even as your father, and say that unless for better reason than gain--aye, however longed for--you would not."

"Aye--maybe I would, after all," he answered, and was silent.

Then he said, "Guthrum and I spoke just now, and he said that your faith must be worth more than he knew, to set you so fixedly on it."

Now I would have told him that it was so, but there came a little sound at the door, and Halfden went and opened it. Across its half darkness came a woman's form, and Osritha spoke in her soft voice.

"Brother, are you here yet?"

"Aye, sister, both of us--come and persuade this foolish Wulfric."

Then I spoke quickly, for it seemed to me that if Osritha spoke and urged me, I should surely give way.

"Nay, but you must not persuade me--would you have had us Christians bid your father choose between death and gain for the sake of winning him to our faith?"

Then said Halfden, "That would I not."

But in the dark Osritha came to my side and clung to me, so that I was between those two whom I loved and must lose, for Halfden held my right hand, and Osritha my left, and she was weeping silently for me.

"Listen," I said, for the speaking must be mine lest they should prevail. "Should I die willingly for one who has given His life for me?"

"Aye, surely--if that might be," said Halfden.

"Now it comes into my mind that hereafter you will know that I do not die for naught. For He whom I worship died for me. Nor may I refuse to spend life in His honour."

Then they were silent, until Osritha found her voice and said:

"We knew not that. I will not be the one to hold you from what is right."

At that Halfden rose up, for he had found a seat of logs and sat by me on it, sighing a long sigh, but saying:

"Well, this is even as I thought, and I will not blame you, my brother. Fain would I have kept you here, and sorely will Osritha pine when you are gone. But you shall not die, else will the justice of Ulfkytel come to naught."

Then I heard again the clank of arms, and Halfden bent down, as I might feel.

"Can you arm yourself in the dark?" he said.

"Why, surely! It is not for the first time," I answered.

He thrust my mail shirt against me, and laid a sword in my hand, and set my helm on my head, all awry because of the darkness.

"Quickly," he said.

Then a new hope that came to me made me clasp Osritha's hand and kiss it before I must see to arming myself; but she clung to me yet, and I kissed her gently, then turning away sorely troubled went to work.

Soon I was ready for Halfden's word, and Osritha buckled on my sword for me, for she had felt and taken it. Halfden opened the door and went out into the night, speaking low to one whom I could not see; and so I bade farewell to her whom I loved so dearly, not knowing if I should ever look on her again.

But she bade me hope ever, for nor she nor I knew what the days to come might bring us.

"Ready," said Halfden; "follow me as if you were a courtman till we come to the outer gate."

Then with Osritha's handclasp still warm on mine I went out and followed him, and she sought the maiden who waited beside the door, and was gone.

When we came to the great gates, they were shut. The sounds of feasting went on in the hall, and the red light glared from the high windows. Forgotten was all but revelling--and the guard who kept the gate was Raud the forester, my friend. He opened the gates a little, and we three slipped out and stood for a moment together. The night was very dark, and the wind howled and sang through the stockading, and none seemed to be about the place.

There Halfden took my hand and bade me farewell very sadly.

"This is the best I may do for you, my brother. Go with Raud to his house, and thence he and Rolf and Thoralf your shield man, who all love you, will take you even to Hedeby, where there are Christian folk who will help you to the sea and find passage to England. And fare you well, my brother, for the days we longed for in your land will never be--"

"Come in the ship to England, that so there may be good times even yet," I said.

"Aye, to England I shall surely come--not to seek you, but at Ingvar's bidding. Yet to East Anglia for your sake I will not come."

Then he grasped my hand again in farewell, and he went inside the gates and closed them, and Raud and I went quickly to his place.

There we found those two other good friends of mine waiting, and they told me that all was well prepared to save them from the wrath of Ingvar, for they had been bidden to carry messages, and other men of the crew who lived far off would do this for them, for I feared for their lives also when the flight was known.

Long was the way to Hedeby, where Ansgar the Bishop had built the first church in all Denmark. But we won there at last and in safety. And there Ansgar's folk received me well, and I parted from my three comrades, not without grief, so that I asked them to take service with us in England. Almost they consented, but Rolf and Thoralf had wives and children, and Raud would by no means leave his brother.

Now in a few days, a company of merchants went from Hedeby with goods for England, and with them I went; and in no long time I came into Ingild's house by London Bridge, and was once more at home as the second week in May began.

CHAPTER XI. THE COMING OF INGVAR'S HOST.

Aught but joy did I look for in my homecoming, but it was all too like that of Halfden, my friend.

No need to say how my kind godfather met me as one come back from the dead, nor how I sent gifts back to Ansgar's people, who sorely needed help in those days.

But very gently the old man told me that Elfric my father was dead, passing suddenly but a month since, while by his side sat Ulfkytel the Earl, blaming himself for his blindness and for his haste in not waiting for the king's judgment, and yet bidding my father take heart, for he had never known his ways of justice fail. And he asked forgiveness also, for there had been a deadly feud concerning this between him and my people, so that but for Eadmund the King there would have been fighting. Yet when one told Ulfkytel that men held that my father's heart broke at my loss, the great earl had made haste to come and see him, and to say these things. So they made peace at last.

When I knew this it seemed to me that I had lost all, and for long I cared for nothing, going about listless, so that Ingild feared that I too should grow sick and die. But I was young and strong, and this could not last, and at length I grew reconciled to things as they were, and Ingild would speak with me of all that I had seen in Denmark.

Now when I told him what I feared of the coming of Ingvar's host he grew grave, and asked many things about it.

"Ethelred the King is at Reading," he said; "let us go and speak to him of this matter."

So we rode thither, and that ride through the pleasant Thames-side country was good for me. And when we came to the great house where the king lay, we had no trouble in finding the way to him, for Ingild was well known, and one of the great Witan {xviii} also.

I told Ethelred the king of England all that I had learned, and he was troubled. Only we three were in his council chamber, and to us he spoke freely.

"What can I do? Much I fear that East Anglia must fight her own battles at this time. Pressed am I on the west by Welsh and Dane, and my Wessex men have their hands full with watching both. And it is hard to get men of one kingdom to fight alongside those of another, even yet. And this I know full well, that until a host lands I can gather no levy, for our men will not wait for a foe that may never come."

I knew that his words were true, and could say nothing. Only I thought that it had been better if we had held to our Mercian overlords in Ecgberht's time than fight for this Wessex sovereign who was far from us; for that unhealed feud with Mercia seemed to leave us alone now.

"Yet," said Ethelred, "these men are not such great chiefs, as it seems. Maybe their threats will come to naught."

But I told him of that great gathering at the sacrifice, and said also that I thought that needs must those crowded folks seek riches elsewhere than at home. Then he asked me many things of the corn and cattle and richness of the land; and when I told him what I had seen, he looked at me and Ingild.

"Such things as crowding and poverty and hardness drove us from that shore hither. I pray that the same be not coming on us that we brought to the ancient people the Welsh, whose better land we took and now hold."

So we left him, and I could see that the matter lay heavily on his mind.

In a week thereafter I rode away homeward, and came first to Framlingham, where Eadmund our own king was. Very glad was he to see me safely home again.

"Now am I, with good Ingild your other godfather, in Elfric's place toward you," he said; "think of me never as a king, but as a father, Wulfric, my son."

And he bade me take my place as Thane of Reedham, confirming me in all rights that had been my father's. With him, too, was the great earl, and he begged my forgiveness for his doubt of me, though he was proud that his strange manner of finding truth was justified. Good friends were Ulfkytel and I after that, though he knew not that in my mind was the thought of Osritha, to whom he had, as it were, sent me.

Now every day brought fear to me that Ingvar's host was on its way overseas to fall on us. And this I told to Eadmund and the earl, who could not but listen to me. Yet they said that the peace between us and the Danes was sure, and that even did they come we should be ready. When I pressed them indeed, they sent round word to the sheriffs to be on the watch, and so were content. For our king was ever a man of peace, hating the name of war and bloodshed, and only happy in seeing to the welfare of his people, giving them good laws, and keeping up the churches and religious houses so well that there were none better to be found than ours in all England.

This pleased me not altogether, for I knew now how well prepared for war the Danes were, and I would fain have had our men trained in arms as they. But my one voice prevailed not at all, and after a while I went down to Reedham, and there bided with my mother and Eadgyth, very lonely and sad at heart in the place where I had looked for such happiness with my father and Lodbrok and Halfden at first, and now of late, for a few days, with Osritha, and Halfden in Lodbrok's place.

For all this was past as a dream passes, and to me there seemed to hang over the land the shadow of the terrible raven banner, which Osritha had helped to work for Lodbrok and his host, in the days before she dreamed that it might be borne against a land she had cause to love.

Ever as the days went by I would seek the shipmen who came to Reedham on their way up the rivers, so that I might hear news from the Danish shore, where Osritha was thinking of me, till at last I heard from a Frisian that three kings had gathered a mighty host, and were even now on their way to England.

I asked the names of those three, and he told me, even as I had feared, that they were called Ingvar and Hubba and Halfden; and so I knew that the blow was falling, and that Ingvar had stirred up other chiefs to join him, and so when the host gathered at some great Thing, he and his brothers had been hailed kings over the mighty following that should do their bidding in the old Danish way. For a Danish king is king over men, and land that he shall rule is not of necessity {xix}.

Again I warned Eadmund, and again he sent his messages to Ulfkytel the Earl and to the sheriffs, and for a few weeks the levies watched along the shore of the Wash; and then as no ships came, went home, grumbling, as is an East Anglian's wont, and saying that they would not come out again for naught, either for king or earl.

Now after that I spent many a long hour in riding northward along the coast, watching for the sails of the fleet, and at other times I would sit on our little watch tower gazing over the northern sea, and fearing ever when the white wing of a gull flashed against the skyline that they were there. And at last, as I sat dreaming and watching, one bright day, my heart gave a great leap, for far off to the northward were the sails of what were surely the first ships of the fleet.

I watched for a while, for it was ill giving a false alarm and turning out our unwilling levies for naught, for each time they came up it grew harder to keep them, and each time fewer came. In an hour I knew that there were eight ships and no more, and that they were heading south steadily, not as if intending to land in the Wash, but as though they would pass on to other shores than ours. And they were not Ingvar's fleet, for he alone had ten ships in his ship garth.

They were broad off the mouth of our haven presently, and maybe eight miles away, when one suddenly left the rest and bore up for shore--sailing wonderfully with the wind on her starboard bow as only a viking's ship can sail--for a trading vessel can make no way to windward save she has a strong tide with her.

She came swiftly, and at last I knew my own ship again, and thought that Halfden had come with news of peace, and maybe to take me to sea with him, and so at last back to Osritha. And my heart beat high with joy, for no other thought than that would come to me for a while, and when she was but two miles off shore, I thought that I would put out to meet and bring the ship into the haven; for he knew not the sands, though indeed I had given him the course and marks-- well enough for a man like Thormod--when I was with him. And there came over me a great longing to be once more on the well-known deck with these rough comrades who had so well stood by me.

But suddenly she paid off from the wind, running free again to the southward down the coast, and edging away to rejoin the other ships. And as she did so her broad pennon was run up and dipped thrice, as in salute; and so she passed behind the headlands of the southern coast and was lost to my sight.

I bided there in my place, downcast and wondering, until the meaning of it all came to me; remembering Halfden's last words, that he would not fall on East Anglia. Now he had shown me that his promise was kept. He had left the fleet, and was taking his own way with those who would follow him.

Yet if he had eight ships, what would Ingvar's host be like? Greater perhaps than any that had yet come to our land, and the most cruel. For he would come, not for plunder only, but hating the name of England, hating the name of Christian, and above all hating the land where his father had been slain.

I climbed down from the tower, and found my people talking of the passing ships, and rejoicing that they had gone. Already had some of them piled their goods in waggons ready for flight, and some were armed. Then, as in duty bound, I sent men in haste to the earl at Caistor to report this, telling him also that the great fleet of which this was a part was surely by this token on its way.

By evening word came back from him. He had sure news from Lynn that the great fleet had gone into the Humber to join the host at York, and that we need fear nothing. Men said that there were twenty thousand men, and that there were many chiefs besides those that I had named. This, he said, seemed over many to be possible, but it did not concern us, for they were far away.

Now, when I thought how the wind had held at any quarter rather than north or east for long weeks, it seemed to me likely that it was this only that had kept them from us, and that the going into Humber was no part of Ingvar's plan, but done as of necessity. For to bring over so mighty a host he must have swept up every vessel of all kinds for many a score miles along the shores. And they would be heavy laden with men, so that he must needs make the first port possible. Yet for a time we should be left in quiet.

Now I must say how things went at home, for my sister's wedding with Egfrid had been put off first by the doubt of my own fate, and then by the mourning for my father's death. Yet the joy of my return had brought fresh plans for it, and now the new house at Hoxne was nearly ready; so that both Egfrid and his folk were anxious that there should be no more delay.

I, too, when the coming of the Danes seemed a thing that might be any day, thought it well that Eadgyth should rather be inland at Hoxne, whence flight southward could be made in good time, than at Reedham, where the first landing might well be looked for. But when the fear passed for a while by reason of the news from Northumbria, the time was fixed for the end of November, just before the Advent season, and not earlier, because of the time of mourning.

So the summer wore through slowly to me, for I was sad at heart, having lost so much. And ever from beyond the Wash and from Mercia came news of Ingvar's host. The Northumbrian king was slain, and a Dane set in his place; and Burhred of Mercia bowed to the Danes, and owned them for lords; and at last Ethelred of Wessex came to himself and sent levies to meet the host, but too late, for Mercia was lost to him. Yet Eadmund our king, and even Ulfkytel, deemed that we were safe as ever behind our fenland barrier, fearing naught so long as no landing was made from across the Wash.

Yet when November came in, and at Egfrid's house all was bustle and preparation, we heard that Bardney was burnt, and Swineshead, and then Medehamstede {xx}. And the peril was close on us, and but just across our border.

"No matter," said men to one another. "It will be a hard thing for Danes to cross the great fens to come hither. They will turn aside into Mercia's very heart, and then the Wessex folk will rise."

But I feared, and two days before the wedding went to Harleston, where the king was, and urged him to have forces along the great wall we call Woden's Dyke even yet.

"Let us see your wedding first, Wulfric," he said. "Eadgyth would be sorely grieved if I were not there."

For he lay at Harleston to be near at hand, as the wedding was to be from the house of Egfrid's father, because Reedham seemed as yet a house of sorrow. And I was glad when the Thane asked that it should take place at Hoxne, and it was safer also.

Surely never moved host so swiftly as Ingvar's, for even as I went, heavily enough, from Eadmund's presence, a man spurred into the town saying that Earl Ulfkytel faced the Danes with a fair levy gathered in haste, between us and Wisbech. They had crossed the fens where no man dreamed that they might come, and were upon us as if from the skies.

Now Eadmund made no more delay, but all that night went forth the summons of the war arrow, and the men mustered in force at last in Thetford town, and I spurred back to Hoxne and found the thane, and spoke to him.

"Let the wedding go on," I said, "for the Danes are yet far, and must pass the earl and us also before they come hither. Now must I be with the king, but if I may, and Ulfkytel holds them back, I shall be at the wedding. And if it must be, I will warn you to fly, and so let Egfrid take his bride and my mother and his own folk southward to Colchester or London."

That, he thought, was well, and no word of fear or haste hindered the wedding gathering. Only some of the great thanes who should have been there were with the king or earl, and it seemed that the number of guests would be small.

I rode to Thetford, bidding Eadgyth look for me on the morrow in good time, and saying that the king would surely come also. But when I came to the town I knew that neither he nor I should be at Hoxne, for the Danes had scattered the levy, and Ulfkytel the great earl was slain, and with him many another friend of mine. And the men said that the Danes were marching swiftly onward, ever nearing Thetford, and burning and wasting all in their track.

We marched out of the town to meet them, for we had a good force behind us, and the men were confident of victory with the king himself to lead them. And he was cheerful also, and said to me, as I armed him:

"I would not have you leave the wedding; howbeit, if we beat back the Danes, which is a matter in the hands of the Lord of Hosts, both you and I will be there in time tomorrow."

Our mounted men met the Danes that evening -- the night before Eadgyth's wedding day--and we slept in our armour on Thetford heath waiting for them. And in the early morning our outposts were driven back on us, and the Danes were close on their heels.

Now Eadmund told me that I should not stand by him today, for so soon as the battle was over I must go to Hoxne, either with news of victory, or to bid them fly, and he would not keep me.

"I will not leave the place that is mine by right," I said.

"Not so," he answered; "I would bid you stand out of the battle for sweet Eadgyth's sake, but that I know you would not obey me."

And he smiled at me as he went on the great white horse he always rode, to draw up the men.

They cheered when he spoke to them, and I thought that they would fight well. Aye, and so they did, in their fierce untrained way. Many a long day it was since we of East Anglia stood in battle array, and the last time was against our own kin, save that now and again the men of some shoreward places would rise to beat off a Danish or Norse ship.

Now were the foes in sight, and they ranged up in close order when they saw we were ready. More than half their force was mounted, for the Lindsey uplands and marshes had given them horses enough of the best in England. And this was terrible, that over the host wheeled erne and raven and kite, as knowing to what feast the flapping of yon Raven banner called them.

Foremost of all rode a mighty chief on a black horse, and I saw that it was Ingvar himself, the king of the Danish host. Well I knew the armour, for it was that which he had worn at the great sacrifice, though now it shone no longer, but was dulled with the stains of many a hard fight. Now, too, round his helm ran the gold circlet of the king.

"Know you yon great man?" asked Eadmund of me; for I would not leave him, but stood before him in my place.

"It is Ingvar the king," I answered; "he who was Jarl Ingvar."

"Speak to him, and ask him to leave the land in peace," he said.

Now I thought that was of little use, but I would do the king's bidding, and asked what I should say.

"Offer him ransom, if you will," Eadmund answered.

So I went forward, and stood at a bowshot's length from our people, leaning on the axe that Lodbrok had made me, and there waited till the Danes came on. And presently Ingvar saw me, and knowing that I was one who would speak with the leader, rode up, looking curiously at me as he came.

"Skoal to Jarl Ingvar!" I said when he was close.

He reined up his horse in surprise, lifting his hand.

"Odin! It is Wulfric!" he said. "Now, skoal to you, Wulfric! But I would that you were not here."

"How is that, Jarl?" I asked; but I had ever heard that the jarl was in high good humour before a fight.

"I would not fight with you, for you have been our guest. And many a man have I questioned since yesterday, and all men say that you were my father's friend. It was a true story that you told me."

"You believed it rightly, Jarl."

"Aye--and therefore I will not fight with you."

Then I asked him to leave the land in peace, and his face darkened.

"I speak of yourself alone," he said, "as for land and king and people--that is a different matter."

"You have had your revenge," I said.

"What?" he asked fiercely. "Is the life of Lodbrok, my father, worth but the death of a hound like Beorn? Stand aside, Wulfric, and let me have my revenge in full."

Now, seeing that our talk was earnest, there rode up another Danish chief, and it was Guthrum, the man who had seemed to take my part at the idol feast. I was glad to see him come at this moment.

"Here is Halfden's friend," said Ingvar to him, "and he, forsooth, would have us go in peace."

And the Danish king laughed harshly.

"Why, so we will, if they make it worth our while," said Guthrum, nodding to me.

"What ransom will you take from us?" I asked them.

"The keeping of Eadmund, your king," answered Ingvar; "nothing more nor less."

"It seems to me that you will have to fight before you take him," I said plainly; for no man in all the Anglian ranks would have listened to that.

"That is too much," said Guthrum. "Tell him to own you as overlord and pay scatt {xxi} to us, holding the kingdom from you, and that will save fighting--and surely the whole land will be weregild enough for Jarl Lodbrok."

Then Ingvar thought for a moment, and said to me, still frowning:

"Go and tell your king those terms, and bring word again."

So I went back and told Eadmund, knowing full well what his answer would be. And it was as I thought.

"Go and tell this Ingvar that I will not give my land into the hands of the heathen, or own them as lords."

Now what I told Ingvar and Guthrum was this only, knowing that to give the full message was to enrage Ingvar:

"Eadmund refuses."

"Your king is a wise man," said Guthrum, "for who knows how a fight will go?"

Ingvar reined round his horse to go to his own men, and he and Guthrum left me standing there. I was turning away also, when the hoof beats of one horse stayed, and Ingvar called me in the voice he would use when most friendly with me.

"Wulfric," he said, "glad was I to find you gone, for I should surely have had to slay you before the shrine; but Thor is far off now, and I have forgotten that, and only do I remember that good comrade to us all you have been in hall and forest. And ere I sailed--one whom you know--that one who stayed my hand from Beorn--made me promise-- aye, and swear by my sword--that you at least I would not harm. And I will not. Stand aside from this fight."

Now, had I not known the great love and reverence in which those three wild brothers held Osritha, I should have been amazed at these words from Ingvar; but there is somewhat of good to be found in every man.

Then I answered:

"I must fight for my land, Ingvar, but I also would fain not fight against yourself. Where stand you in your line?"

"On the right," he said; "Guthrum is on the left."

"Where is Hubba?" I asked, wondering.

"He is not far from us. He will come when I need his help."

"Then we need not meet," I said; "I am in the centre."

Now we both returned to our places, and again Eadmund, after I had told him that we must fight, asked me to stand out.

"For," said he, "you are in her father's place to Eadgyth."

"Until after the wedding, my king," I said; "but you are in my father's place to me always. Should I have left him?"

So I said no more, but stood in my place before him, for I loved him now best of all men in the world since my father was gone, and it seemed well to me to die beside him if die he must.

Now our king gave the word, crying, "Forward, Christian men!" and we shouted and charged with a good will on the Danes, and the battle began. Hard fighting it was on both sides, but our men in their want of order jostled and hindered one another, so that I saw more than one struck down by mischance by his own comrades. But the Danes kept their even line, bent round into half a circle so that we could not outflank them, and our numbers were nearly equal.

Men have said that I did well in that fight, but so did we all, each in his way. All I know of my own deeds is that I kept my own life, and that once a ring of men stood before me out of reach of my axe, not one seeming to care to be first within its swing. And ever Eadmund's clear voice cheered on his men from behind me.

So the battle went on from the first daylight for an hour's space, and then the steadfastness of the Danish line began to strike terror into our men, and the Danish horsemen charged on our flanks and broke us up; and then all at once a panic fell on our levies, and they wavered, and at once the horsemen were among them everywhere, and the field was lost to us. Before I knew what had befallen I was hurried away in a dense throng of our men, who swept me from before the king, and I was soon in Thetford streets, where I thought that surely we should have rallied, for there is no stronger town or better walled in all East Anglia.

In the marketplace sat Eadmund on his white horse, unhelmed that the men might know him yet living, for in the flight word had gone round that he had fallen, and now the men seemed to be taking heart and gathering round him.

But even as I reached him, a fresh throng of flying men came down the street from the gate next the Danes, and after them came a score of the terrible horsemen, driving a hundred like sheep before them. At that sight the few who were gathering fled also, leaving the king and myself and four other thanes alone. I was the only one on foot.

Then one of those thanes grasped the bridle of the king's horse and led him away, crying:

"Come, for our sakes; needs must fly. Let us go to Framlingham."

So they rode, against the king's will as one might see, from the place, and went away towards the southern gate of the town. And seeing that the Danes were in the town I knew that all was lost, and that here I might stay no longer if Eadgyth was to be saved.

I ran to where I had left my horse, and mounted and fled also, following the king, for that gate led to the road along the south bank of the river. I knew not if he had crossed the bridge or no, but over the river was my way, and I had my own work to be done, and some twenty miles to be covered as quickly as might be. Glad was I that I had chosen to fight on foot that day, for my horse was fresh.

Terrible it was to see the panic in the town as the poor folk knew that the Danes were on them. They filled the road down which I must go, thronging in wild terror to the gates, and I will not remember the faces of that crowd, for they were too piteous.

Glad I was to be free from them at last, and upon the road where I could ride freely, for as they left the town they took to the woods and riverside swamps, and save for a few horsemen flying like myself, the road was soon clear. Then, too, these horsemen struck away from the road one by one, and at last I rode on alone.

Now my one thought was for those at Hoxne, and to urge them to instant flight, and I thought that even now Humbert the Bishop would be in the little church, waiting for the bride to come.

Then I would hasten the more, for to reach the church from Egfrid's father's house the river Dove must be crossed; and I would keep them from returning to this side if I could be in time, for we might break down the timber-built bridge and so delay the crossing of the Danes. Yet they might be for days in Thetford before they began to raid in the country.

Swiftly I rode on, for my horse was a good one and fresh, and at last, after many miles were passed, I came to a place where I could see a long stretch of road before me. There rode the king on his white horse, and with him those four thanes. I could not mistake that party, and I thought I knew where they were going. The king would warn my people himself, and so take refuge beyond Hoxne, on the other side of the river, at South Elmham, with Bishop Humbert.

I rode after, but I gained little on them; nor did I care much, for the king would do all that I might. In a few minutes more I should know if he crossed Hoxne bridge, and if he did so they were safe.

I lost sight of the party as they came into a wood, and there my horse stumbled. He had lost a shoe. That was little to me now, but it kept me back; and now I heard the quick gallop of horses behind me, and looked to see who came, for I thought that more fugitives followed, most likely. I had heard the sound coming on the wind more than once before as I rode on the wayside grass.

They were Danes. Twelve of them there were, and foremost of all rode Ingvar on his black horse. Well for the king that they had no change of steeds, but had ridden hotfoot after him from the battlefield. Now their horses were failing them, but they would take me, and delay would give the king another chance; and I was half-minded to stay and fight. Then I thought of Hoxne, and I put spurs to my horse and rode on again.

Now I came in sight of Hoxne bridge, and half feared that I should see the bridal train passing over; but many men were even now leaving the bridge, going towards the church, and I knew that they were there.

But of Eadmund and his thanes I saw nothing--only a lame white horse, that I thought like his, grazed quietly in a field by the roadside, so that for a moment my eyes went to it, thinking to see king and thanes there.

Ingvar was not a mile behind me, and I spurred on. And now I won to the turning that leads to the thane's house whence the company had passed, and a few villagers stood at the road corner. Them I asked how long it was since the bride had gone, and they stared at me in stupid wonder, making no answer. Then I bade them fly, for the Danes were coming; and at that they laughed, looking at one another slyly, proud of their own fancied wisdom. So I left them and rode on.

Even as I came to the hill down to the bridge my horse stumbled and almost fell, and when I gathered him up, not losing my seat, I knew he was beaten. And now I halted for good, unslinging my axe, and waiting to fight and hinder the Danes from going further, as yet. It was all I could do.

Hand over hand they came up to me, and now Hoxne bells rang out in merry peals as the bride and bridegroom left the church. The service was over, and unless our king had warned them, they would be coming back over the bridge in a few minutes. Yet, if he had warned them, surely the bells had not pealed out thus.

Now I heard the music play from across the water, and I heard the shouts of the people--and all the while the hoofs of Ingvar's horses thundered nearer and nearer. Then they came over the little rise in the road and were on me with levelled spears.

I got my horse between them and me, across the narrow roadway, and hove up my axe and waited. But when Ingvar saw who I was, he held up his hand, and his men threw up their spear points and halted, thinking perhaps that I was the king.

"Where is the king?" shouted Ingvar.

I saw that their horses were done, and not knowing which way the king had gone answered truly.

"I know not. The road forks, and that is as far as I know."

Then Ingvar swore a great oath.

"You know not which way he went?"

"I do not," I said.

"Catch a thrall and ask him," he said to his men.

And those silly folk were yet standing at the corner, maybe thinking us belated wedding guests, and the men took one, dragging him to their chief. But the man said that he had seen no horsemen pass. Truly he had heard some, but all men were at the house door waiting for the bride to come forth, and paid no heed.

So the king had passed by before the procession set out, and I knew not what to think.

"What bride?" said Ingvar.

And the music answered him, coming nearer and nearer, and now they were crossing Hoxne bridge--a bright little array of wedding guests, and in the midst I could see those two, Egfrid and Eadgyth, and after came a crowd of village folk.

"See yonder," said a Dane, pointing. "By Baldur, here is a wedding! Gold and jewels to be had for the taking!"

But my horse was across the road, and my axe was in the way, and I cried to Ingvar as the men began to handle their weapons.

"Mercy, Jarl Ingvar! This is my sister's wedding--that Eadgyth of whom your own sister would ever ask so much."

"Hold!" roared the chief, and his men stayed, wondering. "An you touch so much as a hair of any in that company--the man who touches, I will slay!" he said, and the men stared at him.

"Yon is the bridal of Reedham folk," he said, "and the bride is she who befriended Lodbrok. They shall not be hurt."

For he must needs justify himself, and give reason for withholding plunder from Danes as free as himself.

"Aye, King, that is right," they said on hearing that, and Ingvar turned to me.

"For Osritha's sake, lest I should harm you in aught," he said. "Now ask me no more. Let us meet them in peace."

Now I knew that my folk were safe for this time at least, and my heart was light, and so leaving my horse I walked beside the king, as his men called him, until we met the first of the company on this side of the bridge.

Then was a little confusion, and they stopped, not knowing what this war-stained troop might betoken. And I saw that no word had come of the great defeat as yet.

I went forward, calling to Egfrid and the thane his father, and looking at them so that they should show no fear or give any sign to the ladies present that all was not well.

"This is Jarl Ingvar himself, and these are his men," I said. "And the jarl would fain speak with Eadgyth my sister, of whom he has often heard."

And Egfrid, being very brave, although he must have seen well enough what this meant, kept his face well, and answered that Jarl Ingvar was welcome, coming in peace.

"Aye--in peace just now," answered Ingvar, looking at him. "Now, I will say this, that Wulfric's sister has found a brave husband."

Now Eadgyth heard the jarl's name, and knew naught of the terror that that name brought to all the land, and least of all that a battle could have been fought, for we had kept it from her. Nor had I told her of how nearly he had been to slaying me, for I would not make Osritha's brothers terrible to her. So she thought of him only as Lodbrok our friend's son, who had shown me hospitality in his own hall.

So when Egfrid took her hand and brought her forward, looking as I thought most beautiful in her bridal array, she smiled on the great Dane frankly, as in thanks for my sake.

Then Ingvar unhelmed, and spoke to her in courtly wise, even as he was wont to speak to Osritha.

"When I go back to my own land, lady, I shall have many questions asked me by one of whom you have doubtless heard, as to how our friend's sister was arrayed for her wedding. And that I shall not be able to say--but this I know, that I may tell Osritha that Wulfric's sister was worthy of Wulfric."

Now Eadgyth noted not the war stains on Ingvar's mail, but it was strange and terrible to me to see him sitting there and speaking as though the things of a stricken field were not the last, as it were, on which he had looked. But Eadgyth's eyes were downcast, though she was pleased.

"Thanks, Jarl Ingvar," she said; "often have I heard of Osritha. When you return I would have you thank her for her care of my brother--and I would thank you also, Jarl, for your care of him."

Now Ingvar reddened a little, but not with anger, for he saw that I had spoken at least no ill of him to Eadgyth.

"Nay, lady," he answered; "Halfden and Hubba and Osritha have to be thanked--if any thanks need be to us for caring for Jarl Lodbrok's preserver. Little share may I take of the matter."

"Yet I will thank all in your place," she said, and then shrank back to Egfrid's side.

Never had I seen a more handsome couple.

Then Ingvar laid his hand on a great golden snake that twined round his right arm, and I thought he was going to give it as a bridal gift to my sister, for that is ever a viking's way, to give lavishly at times when he might have taken, if the mood seizes him. But as he glanced at the gold he saw blood specks thereon, and I heard him mutter:

"No, by Freya, that were ill-omened."

And he did but seem to put it in place, as if thinking. Then he replaced his helm, bowing, and said:

"Now must I stay your rejoicing no longer. Fare you well, lady, and you, noble Egfrid; I must ride back to Thetford town on my own affairs. Yet I leave you Wulfric. Will you remember hereafter that you spoke with Ingvar the king, and that he was your friend?"

"Aye, surely," answered they both at once.

Then once more the music played, and the little train went on and up the hill, and Ingvar and I stood together for a while looking after them.

"I thank you, King," I said.

"Aye, Wulfric; and maybe you and yours are the only ones who will say that word to me in all this land. Now take my rede, and do you and your folk begone as soon as maybe, for even I cannot hold back men who are not from our own place."

Then I parted from him, going after my people, and thinking that all was well for us, and that surely our king was safe, until I came to where my horse still stood. There over the lane hedge looked that lame white horse that I had seen, speaking as it were in his own way to mine. And when I saw him thus near, it was indeed the king's, and a great fear that he was not far off took hold of me.

CHAPTER XII. IN HOXNE WOODS.

Many of the village folk loitered on the bridge and in the lanes, looking curiously at the Danes, and talking of the wedding and the like. And some of these I saw Ingvar's men questioning, and very soon a knot of them gathered round one man, and there was some loud talking.

Then I would have hastened back, but Ingvar saw me, and waved sternly to me to depart, and slowly enough I went on my way. But I could not forbear looking back when I reached the road to the house.

Only Ingvar was now on horseback, and the men seemed to be swarming over the bridge railings, and climbing under it among the timbers.

Then were shouts, and the village churls began to run every way, and one or two came up the hill towards me.

"What is it?" I asked.

"Oh, master," the first man cried, "when the bridal folk went over the bridge on the way to the church, one man looked over into the water, and cried that he saw somewhat sparkle therein like gold, and others looked, and some saw naught, but others said that they saw in the water as it were the image of golden spurs. And the Danes asked us if we saw the king; but we had not. Only one man laughing, in his fear as I think, said that the nearest thing to a crown that he had seen was the glint of golden spurs shining from the water yonder. Then looked the Danes--and now--oh master!"

The man grew white, pointed, and fled.

Haled and pushed and buffeted by the hands of the Danes, a man was dragged over the rail of the bridge from the network of cross timbers among which he had hidden, and I saw that the armour was that of Eadmund the King.

There, in that seemingly secure place, his thanes must have made him hide when his horse fell lame, for doubtless he would not hinder them in their flight, but would have taken sanctuary in the church. From some point in the road they must have seen their pursuers before I cared to look behind me to see who followed, for there was no mistaking the red cloaks that the Danes of the king's courtmen always wear.

This I thought at the time, and long afterwards learnt from one of those thanes that I was right. And it was their doing, not his, for the king would have gone to the church and there warned my people. But as it chanced there were no men in sight when the king hid, for all were gathered to the thane's house. And I asked that thane if they sent no warning message--and he said they had done so by a certain churl whom they met. But our folk never had it.

Now I knew not what to do, being torn with grief and fear. I dared not cross Ingvar again, lest I should change his mood, mild enough now, to some wild fit of rage, for I had not bided so long in his hall without learning that much of his ways. I stayed till I knew for certain that they had not harmed the king, and so saw him bound, and mounted behind one of the courtmen; and then when I saw them begin to come towards me, I went to the thane's house and told him all, calling him out from the feast.

"Let us mount and rescue the king," I said.

"Then will they kill him--better not. They will but hold him to ransom," the thane said.

I knew his first word was right, and now I left that and urged him to hasten the flight of all the party, bidding him take the road towards the south, ever away from the Danes.

"What will you do?" he asked, for I spoke not of coming with him.

"This," I answered. "I will pledge Ingild's word, as I know I may, for any ransom, going after the Danes and finding Guthrum, who will listen to me."

He thought that well, and then I asked where Humbert the Bishop was. He had gone back to South Elmham at once, and would be far on his road by this time, the thane said.

Then I went out and took a fresh horse from the stables and rode away into the great road. And when I came there, I saw with others the man who told me how the king's hiding place was found.

"How long have the Danes been gone?" I asked.

"Master," he answered, "they have gone back over the bridge, some of them riding forward towards Hoxne."

At that I knew that some plan of Ingvar's was that his men after victory should cross the river at Thetford, and so perhaps strike at Framlingham where the king's household was. But all along the march of the Danish host had been unresting, so that men had no time to prepare for their coming, or even to know what point they would reach next.

Then I sent by this man urgent messages to the thane that they should fly coastwards, crossing the river Waveney, perhaps, so as not to fall into the hands of the host at the first starting, for Ingvar's horsemen would be everywhere south of this and Thetford.

I rode fast over the bridge, for I feared for Humbert our good bishop, and when I came near the church the bells jangled, all unlike the wedding peals that I had heard so lately.

They had found a few late flowers, violets and marigolds and daisies and the like, and had strewn them before the bride as she left the church; and they lay there yet with bright hedgerow leaves to eke them out--but across the path, too, lay the dead body of a poor churl, dressed in his holiday gear, slain by a spear thrust, and the church was burning. Now the men who jangled the bells for help came down in haste, terrified as the fire took hold of the roof, for the church was all of wood and very old.

When they saw me they ran, thinking me yet another of their foes; but I rode after one and caught him, for he would by no means stay for calling, and I asked him what had happened, and where the bishop was.

"Alas, master," the man said, "they have slain my brother and fired the church, and now have ridden after the bishop. They slew my brother because he would not say by which road he had gone; and another told them, being in fear for his life--and our king is taken."

"Did they take the king by the road to South Elmham?"

"Four rode after the bishop with the great man on the black horse who was the leader. The rest went with the king up the track through Hoxne woods, but slowly."

Had I but one or two more with me surely now I should have followed up the king and tried to rescue him. But I think it would have been vain, for Ingvar's men would have slain him rather than lose him. But most of all I wondered at the boldness of these few men, who, with their leader, dared venture so far from their forces. Well did they know, however, how complete is the rout of a Saxon levy; and I too might have guessed it, since I had fled alone after the first five miles, while all those who had left the town with me scattered all ways.

Now the church was blazing from end to end, and one or two more men had gathered to me, seeing who I was.

"Take up yon body," I said, "and cast it into the church. So shall his ashes lie in holy ground at least. For you and yours must even take to the woods for a while. The Danes will be here."

That I think they did, for they were lifting the body as I went away and rode along the way that the bishop had taken, meaning at least to meet Ingvar, for I feared lest the men who had the king should slay him if they were followed.

Hardly a mile had I gone when Ingvar and his men came riding slowly back. Their beaten horses could do no more, and they had left following the bishop. Ingvar's face was black as night, and as he came he roared at me: "You here again! Now this passes all. Did I not bid you stand aside and hinder me not?"

"Aye, King," I answered, coldly enough. "But I cross you not. I have ransom to offer for the king."

"I will have no ransom," he said, very savagely.

"Nevertheless," I said quietly, knowing that his word was not the only one to be spoken on that matter, "let me tell you of it, that you may tell the other chiefs."

"I am the king," he answered, glaring at me.

"Then, King, hear my words, and give them to those under you."

"Speak to this man," he said, pointing to one of the courtmen; for they heard all I said, and he could not refuse to listen altogether to what concerned his fellow chiefs. Then he rode past me, and the men, save that one of whom he spoke, followed him.

Now I was angry as he, but kept that to myself, and waited till he was out of hearing before I looked at the man who waited. And when I did so, the man grinned at me, saying:

"Truly it is like old times to see you stand up thus to the jarl--king, I mean. There is not a man in our host dare do it."

And lo! it was my friend Raud the forester. His beard was gone, and he had a great half-healed scar across his jaw, so that I had not known him even had I noticed any but Ingvar.

Then I was glad, for here was one whom I could trust, even if his help was of little use.

"Glad am I to see you, Raud my friend, though it must be in this way. Why is the jarl so angry?"

"Why, because the bishop has escaped us. We never saw so much as his horse's tail. And if he be like the bishop we saw at Hedeby, I am glad."

"Surely he is," I said. "But now I have come to offer ransom for the king, and you must tell Guthrum and the other chiefs that it would be paid very quickly if they will take it."

At that Raud shook his head.

"I will tell them, but it is of little use. There has been talk of it before, but when we came into East Anglia Ingvar claimed the king for himself, giving up all else."

"Why?" I asked.

"Because when he made Beorn speak, Beorn said that Eadmund the King had set him on to slay Lodbrok. I heard the man confess it."

"But he left that story, telling the truth about himself," I said.

"Aye, so he did. But the tale has stuck in Ingvar's mind, and naught will he hear but that he will have revenge on him."

"What will he do?" I said, looking after the Danish king, who went, never turning in his saddle, with bowed shoulders as one who ponders somewhat.

"How should I know?" answered Raud, carelessly. "Let us go on. Maybe if you come with me we shall hear them speak together."

"Raud," I said, "if harm is done to the king, I shall surely fall on some of you--and Ingvar first of all."

"Not on me with axe, I pray you," he answered laughing, and twisting his head on one side. "I mind me of Rorik."

"Let us be going," I said, for I could not jest.

So we trotted after the party, and when we were near, Raud left me and went to Ingvar's side, speaking to him of what I had said. Then the jarl turned round to me, speaking quietly enough, but in a strange voice.

"Come with me and we will speak of this matter to Eadmund himself. Then will the business be settled at once."

That was all I would wish, and being willing to speak yet more with Raud, I said I would follow. He turned again, and looked no more at me.

Then I asked Raud of his brother, and of Thoralf, my other companion of flight. They were both slain, one at Gainsborough and one at Medehamstede. Thormod was with Halfden in Wessex, where they had made a landing to keep Ethelred, our Wessex overlord, from sending to our help. But as to Halfden, men said that he would not come to East Anglia, for the Lady Osritha had over persuaded him.

Then, though I would not ask in any downright way, I found that Osritha was well, but grieving, as they thought, for the danger of her brothers--and of that I had my own thoughts.

So with talk of the days that seemed so long past, we went on into Hoxne woods, through which Raud said that he had learnt we must go to meet the host in its onward march from Thetford.

"Jarl Ingvar lets not the grass grow under his feet," I said.

We came to a place where the woodland track broadened out into a clearing, and there waited the other Danes, and with them, sitting alone now on the horse, was Eadmund the King.

Pale he was, and all soiled with the stains of war, and with the moss and greenery of his strange hiding place; but his eye was bright and fearless, and he sat upright and stately though he was yet with his hands bound behind him.

I rode past Ingvar and to Eadmund's side, and throwing myself from my horse stood by him, while the Dane glared at us both without speaking.

"Why run thus into danger, Wulfric my son?" said the king, speaking gently; "better have let me be the only victim."

"That you shall not be, my king," I answered; "for if you must die, I will be with you. But I have come to try to ransom you."

"There are two words concerning that," said Ingvar in his cold voice. "Maybe I will take no gold for Eadmund."

"What shall we give you then?" I asked, looking earnestly at him.

"You heard what I said this morning before the battle. I have no other terms but those. And I think they are light--as from the son of Lodbrok whom this king's servant slew."

Now Eadmund spoke, saying to Ingvar:

"Let me hear what are your terms for my freedom. In the slaying of Lodbrok my friend I had no part."

"That is easily said," Ingvar answered, frowning. "I have my own thoughts on that--else had I not been here. But this land is in my power, therefore I will let you go if you will hold it for me, and own me as overlord, doing my will."

"My answer is the same as it was this morning. It is not for me to give over this land into the hands of heathen men to save myself."

That was Eadmund's calm answer, and looking on Ingvar I saw the same bode written in his face as had been when I would not honour his gods. Then he spoke slowly, and his words fell like ice from his lips.

"It seems to me that this land is in the hands of us heathen without your giving."

"So that may be, for the time," answered Eadmund; "but your time of power has an end."

"Has it so?" said Ingvar, and his eyes flashed. "Where is your help to come from? Do you look to Ethelred?--He is busy in Wessex with more of us heathen. Where is Mercia?--It is ours. Will Kent help you?"

"Our help is in the name of the Lord, who hath made heaven and earth," answered Eadmund, lifting his eyes heavenwards so earnestly, that in spite of himself the wild heathen king followed their upward gaze for a moment.

It was but for a moment, and that weakness, as he would deem it, was the spark to light Ingvar's wrath, that as yet he had kept under.

"Hammer of Thor!" he shouted, "you dare throw that in my face! Now will I show you if heathen or Christian is stronger."

Then with his face white with rage he turned to his men: "Bind him to yon tree, and we will speak with him again!"

Now if it is well that I did not die with my king, it was well at that moment for me that my axe hung at my saddle bow, and that my horse--to which I had paid no heed in my troubles--had wandered a little way, for I should surely have fought to prevent this dishonour being wrought. And I sprung to reach the axe, for the short sword I wore was of no use against so many. But Raud was close on me, and he dropped from his saddle on my shoulders as I passed him, so that I fell, half stunned under him, and one of the other men ran up, and ere they had stripped and bound the king to a tree, I was bound hand and foot, and rolled by Raud into a thicket where I might escape Ingvar's eye. And, indeed, he paid no heed to me, but watched the king.

So must I lie there with my heart like to break, seeing all that went on, and I will tell it as best I may.

Ingvar strode to the young oak tree to which they had bound the king and looked fixedly at him. Then he said, "Scourge this man," and his men did so. But the king made no sign by word or motion. I saw Ingvar's rage growing, and he cried as his men forbore, shrinking a little from their quiet victim:

"Ask for mercy, Christian, at the hands of Ingvar the godar, the priest of Odin and Thor, and you shall go free."

But the king met his gaze sadly and firmly, answering:

"That were to own that you have power over me through your false gods."

"Power I have," said Ingvar; "ask for mercy."

Thereat the king answered no word, though his lips moved, and I alone knew what his words might be, for though his hands were bound he moved his noble head in such wise as to make the sign of the Cross. And I think that he spoke to himself the prayer of forgiveness that he had learnt therefrom.

Almost then had the Dane smitten him in the face, but to this cowardice Ingvar the king had not yet fallen. He drew back a few paces, and took his long dagger from his belt, and at that I thought that he was going to slay the king, and I closed my eyes, praying. But he spoke again.

"Ask for peace on the same terms for your people, if you will not for yourself."

Then the king grew pale, but he set his lips close, still gazing at Ingvar. Hard was this for him who loved his people so well.

The Dane's dagger flashed, and he hurled it at Eadmund, but so skilfully that it did but graze his head, sticking firmly into the tree trunk. And he cried in a voice that shook with rage:

"Answer me!"

But the king held his peace, closing his eyes, and waiting for what might come, most bravely.

Then Ingvar turned to his men, and bade them unsling their bows and see if they could make this man find his tongue. Seven of them went to work with a good will, but Raud and the others would not, but turned away.

The men shot, and in many places the king was pierced, and lo! he lifted up his voice and sang gloriously, even as if in the church and on some high festival, the psalm that begins "De Profundis". Nor did his voice falter, though now he might move neither hand nor foot by reason of the piercing of the arrows.

At that the men stayed in amazement, and one threw away his bow and turned aside to where Raud stood, near where I lay. But Ingvar ground his teeth with rage, and stamping on the ground, cried to the men to shoot again.

And again the arrows flew, and now it seemed to me that no more arrows might find mark in the king's body without slaying him; and before my eyes was a mist, and my mouth was dry and parched, yet I could not turn away and look no more. But the men fitted arrows to the bowstrings once more, while Ingvar stood still and silent with his strong hands clasped together behind him, gazing at the king, whose lips moved in prayer, the psalm being ended, and, as I think, his strength ebbing fast from his many wounds.

Now they were about to shoot once more, unbidden, keeping up their torture if they might; but there was one more merciful than the rest. Forward before the bowmen strode Raud, with his sword drawn, and he cried to Ingvar:

"Let me slay him, king, and end this for pity's sake!"

Ingvar turned his eyes gloomily on him for a moment, and then answered:

"What know you of pity? Slay him if you will."

Then when he heard that, Eadmund looked at Raud, smiling on him with a wondrous smile and saying:

"Thanks, good friend."

So Raud slew him in pity, and that was now the best deed that might be done.

Thereat I cried out once, and my senses left me, and I knew no more.

CHAPTER XIII. HOW BISHOP HUMBERT JOINED THE KING.

When I began to come to myself it was late afternoon. At first into my mind came the fancy that I sat on the side of King Eadmund's bed in the king's chambers at Reedham, and that he told me a wondrous dream; how that--and then all of a sudden I knew that it was no shadowy dream, but that I had seen all come to pass, and that through the arrow storm Eadmund had passed to rest.

All round me the trees dripped with the damp November mist that creeps from the river, and the smell of dead leaves was in my nostrils, and for a while I lay still, hardly yet knowing true from false, dream from deed. So quiet was I that a robin came and perched close to me on a bramble, whose last leaves were the colour of the bird's red breast, and there it sang a little, so that I roused to life with the sound. Then swooped down a merlin with flash of gray wings on the robin and took it, and that angered me so that I rose on my elbow to fray it away; and with that the last cloud left my mind and I knew where I was. Then, too, from where he waited my waking came Vig, my great Danish dog, who had been tied at the thane's house, and must have left the flying party to seek me. And he bounded in gladness about me.

Now I found that my bonds were gone, and next that my weapons were left me, and that but for cramp and stiffness I had not any tokens of what had befallen. And at first it seemed to me that Ingvar thus showed his scorn of me, though soon I thought that he had forgotten me, and that it was Raud who had freed me.

I heeded not the dog, looking only in one place. But the body of the king was gone, and his arms and mail were gone. The hoofmarks of Ingvar's horses were everywhere; but at last I made out that they had gone on through the wood.

Presently the dog growled, looking towards the village, and I heard voices coming nearer, and with them I heard the tread of a horse. But soon the dog ceased, and began to wag his tail as if to welcome friends, and when the comers entered the clearing, I saw that they were Egfrid's men, and that it was my horse that they were leading. My axe was yet at the saddle bow.

"Why, master," said the foremost, "surely we looked to find you slain. This is well--but what has befallen?"

For I must have looked wildly and strangely on them.

"Well would it be if I were slain," I said. "Why did you seek me?"

"We found the horse coming homewards, and one knew that you had gone into the wood after the king. Yet we would seek you before we fled."

I saw that all were armed, and I thanked them. But--

"What ails you, master?" said the leader of the group.

"They have slain Eadmund the king," I answered, "and they have taken his body away."

Thereat they groaned, wondering and cast down, and one said:

"They will not have carried him far. Let us search."

We did so, and after a long time we found the king's body in a thicket where it had been cast. But his head we could not find, though now I bade my dog search also. He led us westward through the wood, until we came to a rising ground, and there we could go no further. For thence we saw the Danish horsemen by scores pressing towards us, searching for cattle and sheep as the army passed southward. And the farms were blazing in the track that they had crossed everywhere.

Then said the men:

"We must fly. We who live must save ourselves, and must come back and end this search when we may."

"Let us bear back the king's body," I said, "and find some hiding place for it at Hoxne."

So we did, hurriedly, and hid it in a pit near the village, covering it with boards and gravel as well as we could for haste. Then I asked the men where they would go.

"By boat down the river," they said, "and so join the thane and his party wherever they might be. They have gone to Beccles, for they hear that a ship lies there whose master will gladly take them to London."

That was good hearing, for so would all be safe. The men pressed me to come with them, but I would not do so, meaning to hasten on to the bishop's place and make him fly to Beccles and take ship also, starting this very night. So I bid them go, and on that their leader, a stout freeman named Leof, whom I knew well as one of Egfrid's best men, said that he would come with me. Nor would he hear of aught else.

"What would Egfrid my master say if I left his brother to go alone?" he asked me simply; and so I suffered him, and we two went towards South Elmham together.

Soon Leof saw a horse in a field and caught it, mounting bareback, and after that we went on well enough.

Darkness fell, and all the low clouds were reddened with the light of fires behind us, and ever as we looked back would be a fresh fire and light in the sky, for the Danes were at their work. We pushed on steadily, but the lanes were rough, and the miles seemed very long in the darkness; but at last we crossed the Elmham stream and rode to the stockaded house that was the bishop's, and which stands pleasant and well placed on a little hill beyond the low ground, and with no woodland very near it.

We shouted, and at last men fully armed came and let us in. And as

I looked back once before the gates closed after me, I thought that the fires were nearer. The Danes were not staying their hands for darkness, for so the terror they spread would be the greater. So also was the bishop's peril therefore.

"Where is Bishop Humbert?" I asked.

"Master, he is in the church, nor will he leave it," said the old steward. "He says he must pray for king and land day and night now till this terror is overpast."

"I will go to him--he must fly," I said.

"Aye, pray him to do so, Wulfric; he will listen to you," said the old man earnestly.

"Have all things ready," I said. "See--there is little time."

"What of the king, master?" asked he, looking at the fires with a white face as he once more opened the gate.

"The king has gone where he would wish to be," I answered very gravely; and he understood me, turning away that I might not see his weeping.

Then Leof and I splashed back through the stream that ran between house and church, and came quickly to the porch. The church is very small and more ancient than I can say, for it is built of flint bound together with such mortar as the Romans used in their castles, hard as stone itself, and it stands in the midst of the Roman camp that guarded the ford, so that maybe it was the first church in all East Anglia, for we use wood; and, moreover, this stone church is rounded at the east end, and has a barrier dividing the body of the building into two, beyond which the as yet unbaptized must sit, as men say. And so strong and thick are the walls that I do not know how they can ever fall.

Now through the narrow windows shone lights, and I heard the sound of chanting. Leof held my horse, and I opened the door gently and went in.

At once there was a shrinking together of a group of men, mostly monks, who stood at the upper end of the church where the chancel begins. They were chanting the third psalm, for help against the heathen, and it faltered for a moment. But they were mostly monks of the bishop's own household, and knew me well enough, and they ended it shortly.

Then there was silence, for they were holding none of the set services, but rather as it seemed doing the bishop's bidding, and praying with him in the best way for the ceasing of this new trouble, as in time of pestilence once I remembered that he made litanies for us. And Humbert himself knelt before the altar during that psalm, fully vested, but as in times of fast and penitence.

When he rose, I came up the aisle towards him, and my mail clanged noisily as I walked in the hush. At the chancel steps I stood, helm in hand, and did reverence, not daring to speak first.

"What is it?" asked the bishop, when he turned and saw me. "Speak, Wulfric, my son. Is all well?"

"I have heavy news, father," I answered. "Close on us are the Danes, and you must fly. Then I will tell you all on the way."

"I will fly no more," he answered, "here I will bide. Is the king at my house?"

"He is not there, father," I said; and then I urged him to fly at once, and with me his monks joined, even going on their knees in their grief. Yet he would not be moved.

"Surely the king will come here," he said, "nor will I go without him."

"Father," I said, "the Danes have taken the king."

"Then must I bide here, and pray and scheme for his release."

Now I knew not how to tell him all, but at last I said:

"Eadmund the king has escaped from the hands of the heathen."

At that the bishop looked long at me, judging perhaps what I meant, by my voice. But the monks rejoiced openly, at first, until they saw what was meant also, and then they trembled.

"Where is he?" he asked, speaking low.

"Father," I said, "this twentieth day of November will be the day when England shall honour a new martyr. Eadmund the King is numbered among them."

"How died he?" then said the bishop, folding his hands.

But now the monks bade him fly, and reasoned with and prayed him. But he bade them save themselves, for that there would be work for them to do among the heathen.

"As for me, I am an old man," he said, "and I would fain go the same road as the king."

Still they clung to him, and at last, speaking to each by name, and giving each some message to take to cell or abbey where they must go at his bidding, he commanded them; and so, unwillingly, kissing his hand and receiving his blessing, they went one by one, till he and I and one or two laymen besides were left in the little church. Then he spoke to the other men, and they went also, and we were alone.

"That is well," said the bishop; "tell me all, and then do you fly."

He sat down in his great chair, leaning his head in his hand while I told him all in that quiet place. Never once was there trembling flash from the great jewel of his ring, that shone in the candlelight, to show how moved he was; but when I had ended, the tears were running down his venerable face, and he said:

"Now is there truly one more added to the noble army of martyrs, and he is at rest. Now do you go, my son."

But I had other thoughts in my mind, and I rose up silently from beside him, saying only: "Not yet, father," and I went down the aisle and out into the darkness to Leof.

"See yonder!" said he pointing, and there was a fresh fire not many miles from us. "I think they scour the country for our bishop. We have little time."

"Tell me, Leof," I said, "have you a mind to live?" for there was somewhat in the man's weary voice that seemed to say that he and I thought alike.

"None, master, after today's work, if I may find a brave man or two to die with me."

"Here is a brave man waiting with a like thought in the church. Shall you and I die with him?"

"Aye, surely," said Leof quietly.

"Bide here then," I said, and took the horses from him.

I mounted mine and rode to the house, where the steward and one or two others watched from the gateway. I bade the old man call his folk together, and I told them to fly. Many were already gone, now others went at once.

But a few stayed, and to them I said like words as to Leof.

"Hither will the Danes come presently, but in no great force. We may beat them back, and if we do, then maybe the bishop will fly. But we shall more likely die with him."

"Let us stand by him, come what will," they answered me in steady voices; "better to die with him and our king."

They took their arms and gave me a sword, and we left the horses in the stable, for we might even yet need them. I thought that we could maybe, as I said, beat off the first few Danes, and then that, to save further bloodshed, the bishop would go with us. And if not, we had done our best.

Five men came with me to the ford. When we were at the other side there were but four. One had gone back, and I did not blame him.

Leof sat in the little porch, and so we six went into the church together. The bishop sat where I had left him, but he raised his head when we came up the aisle.

"Nay, my sons," he said, "you must fly. Maybe these men will respect an old man like myself and lonely."

Then I said:

"Father, we would have you say mass for us ere the light comes again."

Now it wanted about an hour to midnight.

"Is there yet time?" he said.

Then I answered that I thought we might wait in peace for so long, and he, knowing nothing of the nearness of the Danes, consented. So we bided there in the aisle benches to wait till midnight was past, and soon one or two of the men slept quietly.

Now, when it may have been almost midnight, and the time for mass would soon be come, the bishop, who had been so still that I thought he slept, lifted his head and looked towards the altar. And at the same time my dog whined a little beside me.

Then Humbert the Bishop rose up and held out both his hands as to one whom he would greet, and spoke softly.

"Aye, Eadmund, I am coming. Soon shall I be with you."

So he stood for a little while very still, and then went to his place again.

Then Leof, who sat next to me, said, whispering:

"Saw you aught, master?"

"I saw nothing, but surely the bishop had a vision."

"I myself saw Eadmund the king stand before the bishop, and he had a wondrous crown on his head," said Leof, speaking as though of somewhat not terrible, but good to think on.

"I also saw him," said the old steward from behind me. "I saw him plainly as in life, and I thought he smiled on us."

But I had had no such sight, and it grieved me. Moreover, two of the other three men whispered, and I thought one of them told of the like vision. And I think, too, that the dog saw it, as the innocent beasts will see things beyond our ken.

Soon the bishop judged that the time was come for mass, and he called softly to me, bidding me serve, for I had often done so for him in the old days when I was a boy and he was at Reedham, and I knew well what to do.

Then was said a most solemn mass with that one aged priest, and us few men present. And all was very quiet round us, for no wind stirred the trees on the old rampart.

The bishop's voice ceased with the benediction, and the hush deepened; but suddenly Leof and I looked in each other's faces. We had heard a shout from no great distance, and the blood rushed wildly through us.

Now the bishop rose from his knees, and I took the holy vessels, as he gave them to me, putting them into their oaken chest in its niche. And when that was done, he said:

"Now I will not bid you fly, my sons, for I think that somewhat has bidden you bide with me. And I have seen the king, so that I know the time is short. Take therefore the holy vessels and drown them in the deep pool of the stream. I have used them for the last time, but I would not have them profaned by the heathen in their feasting."

I knew that this should be done as at Bosham, but already I heard the shouts yet nearer, and I was loth to leave the church, and so paused.

"I know your thoughts," said the bishop. "Yet go, as I bid you; it is not far."

So I took the heavy, iron-bound chest on my shoulder and went quickly, running as well as I might to the stream below the rampart, where it curled deep and still under crumbling banks. There I plunged my burden, hearing it sink and bubble into the depths.

Then I went back, and reached the gap in the rampart that had been the gate next the ford, and that was at the east end of the church, so that the porch was far from me. And before I had gone halfway to the church--over the western rampart spurred a score of horsemen, dimly seen in the half moonlight that was now. And the leader of them saw me, and rode straight at me, calling to me to hold, while I drew my sword and ran to reach the door before he met me; and my dog, which was at my heels, flew at the horse's throat.

But I must fail, and I whirled up my sword to strike--and then a long flash of light from a spear point smote me, and over me the man rode, pinning me to the ground with the spear through my left shoulder. His horse trod on me, and the man wrenched the weapon from me as he passed on, and I had but time to call out to Leof to warn him, when a rushing came in my ears, and a blaze of light before my eyes, and the world passed from me.

Then I seemed to stand in darkness, while past me, gloriously shining, went Leof, and then the old steward and one of those two men who had whispered together, and then Humbert the Bishop himself. But it seemed to me that he paused and looked on me, saying, in a voice that was like music:

"Hereafter--not now. Twice have you offered your life today, and yet there is work for you. Be content to wait."

So he passed, looking kindly at me, and then the blackness came over me again.

When I came round at last it was high day, and the air was full of smoke around me. One sat on a great brown horse looking at me, and by my side cried my dog; and I groaned, whereat the man got off his horse and came to me. And I knew that it was Hubba, and some of the men I knew were there also.

"Why, Wulfric, friend, how is this? I thought you were dead. Who has dared to hurt you? What has happened here?"

"You know well," I gasped.

"Nay, I know not; I have but now ridden this way with our rear guard," he answered, seeming to pity me.

"Look in the church and see," I said, groaning. "You Danes are all one in the matter."

"Now I am not the man to harm you, nor would any of our folk," he said. "Some of our courtmen found you here, and brought me."

"Slay me and have done," I muttered; for that was all I would have him do.

"That will I not, Wulfric," he answered; and he called to some men who were busy about the walls of the church.

The smoke rose thickly from within them, for the burnt roof had fallen in.

"Take this warrior and bind his wound," he said. "It is Wulfric of Reedham, our friend."

The faintness came over me again when the men raised me, though they tended me gently enough, and I could say naught, though I would rather they had cast me into the burning timbers of the church, even as I had bidden men do with that poor churl at Hoxne, that my ashes might be with those of our bishop.

So they bore me far, and at last left me in a farm where they promised all should be safe if they tended me well. And Hubba rode with them, and came to bid me farewell. But I could not speak to him if I would, so he went away sadly. And as in a dream I heard him speak of care for me to the widow and her two sons to whom the farm belonged, and whom his men had taken unawares, so that they had not time to fly.

Presently came the best leech from Ingvar's host and tended me carefully; and I needed it, for besides the spear wound, my right thigh was broken, by the trampling of the horse, as was most likely.

Thereafter I lay for many weeks, as they told me presently, sick and nigh to death; but being young and strong and no high liver at any time, I came through the danger well enough, and began to mend slowly. Yet my sickness, when I could begin to think, was more of mind than body, and that kept me back. For long did it lie heavily on my mind that I should have died with the king, and it was that sorrow and blame of myself that went sorely against me. But after a time the love of life came back to me again, and I began to see things as they really were, untouched by a sick man's fancies. And then the words of the good Prior of Bosham helped me, teaching me that my life was surely spared for somewhat.

These good folk of the farm tended me most kindly, for they knew me by sight as a close friend of both king and bishop, and for their sakes were glad to do all they might for me. But I pined for the touch of that one who had tended me when I was wounded before, Osritha, whom I had learnt to love as she did so.

Sometimes I would think that between her and me had now risen up a barrier stronger than the sea that was washing our shores alike, because that of Ingvar's sister I might not think aught any longer. And then I would set before me how that of these cruel doings nor she nor Halfden had any part, hating them rather, and so would comfort myself. Long are the thoughts that come to a sick man.

Now it was not till February that I might take much heed of anything, but then I learnt that the Danes had wintered in Thetford, and that the land was in peace. The war had passed on to the Wessex borders and then had slackened, as winter came earnest, and now the north and south folk, Dane and Angle, were foes no longer openly. But Ingvar and Hubba were at Nottingham, waiting to fall on Wessex, leaving only strong garrisons in our towns.

Then one of the dame's sons would go to London for me, there to seek Ingild and tell him of my hap, for, the lad said:

"Now that these Danes need fight no more they are decent folk enough, and will not hinder a man who has not whereof to be robbed."

CHAPTER XIV. HOW WULFRIC AND RAUD SEARCHED TOGETHER.

I sat in the warm sun under the wide spread of the farmhouse eaves, dreaming my dreams with the dog at my feet, for so soon as the May time came in I must needs get into the open air, and grow stronger daily.

So it came to pass that one day up the green farm lane came a stranger, at whom the dog barked not, as was his wont, but ran to meet as if he were some well-loved friend. And it was Raud, his old master, who came, lightly mail clad, and with a short hunting spear instead of staff in his hand, and whistling his "Biarkamal" as ever.

Now with Raud I had no quarrel concerning the death of the king, for well I knew that what he had done was truly in mercy, nor had he taken any part in what went before. So I greeted him heartily enough, for all that with the sight of him came back to me, with a sharp pang, the memory of how I saw him last. And he rejoiced to see me again.

"I have half feared that I should find you gone," he said; "for, when I heard of this from Hubba's men, I must needs come and find you, and little hope had I that you would live."

"I have nearly died, they say," I answered; "but I think that I owe it to you that I was not slain in Hoxne woods yonder."

"Why, not altogether," he answered, sitting on the settle by me, and looking me over, from arm yet in sling to lame leg. "Some of the men with Ingvar and me wanted to slay you before they left that place; but Ingvar growled so fiercely that they must let you be, that they said no more, nor even would look your way again. But he himself looked at you, and said strange things to himself."

"What said he?" I asked, wondering.

"He said, paying no heed to me, 'Now, Wulfric--you will hate me forever more, nor do I think that Lodbrok my father would be pleased with this;' after which he spoke words so low that I caught but one here and there, but they were somewhat of the lady Osritha, our mistress. After that he said to me, 'Leave him horse and arms and unbind him,' and then turned away. Yet if I had not bound you at first, maybe they would have had to slay you."

"That is true enough," I said; "surely I should have stood between you and the king. But what came to Ingvar to make him speak thus to me?"

"Why, after the hot fit comes the cold, ever, though Ingvar the King's cold rage is worse at times than his fury. But since that day there has been somewhat strange about the king."

"I wonder not," I said; nor did I. "But how goes it with him?"

"Men say, though they dare not do so openly, that the ghost of Eadmund will not let him rest, and that mostly does he fear him when his rage is greatest. Many a time when the fury seemed like to come on him, Ingvar turns white and stares suddenly beyond all things, as though seeing somewhat beyond other men's ken, and the sweat runs cold from his forehead. Many a man has escaped him through this."

"Surely Eadmund holds him back thus from more cruelty," I thought. And aloud I said:

"What think you of the matter?"

"Why, that I am glad that I was bold enough to save your dying king from more torture--else had I seen somewhat before me day and night. Truly I see him now betimes in my sleep, but he ever smiles on me. Moreover, this is true, that all those seven men who shot the arrows died in that week. Two died in Elmham Church when you were nigh slain."

"Tell me of that," I said.

For no man knew rightly what had befallen there, save that under the charred ruins of the roof lay Bishop Humbert and one or two of his men.

But when he told me, it was as I thought. Those few men had fought bravely until they were slain, themselves slaying three Danes. But one of the bishop's men escaped, cutting through a throng at the doorway and seizing a horse. Then was slain the bishop, who knelt at the altar, not even turning round to face the Danes as they came.

So I hold ever that as I lay for dead I had seen those brave ones pass me even as they were slain. But of this I said naught to Raud, at that time at least.

Now I asked Raud whence he had come, and he said:

"From London."

And at that I feared greatly, asking:

"Has Ingvar taken the city, therefore?"

"Not the king himself, but Guthrum went into London, taking good ransom for peace."

"Where is Ethelred the king of England?" I said, half to myself.

"Ethelred?--he minds naught but Wessex for good reason. For Halfden and Bagsac and the Sidracs are on one side of him, and Ingvar and Hubba the other, waiting for him to make peace. But there is like to be fighting. Alfred, the king's brother, has a brave heart and a hard hand."

"Then all is quiet in London?"

"Peaceful enough; and there Guthrum the King holds court, and I think men are well content with him."

"Of what is Guthrum king?" I asked, for I had not heard him called by that name before. The only other king of the host beside the three jarls was Bagsac.

"Why, of East Anglia. He holds it for Ingvar, while he tries to add Wessex for his own to Mercia. Halfden will be king in Northumbria, maybe, and Hubba over another of the kingdoms."

So they had already parted out the land among them beforehand! Woe for us therefore, for unless a leader was raised up among us, surely all England must own Danish overlords! But I had heard Alfred the Wessex Atheling well spoken of as a warrior.

However, what was that to us of East Anglia? We had been deserted by Wessex at our need as it seemed, and these Danes were as near kin to us as Wessex Saxons.

"How did you come to leave Ingvar's service?" I asked, not being willing to dwell on this matter.

"I think my face spoke to him too plainly of that which was in Hoxne wood--and so he bade me stay with Guthrum. Nor was I loth, for I would find you again."

Then I was touched a little by the kindness of this rough warrior, and thanked him. After that we sat silent for a while, and the good dame brought out food and ale for Raud, and I envied his pleasure therein, for I took little as yet.

Now for many days past a great longing to be away from this place had filled my mind, and now seemed to be the time.

"Take me to London, Raud," I said.

"Why, that is part of my errand here," he answered, smiling. "I have a message to you from Guthrum the King."

"What might that be?"

"He wants to speak to you as one who is known to be friend to Dane and Anglian alike, and being blamed by neither for friendship with the other. So he would have you give him counsel."

"Let me get to London," I said, "and then I will answer. I cannot now."

So Raud bided in the farm with me for a while, and now with new thoughts and with his talk of Halfden and Osritha, I mended quickly, for it was my troubled mind that had kept me back mostly, as I cared for nothing.

One day I felt strong again, waking up and taking delight in the smell of the fresh morning and in the sunlight. And I ate heartily of the brown bread and milk they gave me, and afterwards told Raud of what I had been long thinking.

"All things are quiet in the land now. Let us gather a few of my people and seek the head of our king, if you fear not to go into Hoxne woods."

Raud thought for a while before he answered me.

"I fear not, for the poor king thanked me, smiling at me. Let me go with you."

So that day the dame sent messages by her son to some who had come back to their places, and in the evening when he came home, there were with him two of Bishop Humbert's monks, dressed like churls, for they dared not wear their habits. These two and some others would gladly come with me on my search.

Next day, therefore, they set me on a pony that was quiet, and slowly we went towards Hoxne, coming thither in the afternoon early, seeing no Danes anywhere, while many of our folk were back and at work in the fields.

Then I asked Raud if these poor people were safe now.

"Surely, master," he said, for so he would call me, having heard the farm people name me thus. "There is none so great difference between you and us, and we Danes love to be at peace if we may. I think there will be no more trouble here. And, anyway, we are too wise to hinder a harvesting of that we may eat."

So too thought I, and my heart was less sad after that ride, though there was not one place left unburnt of all that we saw.

When we came to Hoxne I told the two monks where we had bestowed the king's body, bidding them look to see if it was not disturbed. And they said that his bones were safely there.

Now we must seek for the head of the king, and in that Rand could not help us, for one had ridden away with it while he was taken up with me and my plight.

So we went towards that place where the dog had taken us, and searched long, until I, being weak, must get from off the pony and rest. I would ride back to the place where the king had been slain and sit there awhile; but first, knowing that Vig remembered things well, I sent him from me, bidding him search also, hoping that he would not forget his last quest in this place. Yet what we most feared was that the forest beasts had made our search vain.

There were many men from the village with us now, for they had followed the two monks, and they spread about over the wood far and wide, searching, while I sat at the foot of the oak tree to which the king had been bound, leaning my arms and head against the trunk that had been stained with his blood, and thinking and praying, as well I might in that sacred place.

I moved my hand, and felt something sticking from the hard bark and looked to see what it was. It was an arrowhead, such a rough iron spike as men will use when they must make fresh arrows after battle, in all haste, and have to use what they can first find. The shaft was snapped close to the iron and the rawhide lashing that held it, and I could not take it out as I would, for the young oak was sturdy and tough; and so I left it, thinking that I would return some day to cut it out.

That I did in after years, but the arrowhead was hidden, for the tree had grown fast, closing on it, as I think, and I could not find its place. So it will be there for one to find hereafter, maybe long hence, for such a tree has many a hundred years to last yet, if saved from mishap of wind or lightning or axe. Then I think will men still know what that iron is, for Eadmund the King cannot be forgotten.

Presently it seemed to me that the voices I heard in the wood, as the searchers called to each other, drew closer together, crying:

"Where are you?"

"Here--here!"

And then was a sort of outcry, and a silence, and I hoped that maybe they had found what they sought. So I rose up and went slowly and limpingly to the place where they seemed to be.

I met them in a green glade. And foremost came the two monks, bearing between them a cloak, wherein was surely that we looked for, and after them came my dog and Raud, and then the rest. And when they saw me they cried softly to me:

"Master, we have found the head of our king."

So they laid open the cloak before me, and I knelt and looked. And there was indeed the head of Eadmund, seeming whole and fresh as when I had last seen him; and his looks were very peaceful, for on his face was still that smile with which he had greeted death at Raud's hands.

Then, seeing that, the rough Dane was fain to turn away and lean arms and face against a tree trunk, weeping as weeps a child that will not be comforted.

After a little I asked how they had found the head. And one of the villagers, speaking low and holding his cap in his hands as though in the church, answered me.

"When I came to a certain thicket, I heard a crying, as it were, and I turned aside and looked, and at first was sorely afraid, for yon great wolf held the head between his paws, whining over it as in grief. Then I called to the rest, and they came, running, and were afraid also till the good fathers came, to whom the wolf was gentle, suffering them to take that which he guarded. And lo! he follows us even now, as would a dog!"

So the man spoke, not having seen such a dog as mine before, for till more came with the host there were none like him in our land. I told him that it was but my own dog; yet for all that, I know that this tale of a wolf passed for the truth over all the land as it flew from mouth to mouth, so that soon I myself heard from one who knew me not very strange stories of that finding of ours.

Yet would that tale hardly be stranger than was the truth, that not one of the wild creatures, either beast or bird, had harmed our king's sacred head. And how it should be so preserved in that place I cannot tell, but I say what I saw. Yet his body was not so preserved in the place where we had hidden it.

These things are beyond me, nor can I tell all the thoughts that came into my mind as I looked into the face of the king whom I had loved, and who loved me.

Now would we take our treasure, as we must needs think it, to Hoxne, and the monks were about to lift it again. But Raud came forward very solemnly, begging that he might be allowed to bear it, "Because he would make what amends he might."

And I signed to the monks to suffer him to do so, and he took it. None else but I knew what part he had had with the other Danes in this matter, and the monks did but think him grieving for what his comrades had done.

So he bore it to Hoxne village, and we passed the place where the church had been. There, amid the blackened ruins of the walls and roof, stood the font of stone, fire reddened and chipped, yet with the cross graven on its eastward face plain to be seen. And to that place Raud led us, none staying him, yet all wondering.

When he came there he strode over the burnt timber until he came to the font, and there, under the graven cross, he set down his burden very gently, and stood up, looking in my face, and saying:

"Here will I leave the worship of Odin and cleave to that faith for which Eadmund the King died, and for which you, Wulfric, were willing to die both in Jutland and here by Eadmund's side. Will any forbid me?"

Then I knew that the man was in such earnest, that none, save he perilled his own soul, might hold him back, and I took his hand and spoke to the elder monk, saying:

"I will answer for this man, father, as to his will. If he knows enough of our faith, I pray you baptize him straightway."

There was rain water in the font, sparkling and clear, and without any delay or doubt the good man came forward and stood thereby, while I yet held Raud's hand as his godfather.

"What know you of our faith, my son?" said the monk in his gentle voice.

Now of his own accord Raud faced to the eastward, and clasping his hands before him, spoke the words of the Creed, slowly and haltingly maybe, but with knowledge thereof, and all that little company, standing hushed until he ended, answered "Amen" with one voice.

Then again, untaught by us he turned to the west, where the sun was even now sinking, and lifting his right hand very solemnly he put away from him the false gods of his forefathers, and the golden sunlight made his face very glorious, as I thought.

"It is well, my son," said the old monk.

So he was baptized, and I gave him the new name of Cyneward {xxii}, for the memory of Eadmund the King and what he did for him in saving him from torture as best he might. And surely he was the first fruit of the martyrdom of him whose head he had borne.

Then when all was done he took up his burden again, softly and reverently, saying:

"Life I took, and life has been given me. This is not the old way of life for life, but it is better."

So he gave back the head to the monks, and they, wondering at him, but greatly rejoicing, took it, and stood awhile pondering where we might safely bestow it.

Then came one of the villagers, telling of a stone-walled chamber that had been a well in days long gone by, hard by the church porch. That we found after some labour, moving much ruin from over it, and therein we placed the bones and head of our king, covering it again until better days should come. And I, thinking of my riches in the hands of Ingild, promised that when it might be done I would see to raising the church afresh, to be over the ashes of the king.

So our little company parted, and Cyneward, who had been Raud, and I went back with the elder monk and the farm folk to our place, going slowly in the warm twilight, with our hearts at rest, and full of the wonders we had seen that day.

Only one thing would the monk and I ask Cyneward, for we wondered how he had learned our faith so well. And that he answered gladly.

"Ever as Wulfric and I escaped from the vengeance of Ingvar towards Hedeby I wondered that one should be strong enough to defy the Asir and their godar for the sake of the new faith. So I sat in the church of Ansgar among the other heathen and heard somewhat. And again in London of late, where Guthrum will have no man harmed for his religion, I have listened and learnt more. So when I needed them, the words were ready. Now, therefore, both in life and death, Wulfric, my master, I thank you."

But I was silent, knowing how much greater a part in this I might have had. For I thought that, but for the need of proving my faith or denying it, I should have surely been as a heathen among heathen in those days in Jutland. Yet Beorn asked me to pray for him, and that I had done, and it had kept me mindful when I had else forgotten.

So began the work Humbert the Bishop foretold before he died, and that monk of his who saved his own life at Humbert's bidding for the work, saw it, and rejoiced.

After this, in a week's time, Cyneward and I took horse and rode away to London, for the dame's son came back to me, having found Ingild, bringing me messages from him, and also from Egfrid and many more. And all was well. At that time I could not reward as I would those good people who had thus cared for me, but I would send presents when I might. Yet they said they needed naught from me but to see me again at some time, which I promised, as well for my own love of them as for their asking.

We went unharmed and unquestioned, for all the land was at peace. Truly there were new-made huts where farmsteads had been, and at the town gates were Danish axemen instead of our spearmen as of old. Yet already in the hayfields Dane and Anglian wrought together, and the townsmen stood on Colchester Hill beside the Danish warriors, listening while gleeman and scald sang in rivalry to please both.

Little of change was there in London town, save again the scarlet-cloaked Danish guards and watchmen. Few enough of these there were, and indeed the host left but small parties in the towns behind them in our land. Yet those few could hold the country in peace, because men knew that at their back was the might of Ingvar's awful host, which came on a land unawares, marching more swiftly than rumour could fly before it, so that not one might know where the next blow would fall until suddenly the war beacons of flaming villages flared up, and it was too late to do aught but fly.

Yet in our land was none to fight for. No king had we to follow the martyr. Ethelred had left us alone, and already in the hearts of men grew up the thought that the strong hand of the Dane meant peace.

In the house of good old Ingild, my second father, as he would have me hold him, was rest at last. And there I found all whom I held dear gathered to meet me on the night when I came, for they had fled by ship, as they had hoped, and had reached London safely.

CHAPTER XV. THE MESSAGE OF HALFDEN THE KING.

Now when I had been in London for a fortnight, Cyneward, whom Ingild would by no means suffer to live elsewhere than in his house with me, went to Guthrum as was his duty, and told him that I had come. Whereupon he sent to me, asking again that I would speak with him.

On that I took counsel with Ingild and Egfrid, and the thane his father, and they thought it well that I should do so.

"This Dane," said the thane, "is lord of East Anglia by the might of the strong hand, and it seems to us that we might have a worse ruler. At any rate we shall have peace, and no more trouble with Danes while he is here. As for Ethelred, he is no more to us. Even if he overcomes the Danes in the end, it is not likely that we will own Wessex overlords again unless we must."

That was the word of all with whom I spoke, and in the end, when it was certain that the Danes meant to stay, and that help from Ethelred was none, East Anglia owned Guthrum as king quietly and with none to say a word against it, so securing a peace that should last.

But to this I could not bring myself as yet, because of what I had seen, and that the hand of Ingvar was behind Guthrum.

"Go to him at least," said Ingild, "and find what he needs of you. Then will be time to say more."

So at his advice I went, and I found Guthrum in Ethelred's great house, where he sat in little state, doing justice in open hall where many citizens were gathered. And I saw him do even-handed right to both Dane and Saxon, and that pleased me, for already I had liked the man's honest face and free bearing.

He greeted me well, taking me aside presently with Cyneward into a private chamber. And there he told me that he would ask me to do a favour towards him.

I answered that what I might I would do gladly, so that he asked me not to break faith with my own people.

"I would ask no man to do that," he said. "Tell me what I may not ask you."

"Shall I speak plainly?" I said.

"Aye, plainly as you will."

"Then, Guthrum, I may not own Ingvar for overlord. Nor can I allow that you have more than right of conquest over us."

"Plain speaking, in good sooth," he said, laughing a little, "but what I expected from Wulfric of Reedham. However, I am ruler in East Anglia by that right you speak of, and I have a mind to be as fair in it as I may. Now, I think you can help me."

This honest saying warmed my heart to him somewhat, and weary enough of his lawman's work this warrior looked. Yet I was not sure that he would not try to use me to make his hold on the land more sure.

"Tell me in what way that may be," I said, therefore.

"Let me come and ask you of this and that when I am in a strait owing to knowing naught of Saxon ways. Then can I say to a Dane, 'Thus says Wulfric, Lodbrok's friend,' and to an Anglian, 'So says the Thane of Reedham.' Then I think I shall do well, for I would fain be fair."

"I will ever be ready to do that, Guthrum," I said; and I held out my hand to him, for I could not help it.

So he took it and wrung it warmly.

"Now must I go back to Thetford very soon," he said. "Come back that you may be near me."

"I must live here, in London now," I said; for I would by no means live with his court, nor did I think that he should have thought it of me after my words.

"Why not go back to your own place now? I can see you often at Reedham."

"That is an ill jest," I said; for I thought nothing so sad as going back to see that dear home of mine but a blackened heap of ruins, nor would I ever ask any who might have seen the place concerning it, knowing how the Danish ships had burnt all the coast villages.

Guthrum looked at me as if puzzled.

"No jest, Thane," he said; "why not go back?"

"To ruins--what good?" I answered.

"Now I think you mean that you will not take your land at my hands," he said.

"That were to own you king."

"Then, Wulfric, my friend, if I may call you so, that the lands of a friend are not mine to give and take I need not tell you. Nor do we harm the lands of a friend. There is one place in East Anglia that no Dane has harmed, or will harm--the place that sheltered Jarl Lodbrok. And there is one man whose folk, from himself to the least of all, are no foes of ours--and that is the Thane of Reedham. Ah! now I see that I have gladdened you, and I think that you will come."

"This seems almost impossible," I said, in my wonder and gladness.

"Nay, but word went round our host that it was to be so. There you might have bided all unknowing that war was near you. You do but go back of your own free will."

Now I was fain to say that I would at once go back to my place, but there was one thing yet that I would say to Guthrum.

"Will you let the Christian folk be unharmed?"

"Little will our people care," he said, "when once they have settled down, what gods a man worships. Nor would I have any meddled with because of their faith."

"Now am I most willing to help you," I said; "and I will say this--so are you likely in the end to be hailed king indeed."

"That is well," he answered, flushing a little. "But there is one man whom I will never ask to own me as king, and that is yourself. But if you do so of your own will, it will be better yet."

So we parted, each as I think pleased with the other, and I knew that East Anglia had found a wise ruler in Guthrum the Dane.

Straightway now I told my people the good news that Reedham was safe. The longships came up to Norwich time after time now; and there had been but one thought among us, and that was that our place could not have escaped the destruction that had fallen on all the shore and riverside villages.

Then Ingild said:

"These Danes have come as our forefathers came here, to take a new and better country for themselves, but the strife between them and us is not as the strife between alien peoples. They are our kin, but between us and the Welsh was hatred of race. They will settle down, and never will East Anglia pass from Danish hands, even if Ethelred of Wessex makes headway enough to be owned as overlord of England by them. Now therefore is there one place in all England where peace has come, and to that place I would go to end my days. Here in London the tide of war will ebb and flow ever. Let me go down with you to Reedham, my son, that I may die in peace."

So we did but wait until he had set all his affairs in order, selling his house and merchandise and the like. Then we hired a ship that came from the Frankish coast and waited for cargo in the Thames, and sailed at the end of July to Reedham. With us were Egfrid and Eadgyth and my mother and Cyneward, who would by no means leave me, and to whom Guthrum willingly gave leave to go with us.

We came easily to Reedham, and very strange it was to me to see two Danish longships lying in our roads, while our own shore boats were alongside, the men talking idly together on deck or over gunwale in all friendliness. Stranger yet it was to see the black ruins of farms and church on the southern shores of the river mouth, and at Reedham all things safe and smiling as ever.

Then was a wondrous welcome for us on our little staithe, and all the village crowded down to greet us. Nor were the men from the Danish ships behindhand in that matter, for they too would welcome Lodbrok's friends.

So we came home, and soon the old life began again as if naught had altered, but for the loss of loved faces round us. Yet in peace or war that must come, and in a little while we grew content, and even happy.

Soon Guthrum came to Thetford, and many times rode over to me, asking me many things. And all men spoke well of him, so that Egfrid's father and some other thanes owned him as king, and took their lands as at his hands, coming back to rebuild their houses. For as yet none of the greater Danish chiefs chose lands among us, since it seemed likely that in a little while all England would be before them, and in any case the power of Ethelred must be broken before there could be peace.

Now when the first pleasure of return was over, I myself began to be restless in my mind, seeing the quiet happiness of Egfrid in his marriage, and thinking how far I was from Osritha, whom I loved in such sort that well I knew that I should never wed any other. And I would watch some Danish ship when she passed our village, going homewards, longing to sail in her and seek the place where Lodbrok's daughter yet lived beyond the broad seas.

But presently, at the summer's very end, I knew from the Danes that Ingvar had gone back to Denmark, called there by some rumour of trouble brewing at home in his absence; and that made it yet harder for me, if possible, for on Ingvar I would not willingly look again, nor would I think of Osritha but as apart from him.

So the winter wore away. The host was quiet in winter quarters in Mercia, and the Danes in our country grew friendly with us, harming no man.

These men, I could see, would fain bide in peace, settling down, being tired of war, and liking the new country, where there was room and to spare for all.

In early spring Guthrum went to the host on the Wessex borders, taking command in Ingvar's place.

For Hubba went to Northumbria, there to complete his conquests, and Halfden was on the western borders of Wessex. And before he went Guthrum took great care for the good ordering of our land--and that he might leave it at all at that time was enough to show that he feared no revolt against him.

Now as I sat in our hall, listless and downcast, one day in July, Cyneward came in to me.

"Here is news, master, that I know not what to make of."

"What is it?" I said. "Is the war to be here once more?"

"The war is no nearer than Ashdown Heath; but it seems that the Wessex men have found a leader."

Then he told me of the long fighting round Reading, and how at last Halfden had cut his way through Wessex and joined forces with Guthrum after many victories. But that then Ethelred and Alfred the Atheling had made a great effort, winning a mighty victory on Ashdown Heath, slaying Bagsac the king and both the Sidracs, Harald and Osbern the jarls, Frene, and many more with them. Nine battles had they fought that year and last.

"How hear you of this?" I said.

"There has come a messenger from Guthrum with the news, and even now the Danes march in all haste from the towns to fill up the gaps in the ranks of the host, and he says that ships must go back to Jutland to Ingvar for more men from overseas."

Now this news was nothing to us East Anglians for the most part, and to me it was but a turn of the fight between Dane and Saxon for the overlordship of all England. That was not a matter to be settled by one or two victories on either side, nor might one see how it would end. Yet I was glad, for of all things I feared that Ingvar might be our master in the end, and this seemed to say that it was none so certain.

More men came in after that, hastening the going to the front of those who would, for not all the Danes among us would stir from their new homes, saying that they had done their part, and knowing that what they left others might take.

And in ten days' time Cyneward came to me saying that there were two longships coming in from the open sea.

"Let the pilots go out to them," I said; for it was of no use withholding this help from the Danish ships, little as we liked to see them come. So I forgot the matter.

Then again Cyneward ran to me in haste, and with his eyes shining.

"Master, here is Halfden's ship. Come and see!"

Gladly I went out then, and when I saw those two ships my heart leapt up with joy, for it was indeed my own ship that was leading, and I thought that Halfden would be in her.

So soon as she was in the river she made for our wharf, and that was not the wont of the Danes, who mostly went on past us up the river to where the great towns were. And at once when she was alongside I went on board, and at sight of me half her crew came crowding round me, shouting and shaking my hand; for they were our old crew, the same who had fought beside me and had backed me at the Ve. There, too, was Thormod, grim as ever, but welcoming me most gladly. But Halfden was not there.

"What is this, Thormod?" I said, when I had him up to the house, and the men were eating in the great hall. "Why are you not with Halfden?"

"Have you heard no news?" he asked.

"Only a few days ago I heard of the business at Ashdown."

"Well, I have come thence," he said. "Now must I sail home and fetch more men in all haste."

"Why came you in here?"

"Because I came away in haste and need stores. And, moreover, I wanted to see you."

"That is good of you, Thormod, and glad am I to have you here, even if it is only for a day," I answered.

"Moreover, I have a message to you from Halfden," he went on.

Whereupon I asked him about the battle, and long we sat while he told me all. And Halfden's deeds had been great, but could not turn aside defeat. So he ended.

"Then because our ship lay in the Thames, where we had sent her from the west when we broke through the Wessex country and joined Guthrum, he sent me back for men. So I am here. Both sides must needs rest awhile, as I think."

"What of Halfden's message?" I asked.

"Why, I know not how you will take it, but it is this. The night before the battle he slept ill, and at last woke me, saying that he would have me take a message if he was slain. So I said that I hoped he was not fey. That he was not, he told me, but this was going to be a heavy sword play, and one knew not how things would go. Then he told me that ever as he began to sleep he saw Osritha his sister, and she was pale and wrung her hands, saying: 'Now am I alone, and there is none to help me, for Halfden and Wulfric are far away, and I fear Ingvar and his moods'. Then said I, 'That is true enough. It needs no dream to tell one of the maiden's loneliness.' Yet he answered, 'Nevertheless, in some way I will have Wulfric our comrade know that Osritha sits alone and will not be comforted'. So when I must start on this voyage he bade me tell you of this matter, and I have done so."

Now I was full of many thoughts about this, but as yet I would say little. So I asked:

"What of Ingvar's moods? are they more fierce than his wont?"

"Well, between us twain," he answered, looking at Cyneward, who sat apart from us across the king's chamber where we were, "Ingvar is not all himself lately, and all men fear him, so that he is no loss to the host."

I knew somewhat, I thought, of the reason for this, and so did Cyneward, but passed that over. Now nothing seemed more plain to me than that Halfden meant that I should seek Osritha.

"What is Halfden doing?" I asked. "Will he not go back to your own land?"

"Why, no. For he takes Northumbria as his share of what we have won. Hubba is there now. But we fight to gain more if we may, and if not, to make sure of what we have. One way or another Ethelred's power to attack us must be broken."

"So Halfden bides in England. What meant he by his message?"

"Why, Wulfric, if you cannot see I will not tell you."

"What of Ingvar?"

"Now, Wulfric," said Thormod, "if I did not know that you at least were not afraid of him, I should say that he was best left alone. But as neither you nor I fear him, let us go and see what may be done."

"Let me think thereof," said I, not yet daring to make so sure of what I most wished.

"Shall I tell Osritha that Wulfric thought twice of coming to see her?"

"That you shall not," I cried; "I do but play with my happiness. Surely I will go, and gladly. But will she welcome me?"

"Better come and see concerning that also," he answered, laughing a little, so that one might know what he meant.

"Let us go at once on this tide," I said, starting up.

"Not so fast now, comrade," laughed Thormod. "Would you come again half starved, as last time, into the lady's presence?"

Then I called Cyneward, but when he rose up and came to us, Thormod stared at him, crying:

"You here, Raud! I thought you were with Ingvar."

"Aye, Thormod, I am here--at least Cyneward, who was Raud, is with Wulfric."

"Ho! Then you have turned Christian?"

"Aye," answered Cyneward, flushing, though not with shame, for it was the first time he had owned his faith to one of his former comrades.

"Now I thought this likely to happen to some of us," said Thormod, not showing much surprise, "if maybe it is sooner than one might have looked for. However, that is your concern, not mine. Keep out of Ingvar's way, though."

"I bide here with Wulfric," he answered, having paid no heed to our low-voiced talk.

"Wulfric sails with me to find--Ingvar," said Thormod, and at that Cyneward turned to me in surprise.

"Not Ingvar," said I, "but one in his house. Will you come with me?"

Then he understood, and his face showed his gladness.

"This is well," he cried; "gladly will I go with you and return with that other."

"That is to be seen," I answered, though I thought it surely would be so. "Now go and see to the arms and all things needful, and send the steward to me, for we have to victual the ship."

So I left Thormod with the steward and sought Ingild, telling him what I would do. Whereat he, knowing my trouble, was very glad; and then Egfrid would fain come with me also when he heard. That, however, I would not suffer, seeing that there was Ingvar to be dealt with. My mother wept, and would have me not go. But here my sister helped me.

"Bring Osritha back if you can," she said. "Soon will our house be built again, and we shall go, and you will be lonely."

For Egfrid's father had owned Guthrum, and his house and theirs were nigh rebuilt.

In a day's time Thormod and I set sail, and once more I took the helm as we went out over our bar. And the quiver of the tiller in my hands and the long lift of the ship over the rollers seemed to put fresh life in me, and my gloom passed away as if it had never been.

The breeze was fresh, and the ship flew, yet not fast enough for me, though so well sailed ours that when day broke the other was hull down astern of us, and at night we had lost her altogether. And the breeze held and the spray flew, and I walked the deck impatiently, while Thormod from the helm smiled at me. Bright were the skies over me, and bright the blue water that flashed below the ship's keel, but my thoughts would even have brightened such leaden skies as those that last saw me cross along this ocean path. And I thought that I could deal with Ingvar now.

CHAPTER XVI. HOW WULFRIC BROUGHT OSRITHA HOME.

There was a haze far out at sea, and a fog was coming in with the tide when we came to the mouth of Ingvar's haven; and rounded the spit of land that shelters it from the southerly winds. Soon we cleared it and then saw the town and hall above it at the head of the haven, and what my longings were I need not write.

Now by the wharves lay two ships, and I thought little of that, but on seeing them, Thormod, by whose side I was as he steered, seemed to wonder.

"Ingvar has got another ship from somewhere," he said, "or has built one this winter, for he sailed home with one only."

Then, too, the men began to say the like, for the second ship was strange to them also, and, as seamen will, they puzzled over her until we were close at hand. But I leaned on the gunwale and dreamed dreams of my own, paying no heed to their talk.

Out of those dreams I was roused by Thormod's voice.

"Yon ship is no Dane," he said sharply. "Clear the decks and get to arms, men. Here is somewhat amiss."

Then was a growl of wrath from our crew, yet no delay, and in a moment every man was in his place. Down came the sail, and the mast was lowered and hoisted on its stanchions overhead, and in five minutes or less the oars were out, and the men who were arming themselves ran to take them as they were ready, while those who had rowed should get to arms also. Not for the first time saw I that ship cleared for action, but never had I seen it done so swiftly, though we had but half our fighting crew, sixty men instead of a hundred and thirty or so.

I armed myself swiftly as any, and Thormod bade me take Halfden's place on the fore deck, where the men were already looking to bowstrings and bringing up sheaves of arrows and darts.

Then when I came they shouted, and one gray-headed warrior cried:

"Now you have a good fight on hand, axeman."

Then I asked:

"Who are the strangers?"

"It is a ship of the Jomsburg vikings," he said. "They know that our men are all in England, and have come to see what we have left behind--Thor's bolt light on them!"

Now, of all savage vikings these Jomsburgers are the worst. Red-handed they are, sparing none, and it is said of them that they will sacrifice men to the gods they worship before a great fight. Nor are they all of one race, but are the fiercest men of all the races of the Baltic gathered into that one nest of pirates, Jomsburg.

Now a cold thrill of fear for Osritha ran through me, and then came hot rage, and for a little I was beside myself, as it were, glaring on that ship. Then I grew cool and desperate, longing only to be hand to hand with them.

Swiftly we bore down on the ship, and now from her decks came the hoarse call of uncouth war horns, and her crew came swarming back from the streets with shouts and yells, crossing Ingvar's ship to reach their own, for she lay alongside, stem to stern of the Dane, and next to the open water.

Now I could see that men fought with the last of the Jomsburgers as they came down the street to their ship, and there were no houses burning, so that they could have been for no long time ashore. And that was good to know.

We came into the channel abreast of her, and then Thormod roared to me:

"Now I will ram her. Board her as we strike if we do not sink her!"

Then he called on the oarsmen, and they cheered and tugged at the oars, the men in the waist helping them, and my fore deck warriors gripping the bulwarks against the shock. Down we swooped like a falcon on a wild duck, and as we came the Jomsburgers howled and left their own ship, climbing into Ingvar's to fly the crash, while some tried to cast off, but too late.

"Shoot!" I shouted to my men, and the arrows flew.

Through skin-clad backs and bare necks the arrows pierced, and the smitten pirates fell back into their own ship, as they swarmed the higher sides of Ingvar's, like leaves from a tree.

Then with a mighty crash and rending of cloven timbers our dragon stem crushed the Jomsburg ship from gunwale to gunwale, splintering the rail of the other ship as the wreck parted and sunk on either side of our bows, while above the rending of planks and rush of waters rose the howls of the drowning men.

I clung to the dragon's neck, and the shock felled me not. Yet my men went headlong over the oarsmen as we struck, rising again with a great shout of grim laughter, to follow me over the bows as I leapt among the pirates who thronged on Ingvar's deck before me.

Then was the sternest fight I have ever seen, for we fought at close quarters, they for dear life, and we for those even dearer than life. There was no word of quarter, and at first, after our cheer on boarding, there was little noise beyond the ringing of weapon on helm and shield and mail, mixed with the snarls of the foul black-bearded savages against us and the smothered oaths of our men.

Then came a thickness in the air and a breath of chill damp over me, and all in a moment that creeping sea fog settled down on us, and straightway so thick it was, that save of those before and on either side of him no man might see aught, but must fight in a ring of dense mist that hemmed him round. And for a while out of that mist the arrows hissed, shot by unseen hands, and darts, hurled by whom one might not know, smote friend and foe alike, while if one slew his man, out of the fog came another to take his place, seeming endless foes. And as in a dream the noise of battle sounded, and the fight never slackened.

All I knew was that Cyneward was next me, and that my axe must keep my own life and take that of others; and I fought for Osritha and home and happiness--surely the best things for which a man can fight next to his faith. And now men began to shout their war cries that friend might rally to friend rather than smite him coming as a ghost through the mist. Then a man next me cried between his teeth:

"It is Ragnaroek come--and these are Odin's foes against whom we fight."

And so smote the more fiercely till he fell beside me, crying: "Ahoy! A Raven!--a Raven!"

Then was I down on the slippery deck, felled by a blow from a great stone hammer that some wild pirate flung over the heads of his comrades before me, and Cyneward dragged me up quickly, so that I think he saved my life that time. And I fought on, dazed, and as in a dream I fancied that I was on the deck of my father's ship fighting the fight that I looked for in the fog that brought my friend Halfden.

When my brain cleared, I knew not which way we faced. Only that Cyneward was yet with me, and that out of the dimness came against us Jomsburgers clad in outlandish armour, and with shouts to strange gods as they fell on me.

"Hai, Wainomoinen! Swantewit, ho!"

Then I cast away my shield, for I grew weary, and taking both hands to my axe, fought with a dull rage that I should have fallen, and that there were so many against me. And all alone we two seemed to fight by reason of the fog, though I heard the shouts of our crew to right and left unceasingly.

Then I felled a man, and one leapt back into mist and was gone, and a giant shape rose up against me out of the thickness, towering alone, and at this I smote fiercely. Yet it was not mail or hardened deerskin that I smote, but solid timber, and I could not free my axe again, so strongly had I smitten.

It was the high stem head of the vessel. For I and my men had cleared away the foe from amidships to bows, and still the noise of fight went on behind us, while the fog was thick as ever.

Then Cyneward leaned against the stem head and laughed.

"Pity so good a stroke was wasted on timber, master," he said.

"Pull it out for me," I answered, "my arm is tired."

For now I began to know that my left shoulder was not yet so strong as once.

He tugged at the axe and freed it, not without trouble.

"What now?" said one of the men.

But a great shout came from aft, and then a silence that seemed strange. We were still, to hear what we might, and I think that others listened for us.

"Surely we have cleared the ship?" I said. "Let us go and see."

Then I hailed our men, asking how they fared--and half I feared to hear the howl and rush of pirates coming back on us. But it was a Danish voice that called back to me that the last foe was gone.

We stumbled back now along either gunwale, over the bodies of friend and foe that cumbered all the deck, and most thickly and in heaps amidships, where our first rush fell. One by one from aft met us those who were left of the men who had fought their way to the stern. Well for us was it that the darkness had hindered the Jomsburgers from knowing how few we were and how divided. But shoulder to shoulder we had fought as vikings will, never giving back, but ever taking one step forward as our man went down before us.

Now I called to Thormod, and his voice answered me from shoreward.

"Here am I, Wulfric. How have you sped?"

"Some of us are left, but no foemen," I answered.

"Call your names," he said. And when we counted I had but sixteen left of my thirty, so heavy had been the fighting. Yet I thought that the Jomsburgers were two to our one as we fell on them, and of them was not one left.

"What now?" asked Thormod. "There are more of these men in the town. Here have I been keeping them back from the ship."

"Let us go up to the hall," I answered. "We could find our way in the dark, and they cannot tell where they are in this fog."

So I and my men climbed on to the wharf, and there were the rest of the crew with Thormod, who had crossed the decks as we cleared a passage, even as the fog came down, and had driven the rest of the Jomsburgers away from the landing place before they could join those in the ship. Well for us it was that he had done this, or we should have been overborne by numbers, for the ship was a large one, carrying maybe seven score men.

"We must leave your tired men with the ship and go carefully," said Thormod. "Likely enough we shall have another fight."

We marched up the well-known street four abreast, and as we left the waterside the fog was thinner, so that we could see the houses on either side of the way well enough. And as we went we were joined by many of Ingvar's people, old men and boys mostly, who had been left at home when the fleet sailed. And they told us that the Jomsburg men were round the great house itself.

Yet we could hear no sound of them, and that seemed strange, so that we feared somewhat, drawing together lest a rush on us were planned. But beyond a few men slain in the street we saw nothing till we came to the gate of the stockade. And that was beaten down, while some Danes and Jomsburgers lay there as they had fallen when this was done.

Now when we saw this I know not which was the stronger, rage or surprise, and I called one of the old men.

"Where is the king?" I asked.

"He is not in the town," he said; "he is away with his own courtmen, fighting against these pirates for Jarl Swend, who is beset by them."

Now it was plain that this ship came from that place; either beaten off, or knowing that Ingvar's haven lay open to attack while his men were away thus. And a greater fear than any came over me.

"Where is the Lady Osritha?" I said.

"She was here in the town this morning."

"So, Wulfric," said Thormod quickly, "she will have fled. The steward will have seen to that. No use her biding here when the ship came."

So I thought, but I was torn with doubt, not knowing if time for flight had been given, or if even now some party of Jomsburgers might not be following hard after her. I must go into the hall and find out, whatever the risk, for it was certain that it held the rest of the pirates.

"Leave men here to guard the gates," I said to Thormod. "Needs must that we see more of this."

Ten men stayed at the gate, lest Jomsburgers lurked in the houses to fall on us, and we went across to the great porch. The door was open, nor could we see much within; and there was silence.

"Stand by," said Thormod, and picked up a helm that lay at his feet.

He hurled it through the door, and it clanged and leapt from the further wall across the cold hearthstone. Then there was a stir of feet and click of arms inside, and we knew that the hall was full of men.

I know not what my thoughts were--but woe to any pirate who came within my reach.

"Show yourselves like men!" shouted Thormod, standing back.

Then, seeing that there was no hope that we should fall into this trap they had laid, there came into the doorway a great, black-haired

Jomsburg Lett, clad in mail of hardened deerskin, such as the Lapp wizards make, and helmed with a wolf's head over the iron head piece. He carried a long-handled bronze axe, and a great sword was by his side.

"Yield yourselves!" said Thormod.

The savage hove up his axe, stepping one pace nearer into the porch.

"What terms?" he said in broken Danish.

"Give up your prisoners and arms, and you shall go free," answered Thormod, for he feared lest if any captives were left alive they would be slain if we fought.

"Come and take them!" spoke back the Jomsburger in his harsh voice, and with a sneering laugh.

Now I could not bear this any longer, and on that I swung my axe and shouted, rushing on the man. Up went his long weapon overhead, and like a flash he smote at me--but he forgot that he was in the porch, and as his blow fell the axe lit on the crossbeams and stuck there. The handle splintered, and he sprang back out of reach of my stroke.

Then I dropped my axe and closed with him, and I was like a Berserk in my fury, so that I lifted him and flung him clear over my shoulder, and he fell heavily on the threshold on his head. Nor did he move again.

Cyneward thrust my axe into my hand, as past me Thormod and the men charged into the doorway. The hall was full of the pirates, and now we fought again as on the decks, hand to hand in half darkness. But it was no long fight, for those of our men who had been at the gate, finding they might leave it, came round and fell on the Jomsburgers from the back of the hall, coming through the other doors. So there was an end, and though many of us were wounded, we lost there but three men, for there were ale casks lying about, and the pirates fought ill.

Now we stood among the dead and looked in one another's faces. There were no Danes among the Jomsburgers, and they had, as it seemed, found the place empty. Then I thought:

"Those men who fell at the gate should be honoured, for they have fought and died to give time for flight to the rest."

And I called Cyneward to me, and we went through the house from end to end. Everywhere had been the pirates, rifling and spoiling in haste, so that the hangings were falling from the walls, and rich stuffs torn from chests and closets strewed the floors of Osritha's bower.

But we found no one.

Then said Cyneward:

"They are safe--fled under cover of the fog."

But now broke out a noise of fighting in the streets, and we went thither in haste. Some twenty Jomsburgers had sallied from a house, and were fighting their way to the ships, for now one could see well enough. They were back to back and edging their way onward, while the boys and old men tried to stay them in vain.

When they saw us, they broke and fled, and were pursued and slain at last, one by one. Then were no more of that crew left.

Now Thormod and I went back to the hall, and in the courtyard stood a black horse, foam covered, and with deeply-spurred sides. It was Ingvar's.

And when we came to the porch, the axe still stuck in the timbers overhead, and the Jomsburg chief's body lay where I had cast him--but in the doorway, thin and white as a ghost, stood Ingvar the king, looking on these things.

He saw me, and gave back a pace or two, staring and amazed, and his face began to work strangely, and he stepped back into the dim light of the hall, and leant against the great table near the door, clutching at its edge with his hands behind him, saying in a low voice:

"Mercy, King--have mercy!"

Now, so unlike was this terror-stricken man to him who stood in Hoxne woods bidding that other ask for mercy, and gnashing his teeth with rage, that I could hardly think him Ingvar, rather pitying him. I would have gone to him, but Thormod held me back.

"Let him bide--the terror is on him again--it will pass soon."

"Aye, I saw him thus once before in Wessex," said one of our men; and I knew that this was what Cyneward had told me of.

Very pitiful it was to see him standing thus helpless and unmanned, while his white lips formed again and again the word of which he once knew hardly the meaning--"Mercy".

Presently his look came back from far away to us, and he breathed freely. At last he stood upright and came again to the doorway, trying to speak in his old way.

"Here have you come in good time, comrades. Where are the Jomsburgers?"

"Gone," said Thormod, curtly. "Where were you, King?"

Now Ingvar heeded me not, but answered Thormod.

"With Jarl Swend beating off more of this crew. Then I saw the ship leave, and I knew where she would go. Hard after me are my courtmen, but I was swifter than they."

Now all this was wearisome to me, for I would fain follow Osritha in her flight, if I could. So I left Thormod, without a word to Ingvar, and went to the stables. There were but two horses left, and those none of the best; but Cyneward and I mounted them, and rode as fast as we might on the road which he said was most likely to be taken by fugitives.

We had but two miles to ride, for in the fog that frightened crowd of old men, women, and children had surely circled round, and had it lasted would never have gone far from the town.

When they saw us the women shrieked, and what men were with them faced round to meet an attack, thinking the pirates followed them; but we shouted to them to hold, as we were friends, though not before an arrow or two flew towards us.

At my voice, Osritha, who sat on her own horse in the midst of the company, turned round, saying quickly:

"Who is it speaks?"

And I took off my helm, and she saw me plainly, and cried my name aloud, and then swayed in her saddle and slipped thence into her old steward's arms, and one or two of the maidens went to her help.

But the men cheered, knowing that now help, and maybe victory, had come with us.

"Is all well?" they said in many voices.

"All is well," I answered; "let us take back your mistress."

Now Osritha came to herself, and saw me standing looking on her, for I feared that she was dead, and she stretched her hands to me, not regarding those around her in her joy and trouble.

"Wulfric," she cried, "take me hence into some place of peace."

I raised her very gently, holding her in my arms for a moment, but not daring to speak to her as yet. And I lifted her into the saddle again, telling her that all was well, and that we might take her back to the town in safety. Then she smiled at me in silence, and I walked beside her as we went back.

Then rode forward Cyneward and the steward to deal so with matters that the women might be terrified as little as possible with sights of war time, and we followed slowly. Naught said Osritha to me as we went, for there were too many near, and she knew not what I might have to tell; yet her hand sought mine, and hand in hand we came to Ingvar's house, and to the lesser door. There I left her, and went to seek Thormod.

The large hall was cleared, and little trace beyond the dint of blows on walls and table showed what fight had raged therein, but only Thormod and Cyneward and Ingvar were there; and Ingvar slept heavily in his great chair.

"This is his way of late," said Thormod, looking coldly at him; "fury, and terror, and then sleep. I fear me that Ingvar the King goes out of his mind with that of which he raves. Nor do I wonder, knowing now from Cyneward here what that is. Little help shall we take back from Ingvar, for he has bestirred himself to gather no new host since he came back."

"Men said that trouble at home brought him from England. I suppose he judged it likely that the Jomsburgers might give trouble," I said.

"The foes that sent him back were--ghosts," said Thormod bitterly. "Come and let us see to the ship."

So we went down to the wharf, and found the ship but little hurt by that business. And I stayed on board her that night, for I would not see Ingvar again just yet.

But in the early morning he sent to beg me to speak with him, and I came. He sat in his great chair, and I stood before him.

"You have brought me a quiet night, Wulfric," he said. "Tell me how you came here, for I think it was not that you would wish to see me again."

So Thormod had told him nothing, and I answered:

"I came with Thormod for more men, for Ethelred the King is growing strong against you. Have you heard no news?"

"None," he said; "but that is not your errand, but his."

"That will Thormod tell you, therefore," I answered. "As for me, I came at Halfden's bidding, which Thormod told me."

"What did Halfden bid you come here for?"

"To take Osritha his sister into safety and peace again. Suffer me to do so," I said, boldly enough, but yet quietly.

Now Ingvar looked fixedly at me from under his brows, and I gave back his look. Yet there was no silent defiance between us therein.

"Take her," he said at length; "you have saved her from these Jomsburgers, and you have the right. Take her where you will."

"Do you come back with us, King?" I asked him, giving him no word of thanks, for I owed him none.

"Tell Guthrum from me that I shall never set foot in England again. Tell him, if you will, that our shores here need watching against outland foes, and that I will do it. Let him settle his kingship with Hubba and Halfden."

Then he paled and looked beyond me, adding in a low voice: "Eadmund is king in East Anglia yet."

Now I answered him not, fearing lest his terror should come on him again. And slowly he slipped from his arm the great gold bracelet that he had so nearly given Eadgyth.

"Tell your people that never should a bridal train cross the Bridge of the Golden Spurs on the way to the church while the brook flows to the sea, lest ill should befall both bride and groom, because thus found I Eadmund the King, whose face is ever before me by night and day. Take this gold, I pray you, Wulfric, and lay it on the tomb where his bones are, in token that he has conquered--and let me fight my shame alone till I die."

Wondering, I took the bracelet, pitying the man again, yet fearing what he might say and do next, for I thought that maybe he would slay himself, so hopeless looked he.

"Fain would I have been your friend," he said, "but pride would not let me. Yet Eadgyth your sister and Egfrid called me so, and maybe that one deed of ruth may help me. Now go, lest I become weak again. Lonely shall I be, for you take all that I hold dear--but even that is well."

So he turned from me, and I went out without a word, for he was Ingvar. Yet sometimes I wish that I had bidden him farewell, when the thought of his dark face comes back to me as I saw him for the last time in his own hall, leaning away from me over his carven chair, and very still.

I sought Thormod, and told him that he must see the king with his tidings, for I would not see his face again.

"Nor shall we see Jutland again," he said, pointing to the ship, which lay now in the same place where the pirate had been, alongside Ingvar's. And the other ship had come in during the night, and was at anchor in the haven.

"Shall we sail home at once?" I asked him.

"Aye; no use in waiting. We are wanted at Guthrum's side, and can take no men, but a few boys back. Yet the other ship will stay while I send messengers inland, if Ingvar will not. But I shall return no more."

"Then," said I, "I will speak to the Lady Osritha."

"Go at once," he said, smiling; "bid her come with us to the better home we have found."

I had not seen Osritha since I left her yesterday, and now I feared a little, not knowing how she would look on things.

Yet I need not have feared, for when they took me to her bower she rose up and came to me, falling on my neck and weeping, and I knew that I had found her again not to part with her.

When she grew calmer, I asked her if she would return with us to Reedham, telling her how there would be no fear of war there in the time to come. And she held her peace, so that I thought she would not, and tried to persuade her, telling her what a welcome would be to her from all our folk, and also from the Danish people who loved her so well.

So I went on, until at last she raised her head, smiling at me.

"Surely I will follow you--let me be with you where you will."

So it came to pass that next day we sailed, Osritha taking her four maidens with her, for they would not leave her; having, moreover, somewhat to draw them overseas even as I had been drawn to this place again. And with us went close on a score of women and children whose menfolk were settled already near to Reedham. These were the first who came into our land, but they were not to be the last.

I had seen Ingvar no more, busying myself about fitting the ship with awnings and the like for these passengers of ours; and what Thormod did about the men he sought I know not, nor did I care to know.

There is a dead tree which marks the place where I had been cast ashore in Lodbrok's boat, and which is the last point of land on which one looks as the ship passes to the open sea from the haven. And there we saw Ingvar the king for the last time. All alone he stood with his hands resting on his sword, looking at our ship as she passed. Nor did he move from that place all the time we could see him.

Silently Thormod gave the tiller into my hands, and went to the flag halliards. Thrice he dipped Halfden's flag in salute, but Ingvar made no sign, and so he faded from our sight, and after that we spoke no more of him. But Osritha wept a little, for she had loved him even while she dreaded him, and now she should see him no more.

Very quietly passed the voyage, though the light wind was against us, and we were long on the way, for we were too short handed to row, and must beat to windward over every mile of our course. Yet I think of the long days and moonlit evenings on the deck of Halfden's ship with naught but keenest pleasure, for there I watched the life and colour come back into Osritha's face, and strove to make the voyage light to her in every way. And I had found my heart's desire, and was happy.

Then at last one night we crossed the bar of our own haven, and the boats came out to meet us, boarding us with rough voices of hearty welcome; and from her awning crept Osritha, standing beside me as I took the ship in, and seeing the black outline of hill and church and hall across the quiet moonlit water. And when the red light from wharf and open house doors danced in long lines on the ripples towards us, and voices hailed our ship from shore, and our men answered back in cheery wise, she drew nearer me, saying:

"Is this home, Wulfric?"

"Aye," I answered. "Your home and mine, Osritha--and peace."

Now have I little more to say, for I have told what I set out to tell-- how Lodbrok the Dane came from over seas, and what befell thereafter. For now came to us at Reedham long years of peace that nothing troubled. And those years, since Osritha and I were wedded at Reedham very soon after we came home, have flown very quickly.

Yet there came to us echoes of war from far-off Wessex, as man after man crept back to Anglia from the great host where Guthrum and Hubba warred with Alfred the king. And tired and worn out with countless battles, these men settled down with us in peace to till the land they had helped to lay waste and win. Hard it was to see the farms pass to alien owners at first, but I will not say that England has altogether lost, for these Danes are surely becoming English in all love of our land; and they have brought us new strength, with the old freedom of our forefathers, which some of us had nigh forgotten.

Now today I know that all the land is at peace, for Alfred is victor, and Guthrum is Athelstan the Christian king of Eastern England; and I for one will own him unasked, for he has governed well, and English is our overlord.

But Hubba is dead in far-off Devon, slain as he landed as Halfden had landed, to hem Wessex in between Guthrum and himself, and his dream of taking the Wessex kingdom is over. And the Raven banner that my Osritha made flaps its magic wings no more, for it hangs in Alfred's peaceful hall, a trophy of Saxon valour.

Thormod, my comrade, lies in his mound in wild Strathclyde, slain fighting beside Halfden my brother, the king of Northumbria. Him I have seen once or twice, and ever does he look for peace that he may sail to Reedham and bide with us for a while. Well loved is Halfden, and he is English in every thought.

Many of our old viking crew are here with me, for they would fain find land in our country, and I gave them the deserted coast lands that lie to our northward, round the great broads. Good lands they are, and in giving them I harmed none. Filby and Ormesby and Rollesby they have called their new homesteads, giving them Danish names.

Now as to our own folk. My mother is gone, but first she stood for Osritha at the font, naming her again with the name by which I learnt to love her, for I would not have it changed.

Gone also has good old Ingild; but before he went he and I were able without fear of hindrance to build a little church of squared oaken timbers at Hoxne, for the heathen worship died quickly from among our Danes. On that church, Cyneward, who was Raud, and is our well-loved steward, wrought lovingly with his own hands side by side with the good monk who baptized him. And he has carved a wondrous oaken shrine for the remains of our martyred king, whereon lies the bracelet that Ingvar sent in token that Eadmund had conquered him who was his slayer.

How fared Ingvar I know not, for soon the incoming tide of Danes slackened, and I heard no news of him; and, as he said, never did he set foot on English shores again.

Egfrid and Eadgyth are happy in their place at Hoxne, and on them at least has fallen no shadow of misfortune from that which came of their passing over the Bridge of the Golden Spurs--the Golden Bridge as our folk call it now.

Yet it needed no words of Ingvar's to keep the memory of that day's work alive in the minds of our people. Never so long as the Gold Brook flows beneath that bridge will a bridal pass churchwards over its span, for there, but for such a crossing, Eadmund the king might have bided safely till Ingvar the Dane had passed and gone.

Little use is there in grieving over what might have been, but this I know, that in days to come forgotten will be Ingvar, and English will have become his mighty host, but in every English heart will live the name of Eadmund, who died for faith and country.

NOTES.

i Ran: the sea goddess or witch of the old mythology, by whose nets drowning men were said to be entangled.

ii The Jarl ranked next to the king, and was often equally powerful. Our English title "Earl" is derived from this.

iii A small wharf.

iv A lay brother of the monastery of Hackness, near Whitby, who rendered the Sacred Histories into verse about A.D. 680.

v Now Whitby. The present name was given by the Danish settlers.

vi As if under the shadow of coming death.

vii The Viking ship of war, or "long ship".

viii The usual Scandinavian and Danish greeting: "Health".

ix After expulsion from his bishopric of York by King Egfrid.

x Mail shirt.

xi The fine allowed as penalty for killing an adversary in a quarrel, or by mischance. The penalty for wilful murder was death.

xii Nidring, niddering, or nithing, may be beet expressed by "worthless ". It was the extreme term of reproach to a Saxon.

xiii The "Lodbrokar-Quida", which is still in existence. By some authorities Ragnar is said to have been the father of Ingvar and Hubba, but the dates are most uncertain.

xiv "The Fates" of the Northern mythology.

xv St. Ansgar, or Ansgarius, built the first church in Denmark at Hedeby, now Slesvig, in 840 A.D.

xvi The "twilight of the Gods", when the Asir were to fight against the powers of evil, and a new order should commence.

xvii The Danes traced their origin back to a great migration from the East, under Odin. Their priesthood was vested in the head of the tribe after the ancient patriarchal custom.

xviii The great representative Council from which our Parliament sprang.

xix Four degrees of kingship are spoken of in the Sagas, the highest being the overlord, to whom the lesser kings paid tribute. The "kings of the host" came third in rank, the "sea kings" last, these being usually sons of under kings, to whom a ship or two had been given.

xx Now Peterborough.

xxi Tribute.

xxii "The King's Guardian."

Lightning Source UK Ltd.
Milton Keynes UK
UKHW041822280219
338221UK00001B/102/P